the POCKET PAIR

the POCKET PAiR

EMMA ST. CLAIR

To the REAL Chevy, who is sadly not here to read this. And a special thanks to Brooke, for honoring her brother and allowing me to use his name.

CONTENT WARNINGS

This is a light and funny romcom, but I want to help readers feel safe! Here are some topics that are touched on in the book:

- Death of parents to cancer (past)
- Parental abandonment & parents having affairs (past)
- Mentions of pregnancy
- Disparaging remarks about mullets and the name Jaxon (which do not necessarily reflect my personal beliefs)
- A leading man withOUT six-pack abs

Spoiler alert: No one dies. There is no sex in this book. You will get a happy ending with no cheating and minimal angst.

POCKET PAIR:
when a player is dealt a set of two matching cards in his hand
from the very start of a game

CHAPTER 1

Chevy

"ANY CHANCE you want to put that weapon down, Mrs. Fleming?" I ask, patient as can be.

Even though this is the fourth time in as many months I've been called out to her house for disturbing the peace. Such is the life of a police officer in a small town like Sheet Cake, Texas: lots of domestic calls, sadly (same as anywhere else), the occasional car or tractor accident, and then a whole lot of weird. Like today.

"This isn't a weapon." Mrs. Fleming has on what my mama used to call a house dress, curlers in her pouf of white hair, and she holds a tire iron loosely in her weathered hand. She's chewing gum with the vigor of a woman who still has all her own teeth.

Oh, and she also has a possum—sorry, technically an *o*possum—on a leash. *As one does.*

"Maybe I was fixing to change my oil."

I ignore the ridiculousness of *that* statement because I'm sure even Mrs. Fleming knows you don't need a tire iron for changing the oil. She also very well knows her opossum is not a cat, though she tells anyone who asks that Georgina is a special semi-hairless breed, like a sphinx. Its pink bedazzled leash is looped around one of Mrs. Fleming's wrists while the thing stares at me with a deeply disturbing intensity. If we were to have a staring contest, I feel sure the possum would win.

"Come on, now. Let's just put down the tire iron and have a chat."

She *tsks* but does as I ask, leaning it against the front of her house. Almost immediately, it tips over, making a loud clang as it hits the wooden porch. The opossum falls right over, playing dead. Guess I won our staring contest by default.

"Oh, poor Georgina. Don't worry," Mrs. Fleming assures me, despite my notable lack of worry. "She'll be all right in a minute. She suffers from narcolepsy, the poor thing."

Is that *what the kids are calling it these days?* I bite back this response.

Mrs. Fleming switches gears, circling back to the reason for my visit. "Those horrible teenage vandals were stuffing trash in my cannons again."

Her craftsman-style bungalow has two cannons on either side of the front steps. Yes—cannons. They're rusted but real, and legend has it they were stolen off a pirate ship, though our town is hours from any ocean. Because we just moved into January, they're both still wrapped in blinking white lights. And sure enough, I can see the edge of a crushed soda can glinting inside one of the two cannons.

"Next time, call me rather than making threats," I admonish her gently. "We've talked about this."

She blinks innocently and cups one hand around her ear. "What's that?"

I raise my voice, despite knowing she has no problems with her hearing. Just as she doesn't have the kind of vision problems or mental impairment that would make her think Georgina—who is now emerging from her fake death—is actually a feline. "You cannot make threats while holding something which could be construed as a weapon, even for dramatic effect."

Her expression turns stormy, and I don't miss the way her fingers twitch as she steps closer to the tire iron. "Did you call me dramatic, son?"

I place a hand over my heart. "I would never."

I like to think of myself as a fairly smart man. Smart enough, anyway. And smart men know *never* to call a woman dramatic. Especially not a woman with a tire iron and pair of actual cannons on her front porch, even if they don't—probably?—still fire.

"What, exactly, defines a weapon?"

I begin to tick off options on my fingers. "Weapons may include but are not limited to, tire irons, baseball bats, cannons, or firearms."

"Did you say forearms?"

"*Firearms.*"

She sighs. "I love a good set of forearms. My Nate had lovely forearms. Not too much hair and a Navy tattoo."

She pauses, chewing her gum with a little more vigor as her eyes cloud over with memory. I listen, because at times, listening is an easy kindness to offer. Especially to someone who's lonely.

"Is that right?" I ask.

"He didn't get the tattoo until after he was out of the service. The Navy didn't allow them below the elbow until 2016." She frowns, managing to look angry and sad at the same time. "Nate would have hated that. The man didn't like change."

"Your husband and I both." I clear my throat as I hear my watch beep, signifying the start of a new hour and, more importantly, the end of my shift.

"When are you going to settle down for good with a nice girl?" Mrs. Fleming asks.

I resist the urge to tell her she should use the term *woman*, not *girl*. The short answer is *never*, but I don't say that either.

"Will you please call me next time?" I ask. "You know I'd be here in half a heartbeat."

If gum-chewing can have a vibe, hers turns vindictive. "Next time, I'll throw eggs. See how they like that."

To be honest, a lot of teens could do with a good egging. Some adults too, for that matter. I make a note to check for what kind of charges egg-throwing might carry. Tipping my cowboy hat, I promise to come back soon and clean the trash out of Mrs. Fleming's cannons.

But not at this moment. Because as of now, I'm off-duty.

"I'll come back sometime this week or next and clean out those cannons for you," I promise.

Her expression softens. "Your mama would be proud of the boy she raised."

I sure hope so. I swallow thickly. "Thank you, ma'am. It means a lot."

I'm halfway to my cruiser when she calls, "And aren't you just the spittin' image of your daddy. He'd be proud too."

I sure hope *not*.

I don't pause, though my steps falter, my cowboy boots

kicking up a little cloud of dust in Mrs. Fleming's gravel driveway. I'd love to take the first compliment, to let it wrap around my heart like a warm blanket on this cool January day. But she had to go and ruin it by comparing me to the last man I would ever want to resemble in looks or any other way. Making him proud is the last thing I'd want to do.

Because if a man like my father were proud, I must be doing something wrong. Too bad only a tiny percentage of the population—me, my sister, Winnie, her best friends and boyfriend—know the truth about my father. Who he was. What he did.

"He was such a good man," Mrs. Fleming goes on, and, as I do anytime someone says something positive about my father, I bite my cheek so I don't burst their bubble with the truth.

I can't seem to escape the pale ghost of a man I looked up to for half my life—until I didn't look up to him at all. He clings to me like the smoke from the cigars he sometimes covertly lit up in the backyard, the stink clinging to his hair and clothes for days after.

As much as I'd love to shower or scrub or bleach his stink off me, I don't think that's how it works. I share the man's DNA. Which means I might share in his epic failures too.

"We're not going to torpedo our relationships because of Dad's mistakes," my obviously much smarter-than-me sister said when we visited our parents' graves around Thanksgiving. At least one of us is holding up the bargain we made by way of a pinky promise.

Me? I had the fingers of my other hand crossed behind my back. Figuratively, that is. Because Winnie definitely would have noticed otherwise. She can happily settle down for good with her boyfriend, James. And I'm glad for her. But it's not for me.

And yet ... I swear, ever since then, it's like making the promise has cursed me. Dating has become a chore. Like heading to the mechanic when the check-engine light comes on. Tomorrow night is the first date I've scheduled for months, and I've considered canceling more than once. Instead, I keep finding myself watching Winnie so happy with James and feeling this weird pinch in my chest.

Better get over *that* quick.

My phone dings with a text, and I'm more than grateful for the chance to shove all thoughts of my father and longing for things I can't have into a mental trash compactor in my mind.

Mari: Can you stop by the diner this afternoon? It's important.

If it were most people, I'd put this off until tomorrow, using my date as an excuse. But I'm not all that eager about the date. Plus, it's Mari—the woman who was like a second mother to me after mine died. Just like she stepped in to care for Val and her sisters when their mom ran off that same summer. I'd do just about anything she asked.

Is this about Val? I can't help but wonder. *Is she okay?*

As one of my sister's best friends, Val falls under the umbrella of my protection.

That's why I care, I tell myself. *The only reason.*

Not because of the way her dark eyes sparkle when she laughs at my dumb jokes or the way she always manages to have paint somewhere on her skin or the way she somehow manages to look feminine in a pair of Dickie's coveralls and a tank top. None of those reasons are why I'm hustling to get to the diner. Because those reasons would get me in trouble with my sister, even if I were the kind of guy to date someone like Val.

Nope—I'm going for Mari. Just Mari.

I almost believe it.

———

The diner, as always, is busy. The Bobs, three old-timers who share the same name and an unparalleled love for Sheet Cake High School football, toss me a wave. I help coach the team, but I'm gladly taking a brain break from it in the off-season, while I bet they're already talking about next fall's lineup. They'll rope me into a whole conversation about it if I let them.

Kitty Bishop is at the counter with one of her three teenage daughters—I can never tell the girls apart—and Judge Judie and her husband, Burt, are sharing an enormous slice of cake.

Mari winks at me while taking plates back to the kitchen, mouthing, *Give me a sec.* And there, at the farthest back table, I spy Tank Graham across the table from Val, whom I'd know even from the back. Her dark hair is twisted up into a messy bun, held in place by two thin paintbrushes and obviously some form of magic.

A smile tugs at my lips as I slide into the booth next to theirs, my back to Val's. If I'm eavesdropping, it's because I'm trained to pay attention to details. Not because I'm a nosy gossip like the rest of the town. I quickly pick up on the fact that they're talking about Val's paintings.

"Do you need me to send you pictures for approval, or do you want to come to the studio and look?"

"Winnie's shown me pictures. You're talented, and any of your work is good enough for me, Val."

I can hear the smile in Tank's voice, and I realize I'm smiling too. *That's my girl.* Not that Val's mine, per se. I'm proud of her the same way I was proud when my sister developed and sold an app—something I wouldn't begin to know how to do.

Even when Val was a kid, she made these amazing crayon and colored pencil drawings. I know she's had a hard time since college figuring out how to support herself as a full-time artist, but she's talented. I'm happy to hear Tank thinks so too. Even happier that it sounds like he'll be buying some of her paintings.

"What's your timeline?" Val asks, and I hear her shifting behind me. "Because I actually have something coming up and may not have much time to—"

"Thanks for coming." Mari chooses this moment to show up with a smile and a to-go cup of coffee.

I hold back a groan. *What exactly does Val have coming up? She won't have much time before* what?

"You ask, I'll answer," I tell her. "Anytime."

Mari's eyes sparkle, but before she can respond, I feel movement against the back of my booth.

"Chevy?"

I swivel at the question and find myself face to face with Val, her surprised brown eyes inches from mine.

"Hey, Tiny. How's it going?" I glance past her, tilting my head in greeting to Tank. He grins in return.

"Finish your talk," Mari tells Val. "Then you can join us."

Val gives me a small smile before we both turn back to our respective conversations. Though, if I'm being honest, my attention is not fully on Mari. I keep straining to hear what Val and Tank are talking about, wondering what she has coming up that would limit her time. A new job, maybe? I know she can't stand her job at the art gallery. More specifically, her boss. Maybe this town has rubbed off on me, and I *am* just a nosy gossip.

"I need a favor." Mari lowers her voice and leans across the table. Per the usual, she's got a fresh flower tucked behind one ear, the pink bloom bright against her white hair.

However, *not* per the usual, Mari isn't smiling.

"It's regarding ..." As she trails off, Mari juts her chin toward the table behind us. Toward Val.

Worry sprouts twenty heads inside my belly, all of them fire-breathing. "Is she okay?" I ask quietly.

"She's fine," she says.

"So, what's the favor?"

Mari purses her lips. "I'd like for you to look out for ..." Once more, Mari tilts her chin toward Val.

In a lot of ways, I've already been watching out for Val. Just like I would my sister. This feels ... different. Unease squirms in my belly.

"Shouldn't her boyfriend do that?" I have trouble not sneering when I say *boyfriend*.

Honestly, I'm surprised Val's latest boyfriend lasted more than a week. The man might as well have *loser* tattooed on his forehead. I don't need to spend quality time with Jared —*Jason? Jensen?*—to dismiss him. It took one look at the mullet he sports in a completely non-ironic way paired with a polo shirt and popped collar. Val's fatal flaw seems to be her penchant to date men who are never good enough for her.

Winnie likes to say Val's bad taste in men rivals my bad taste in women. My ALLEGEDLY bad taste in women. Aside from being surface deep, I don't see what's wrong with the women I date. The name of my dating game is casual. Surface-level women are just fine when we don't ever dive deep. Or they were. Until Winnie cursed me with the pinky promise.

Mari's smile stretches wide. "They broke up."

"Did they, now?"

"She's single," Mari says, her smile growing wider. "Which is why I'm asking you. Not that I would have trusted that fool to take care of her anyway."

"Okay," I say slowly. "Is there a particular reason she needs looking out for?"

Mari leans back, crossing her arms. "Not one I'm at liberty to say. Yet."

I scratch my jaw. Ever since Mom died, Mari has been like an honorary aunt to me and Winnie, bringing meals over, offering little maternal things, and just generally racking up points she can cash in any way she likes. I *will* say yes. Mari knows it. I know it. But I want more info. I'm a planner. Going into things blind is not my strong suit. And the many-headed worry monster just sprouted a few new ones. Because there's obviously a secret I'm not privy to that has Mari asking me.

"So, there is a reason, but not one you want to tell me."

The tiniest of smiles appears. "Are you hungry?"

"Always. But I just got off work and want to head home. Maybe a burger to go?"

"Of course." She pauses and then grabs my hand, holding it with surprising strength. "You shouldn't spend your life fighting ghosts."

It's been a long time since my mama was around to scold me, but I still remember the feeling. My stomach squirms just as much under Mari's scrutiny. And under the weight of what she said, which hits me like some kind of battering ram to the sternum. I'm not sure how she made the leap from dinner to me fighting ghosts or how she managed to hit me right where I didn't know it hurt, but she did both with one sentence.

I give her an easy grin that feels like trying to swim against the current in a flash flood. Because her words, like Mrs. Fleming's, strike a little too close to home. Is there some kind of secret thread on the Neighborly app where all the older women of the town are discussing me today?

"Fighting ghosts?" I say, casual, casual, casual. "I don't know what you mean."

Mari squeezes my hand so hard my bones feel on the verge of breaking. "I want to see you happy, Chevy."

"I *am* happy," I tell her. And up until I say the words and hear how hollow they sound, I *thought* it was true.

Aren't I happy? Why wouldn't I be?

I've got a job I enjoy, my own home, and a bunch of friends in this sometimes cloyingly close-knit community. No, there's no steady woman in my life. But being the kind of man who isn't sure he can be steady himself, I'm not looking for one. I don't want a wife and two-point-five babies or whatever the number is. I just want …

I want …

Well. I guess right at this moment, I'm having some kind of existential crisis in a diner because *I don't know what I want anymore*.

Mari releases her crushing grip on my hand just as Val slides into the booth next to me. I scoot in a bit, but our thighs are still touching, our arms brushing as she waves animatedly. It's closer than we usually sit, more touching than we usually do. I could slide away a few more inches, but I don't.

"Speaking of happy," Val says, making me wonder just how much of our conversation she heard, "Tank is buying some of my paintings to decorate the lofts. Isn't that great?"

She's beaming, and so is Mari when she zips over to hug Val. "So proud of you, princesa," Mari whispers.

"You should be proud. I couldn't be more thrilled to have Val's work hanging in the lofts," Tank says, and Mari hugs him too. She barely comes up to the big man's chest.

Back in September, the Graham family rolled into Sheet Cake after Tank purchased the whole downtown area. Faster than I would have thought possible, he's been renovating the abandoned storefronts and getting new tenants. The second story of nearly every building has been converted into modern loft living spaces. He and James currently share one; my sister is in another. Probably a dozen others are nearing completion. This is a big job for Val.

I nudge her with my shoulder. "I'm proud of you too, Tiny."

Her cheeks turn pink and she grins down at her hands, twisting in her lap. "Thanks."

Tank says his goodbyes, and Mari heads off to refill the Bobs's coffees.

Which leaves me and Val awkwardly sharing the same side of the booth. I clear my throat, trying to catch her eye without turning my head. That would put our faces far too close.

"Everything good?" I ask her, my mind still stuck on the part of the conversation I missed about why Val might be on a time crunch.

"Yep. All good," she answers. A little too quickly if you ask me.

Mari reappears with a to-go box. "That was fast," I tell her.

"Big Mo started fixing it as soon as you walked in," she says with a laugh.

"Guess I'm pretty boring."

"Hardly," Mari says. "You're constant. Steady. Trustworthy. Isn't he a good man, Val?"

Val gives me a conspiratorial look, letting me know she, too, gets how Mari seems to be playing matchmaker. Not for the first time. "I guess he's okay," Val says.

"Thanks for the high praise, buddy."

Buddy? Val's nose wrinkles the slightest bit at the term, which is almost as dorky as if I'd called her *pal*. But Mari's not-so-subtle words have me wanting to make it clear what Val and I are: Friends. I'm not sure who, exactly, the reminder is for. Mari? Val?

Me?

Val is, and always has been, completely off-limits. When I was a senior in high school and they were freshmen, Winnie threatened to castrate me in a number of colorful and terrifying ways if I ever hurt Val. That has made it really easy to shut down any feelings other than friendship, which is where we need to stay.

I knock my shoulder into her again and shoot her a grin. "You wanna stop blocking my exit?"

Val scoots to the end of the booth, losing the paintbrushes from her hair as she does. The long curtain of her hair falls. A sweet scent hits my nostrils as a few strands whisper against my cheek, the ends marked with purple paint. I grab her brushes from the floor, handing them back as I stand.

"Thanks, Chev." She puts them between her teeth, grinning as she winds her hair back up in a knot and sticks the brushes through. It feels strangely intimate to watch, though it's a simple movement and something I've seen dozens of times before. I swallow and take a step away.

"I'll see you around, Tiny."

Grabbing my box, I make a quick exit and head for home, my head full of loud thoughts, like a bunch of toddlers have been set loose with cymbals in there.

Why does Mari need me to take care of Val?

What does Val have coming up?

Would my mama be proud?

Am I really like my daddy?

Why does Val have a time issue?

And finally, the one that's clanging loudest of all—*AM I happy?*

CHAPTER 2

Val

When you live in a tiny, nosy town, buying a pregnancy test for one of your best friends requires stealth. Which tonight, looks like driving halfway to Austin in order to find a CVS where you don't know everyone inside the building.

I mean, unless you WANT all of Sheet Cake to hear about your potential bun in the oven on the Neighborly app, right alongside complaints about Harvey Woodward leaving his trash cans out by the curb all week. Lindy *definitely* doesn't want the rumor mill on Neighborly knowing anything. Honestly, I'm not even sure Lindy herself is ready to know if she's pregnant.

"I'm only a couple of days late," Lindy says, staring wide-eyed at the rows of pregnancy tests like she's looking at a venomous snake exhibit.

She's been running her hands through her dark hair so much that it's starting to look like the end of a well-used broom. Meanwhile, Winnie, who drove and is leading this misadventure, still looks like the picture of a perfect punk pinup with her high blond ponytail, black-rimmed glasses, and boots under a flouncy polka-dot dress.

"Maybe I should wait a few more weeks. I'll probably get my period tomorrow. No need to waste time."

"Nope. You've totally got baby boobs," Winnie says, pointing at Lindy's chest. "Back me up, Val."

I can't see a difference, but then I don't spend much time examining my friends' chests.

Lindy pulls her long-sleeve shirt away from her body, effectively hiding any baby or non-baby boobs and starts to slowly back away.

"They are extra sensitive ... but that could be a PMS thing. I'm sure that's it."

"Val, grab her before she bolts." Winnie hasn't looked up from the box she's holding, but she obviously sensed Lindy's fight-or-flight urge heading quickly toward flight.

I'm not usually the enforcer—I'm the least likely candidate compared to my two fierce friends—but I step in front of Lindy, giving her an apologetic smile. "Sorry, chica."

Lindy frowns. "We should just go. I don't want to be late to the meeting."

We have about an hour until the monthly meeting of the Ladies Literary and Libation Society. Considering the annual Sheet Cake Festival is about a month away, there is a lot to discuss. Usually, I enjoy the meetings, which involve town business, alcohol, and very little of the literary nature.

But I've got an inescapable feeling of dread coiling in my belly about tonight's meeting. I know what my aunt Mari is going to announce, and it's not something my friends—or anyone else for that matter—will embrace. Especially since I've been keeping them in the dark. I planned to tell them Mari's big news—and mine—tonight, but when Lindy mentioned her late period, our plans were derailed, and now we're here.

I did *try*. My voice wobbled only a little when I said I needed to tell them something. But they jumped in, congratulating me, thinking that I meant Tank buying my paintings. Which is a big deal. Just … not as big as the other thing I was planning to tell them.

My news seems like small potatoes compared to Lindy potentially being pregnant. Somehow, I don't think my two best friends will see it that way. Now I'm the one trying to stuff down a sudden urge to flee.

"We could always skip tonight," I suggest.

"If we skip, they'll stick us with some terrible job for the festival, like making sure the portable toilets stay stocked with toilet paper." Winnie holds out a box to Lindy. "Take this one."

Lindy shoves her hands in the back pockets of her jeans. "No, thank you."

Rolling my eyes, I take the box from Winnie. "I've got it."

"Can we just go, please?" Lindy begs.

"We'll go after you buy a test," Winnie says. "Or a *few* tests. I can't force you to pee on a stick, but this way we won't have to make a second trip out here." Winnie picks up another test, frowning as she reads the back of the box.

"How did Julian take the breakup?" Lindy asks me, an obvious ploy to direct attention away from herself.

"His name is *Jaxon*. With an X. Not *that* hard to remember."

"Right—Jackwagon," Winnie says, pushing her black-framed glasses up her nose. "Still can't believe you dated him so long."

"He didn't deserve you," Lindy says.

"And he has a mullet," Winnie adds. "On *purpose.*"

Is there such a thing as an accidental mullet? Even if so, Jaxon's mullet is absolutely intentional. And gross. Which I tried to overlook because I'm not that shallow, but it turns out I am *exactly* that shallow. I know they're coming back in style, but they *shouldn't.*

How did I even get to be in the position where I'm dating a guy with a mullet?

Oh, right. Because the actual guy I like, whom I don't talk about because he happens to be Winnie's brother, is off-limits. And also not at all interested. In order to kill my long-time crush on Chevy, I've been desperately dating any guy—including ones with unfortunate throwback hairstyles—for longer than I care to admit. Even the thing I still haven't told Winnie and Lindy was partially motivated by my feelings for Chevy. Or, more to the point, my desire to get rid of those feelings.

"He was surprisingly upset about the breakup," I admit. "I mean, he was the one who said he didn't want to be exclusive. He'll get over it."

Movement catches my eye, and I realize that Lindy used talk of Jaxon to distract me. Once again, she's edging away toward the end of the aisle. I hook an arm around her waist, and pull her back toward Winnie. Sighing heavily, Lindy leans her head on my shoulder. I swear, I feel the tiniest tremor, like she's barely holding in a serious cry. Winnie is still task-focused, reading every label of every pregnancy test on the shelf, and doesn't notice.

"Hey—it's fine," I whisper, giving Lindy a squeeze. "Pregnant, not pregnant—it will be okay. You and Pat want to have kids, right?"

Lindy has mentioned wanting a big family before, or I wouldn't have assumed. Despite what society seems to think, not every woman *wants* to get pregnant. Even if they're happily married and have the means and support. Frankly, the idea of having a baby terrifies me, though Jo, Lindy's daughter, is pretty amazing.

I can barely be trusted to remember my own schedule. Who would trust me with a whole human? Wasn't I just a kid myself? Weren't we all?

Though Lindy, Winnie, and I weren't friends back when we were in diapers, it was pretty soon after that we became inseparable.

The very first picture of the three of us was taken in first grade, and we each have a framed copy. Winnie has two blond pigtails instead of the single high ponytail she sports most days. She's squinting at the camera because no one realized she needed glasses yet. Lindy has her eyes crossed and her tongue stuck out, her dark hair in a bowl cut we still make fun of to this day. And me? I'm wearing overalls with one strap undone and a closed-mouth smile because I was self-conscious about missing a tooth. My thick, brown hair is lighter than it is now, but it's just as unruly and long, hanging almost down to my waist.

And now … Lindy might be pregnant. She was the first to get married, just last fall, and now could be the first one going through this particular milestone. It's hard to believe.

"I just didn't plan for it to happen so soon," Lindy says. "Pat and I have only been married a few months and then there's Jo …" She trails off as her voice gets wobbly.

When Lindy came home the last semester of college, her troubled sister, Rachel, had abandoned her infant daughter.

Lindy's mom had taken Jo in but was showing the first signs of dementia and couldn't care for a baby, much less herself. All this meant Lindy suddenly became a capital-A adult in ways few college grads have to. At least, not so quickly or in such huge ways. Jo is so much better off with Lindy and Pat, who *adores* her, but I can understand how a new baby might really change the dynamics. Especially since they're practically still newlyweds.

"I don't want Jo to feel *less than* if we have a biological child," Lindy says, looking dangerously close to crying.

If she cries … I'm going to cry. So, selfishly, I really *need* her to hold it together.

"No kid is as loved as Jo," Winnie says, pausing in her box-reading to give Lindy's shoulder a squeeze. "She won't feel that way. *If* you're pregnant."

"If," Lindy agrees. "I'm probably not."

Winnie pushes up her glasses, giving Lindy's chest a pointed look. "Yeah. *If.*"

"Whatever happens, we're here," I tell Lindy. "Okay?"

She nods emphatically, but her eyes are still glistening. My own eyes start stinging, and I bite the inside of my cheek. *MUST. NOT. WEEP. IN. CVS.*

"You know," Winnie says, glancing up and down the aisle with narrowed eyes, "it's ridiculous how they lump these items together: tampons, condoms, and pregnancy tests. Doesn't this seem darkly ironic somehow?"

It's clear she's trying to lighten the mood a little, and at least for me, it's working. Lindy snorts out a laugh, and I feel her relax against me.

"I'm not sure this is irony," I say. "But let's not forget the adult diapers."

Lindy giggles. "This is not aisle seven. It's the aisle of embarrassment."

A throat clears nearby, but before any of us even has a chance to turn, a deep and familiar voice says, "Periods, pregnancy, and peeing your pants are not things to be embarrassed about, ladies."

Winnie gasps, Lindy lets out a little scream, and I hurl the pregnancy test I'm holding at the man standing at the end of the aisle. It's only as the box hits him in the center of the forehead that I realize the man is Chevy. Winnie's brother.

AKA my longtime, semi-secret, super impossible crush.

Annnnd I just beaned him in the face with a pregnancy test.

This truly is the aisle of embarrassment.

"Nice arm, slugger," Chevy says with a grin that makes my heart thump unsteadily. "I suppose I might have deserved that." He bends to pick up the box.

Oh, no. Don't look at the box. Do. Not. Look. At. The Box.

Lindy clutches my elbow, and I swear the three of us all hold our breath as Chevy picks up the pregnancy test. But casual as can be, he sets it on a shelf. When he offers us the same crooked smile that makes my knees feel wobbly, my breath leaves my chest in a whoosh, and Lindy loosens her death grip on my arm.

Just act casual, I tell myself. *There's nothing to see here! Definitely no potential pregnancies. Nope! We're just three friends, driving out of town to hang out next to adult diapers in CVS. A typical Tuesday night!*

Even if Chevy finds out why we're here, he wouldn't say anything. Probably. Though he is Pat's best friend, and has basically worked his way into being the unofficial fourth Graham son. Surely, he would be loyal to his sister and her best friend.

Wouldn't he?

"Are you following us?" Winnie demands.

"Y'all aren't that interesting," Chevy says with a wink. "I was just picking up some snacks for the drive back home from Austin."

Winnie crosses her arms. "Where are the snacks?"

Chevy might be the cop, but he's the one being interrogated. And it's a solid question. Where *are* these alleged snacks?

He tilts his head toward the front of the store. "Left them at the self-checkout when I heard the telltale sounds of a few shady characters up to no good."

I know he's teasing. I know it because I've known him my whole life and have made studying him a hobby. A tortuous one, considering my crush and the lack of any observable evidence that he sees me as anything more than a friend. More specifically, his sister's friend, which is somehow worse.

Anyway, I know from his tone he's joking, but we actually *are* being shady. Or, at least, *secretive*. His words hitting so close to the truth make my paranoia grow roots and sprout like a field full of weeds.

"And on your way home from *what*, Chevrolet?"

He shrugs, leaning on a shelf with a casualness that seems a little *too* casual. "I needed some fresh air, *Winchester*."

"Austin air isn't as fresh as Sheet Cake air."

Chevy inhales audibly. "I don't know. Smells fresh to me."

"It smells like CVS." Winnie pauses, then pokes a finger into her brother's chest. "Were you on another date with another horrible woman?"

My reaction to Winnie's words is instant and visceral, like someone just took a blowtorch to my gut. Chevy's blue-gray eyes meet mine over Winnie's shoulder. Can he tell what I'm feeling by whatever look is on my face? I sure hope not.

I can't help it if the thought of him dating other women—

even though he does date other women and dates them a lot —makes me want to find the aisle for anti-nausea meds. He certainly has never shown any sign of jealousy over any of the guys I've dated. None of whom have even remotely helped eradicate the feelings I have for Chevy.

The feelings I don't think he knows about. I mean, the whole town seems to, but Chevy never treated me differently than Lindy. Honestly, he treats the three of us as though we're ALL his sisters.

Gross.

If Chevy knows about my feelings, he would avoid me, right? Or keep more of a distance, put me more at arm's length.

But with the way he's still staring at me now, looking almost apologetic, I have to wonder.

Does he know?

And if so, HOW EMBARRASSING. I'm going to need more than anti-nausea meds. I'm going to need a new identity.

Do they sell those at CVS?

"Well?" Winnie demands.

"I was on a date, but it's over."

So, it *was* a date. *Triple ugh*. The blowtorch to my guts feeling is now more of a rusty chainsaw to the heart.

And now I'm picturing Chevy in his faded jeans and boots, tousled brown hair, tucked in shirt stretched wide across his broad chest, on a date with someone else. He's flashing that crooked smile at her across a candlelit table, his teasing voice turning flirtatious. He's wrapping her in a hug against his big frame, maybe leaning in for a kiss at the end of the night ...

"But it's only six-thirty." I didn't mean to say this out

loud. I definitely don't want more details about this date. But aren't most dates *starting* right now, not ending?

"We didn't click," Chevy says with a shrug. "Ended before it began."

Is it bad that I feel a swell of triumph? In my mind, I'm blowing celebratory horns and shooting confetti cannons. Even though I'm still slightly ill at the idea of him having a date planned at all. Which is stupid. Sometimes I wish my imagination weren't so vivid, that my feelings for everything weren't so BIG.

Winnie stretches out her fist toward Chevy, then slowly extends her pinky finger. "You remember this?"

Chevy glances away, his jaw tight. Knowing Winnie and her penchant for treating pinky promises like treaties signed in blood, I'm guessing there's some promise she's holding her brother to. A promise about ... dating?

"You said you'd try," Winnie says, waving her pinky finger. "*We'd* try."

"What are they trying?" Lindy hisses from behind me.

"I don't know," I whisper back. But oh, how I wish I did.

Chevy's eyes meet mine, briefly, like the brush of a fingertip over my skin. It has the same effect, sending a wave of goose bumps along my arms. If I'm not imagining it, the tops of his cheeks flush as he returns his full focus to his sister.

Recovering, Chevy's features relax, and he locates his signature crooked grin. I wonder if I'm the only one who notices how it doesn't quite reach his eyes.

"I'm here, aren't I? In CVS and not on a date? So, you can put that pinky away." Chevy reaches out and folds Winnie's finger down with the rest, then pats her hand.

"You're still an idiot, making idiotic choices." Winnie

reaches out and flicks her brother right in the forehead. He blinks, looking momentarily stunned.

Growing up, my two older sisters mostly ignored me, saving the sisterly bonding *and* sisterly bickering for each other since they were only a year apart and I was the baby of the family. Usually, I tried to worm my way into the middle of their fights, desperate for attention, but I could always tell when things were about to get vicious. It was a subtle shift in the air when things turned sharp and dangerous.

It's memories of those for-real fights that have me stepping forward. Only, instead of pulling Winnie back the way I normally might, I grasp Chevy's arm and give it a quick squeeze.

I almost never touch him, even casually like this. And right now I'm aware of exactly why I try to avoid it. Being close to him, touching him, only makes me want *more*. More touching. More of him.

More, more, more.

Focus, Val. You're breaking up a fight before Chevy and Winnie get arrested for a brawl in CVS.

"Hey there, you two," I say, glancing between them. "Let's all calm down. Win, why don't you let me handle this? I'll meet you and Lindy in the car."

Winnie nods. "Fine." She stomps on her brother's cowboy boot before walking away, leaving me in the aisle of embarrassment, nose to nose with Chevy.

CHAPTER 3

Val

I WAVE A HAND, snagging Chevy's attention. "Hey, Chev."

The goal is to distract him, allowing Winnie to grab a pregnancy test—or five—without him seeing.

"Tiny," he says, and I can't smother my smile.

I can't remember how long ago Chevy gifted me with this nickname, but I love it.

Winnie tried to tell him once that Tiny was insulting. I mean, yeah—I clock in at about five-two, so I can see where she's coming from. But I'm proud of my size. As Mari— who's the same height as me—always says, "Fierce things come in tiny packages." Plus, it's a play on my full name, Valentina. It's cute. It's sweet.

It's *mine*. A gift from Chevy to only me.

Trying to avoid looking like the lovesick human I am, I

glance down and notice his knuckles are all torn up. "You're bleeding!"

I lift his hand, giving the broken skin and tiny cuts a closer look. He doesn't fight me, and I take my time, loving the feel of his warm skin on mine, even as I'm telling myself to focus on his injury. I can't help but revel a little in the physical contact.

Chevy's skin isn't split so much as riddled with shallow cuts and scrapes. Almost like a skinned knee. Despite trying to keep myself focused on the man's injury, I can't stop my greedy little thumb from swiping across his soft palm.

Chevy sucks in a breath, and I meet his gaze again, feeling a little woozy.

"It's nothing," he says, acting like he's going to take his hand back.

Oh, no you don't, sir! I've got you in my clutches now.

Avoiding the bloody scrapes, I hold on tighter. "You're hurt."

"I'm fine. Nothin' a little time won't heal."

I roll my eyes. "Come on, tough guy. Let's get you fixed up."

My grip on his hand is light, but I drag Chevy away to find the first-aid aisle. It's nice to feel needed, to have a purpose.

It's also nice to have an excuse to keep touching Chevy. He doesn't resist again, though he sighs deeply as I scan the bandages and ointments to see what we need. Am I going slower than necessary to prolong this moment? Maybe.

Am I determined to memorize the feel of Chevy's skin on mine? Heck yes.

"Animate or inanimate object?" I ask, grabbing a tube of off-brand antibiotic cream.

"Hm?"

"What did you punch, Chevy? That's usually how big, dumb men hurt their knuckles."

"Big and dumb, huh? Is that all I am to you?" he teases.

"Hardly." A blush creepity-creeps up my cheeks as I'm thinking of all the things he is to me. If he only knew.

When you have a crush, sometimes every word feels like a tell-tale heart, beating out the truth. Displaying your secret. Loudly announcing to everyone I HAVE FEELINGS.

I mean, *sure*—this is a little less morbid than the heart of a murdered person beating under the floorboards. But no less obvious.

"Thank you," Chevy says, and thankfully, he doesn't seem to hear the tell-tale truth in my voice.

There are too many choices for bandages, too many boxes and brands, and I'm feeling all fuzzy from Chevy's proximity and his hand still in mine. But when I see the light pink bandages with hearts and sheep, I grin. *Perfect.*

Not wanting to let go of Chevy yet, I rip open the box with my teeth, careful to keep my gaze trained on his hand, lest my eyes reveal all my secrets.

"Really, Tiny? Do you care nothing for my reputation?"

I grin. "I think it's nice when a man has a softer side."

Opening the wrapper one-handed is harder than it looks, but I manage, still keeping Chevy's warm hand tucked in mine. It might need to be surgically removed by the time this is said and done.

"So, you won't tell me how it happened? I thought you trusted me. I'm wounded, Chevy. *Wounded.*"

"I was vanquishing a dragon."

I snort, shaking my head. My hair starts to fall out of the messy bun I put it in earlier, but fixing it will have to wait. My hands are occupied with something much more pressing. "Try again," I say, opening a second bandage.

Overkill? Absolutely. But you better believe I'm going to use at least five.

"I was on official police business," he says.

I skim my eyes over his broad chest. "Nope. You're not in uniform."

"Defending a woman's honor, then."

NOT the mental image I want to have. I glance up at him, only to find that his blue eyes are sparkling with amusement. Meanwhile, my eyes are sparking with a totally different emotion, a jealous fire I *really* hope isn't obvious.

"Were you?" I ask.

He shakes his head. "Nope."

"Why won't you tell me?"

I don't mean to sound so sad. So desperate for him to open up to me. But it seems like the dam hiding my emotions from Chevy has sprung a leak. Or several. And when he leans forward, his lips brushing my ear, I'm afraid the whole dam is crumbling down.

"The truth, Tiny, is that I got into a fistfight with a brick wall," he murmurs.

What is happening in this moment? I feel like I've stepped into an alternate dimension because Chevy is standing VERY close, and he isn't moving away. He isn't giving me the kind of space you give friends.

In fact, is he ... *flirting?*

"Now, why would you get in a fight with a wall?"

My voice is husky and low. I wobble a little, my whole axis knocked off-kilter by Chevy's stubble grazing my cheek, but manage to stay in place and on my feet. Barely.

Had this been the regency era, my bodice would be heaving. I'd pull out a fancy pocket fan and cool my flaming cheeks. As Chevy smiles, those impossibly adorable dimples popping, his lips brush my ear. Regency-me would be swooning.

Chevy speaks again, his breath a warm tickle on my skin.

"I didn't like the way the wall looked at me," he says. "All judgmental and bricky."

It's all I can do to utter a single word. "Liar."

He sighs. "You're right. Truth is, I didn't have any good reason. I felt frustrated, and thought maybe it would help."

"You need to take better care of yourself, Chevy."

Or find someone to take care of you.

I VOLUNTEER AS TRIBUTE!

"And who's taking care of you, Tiny?"

Unless I'm reading this wrong—*please don't let me be reading it wrong!*—it feels almost like Chevy is offering to take care of me. Or hinting at an offer. I have to be imagining this. Hearing what I'd LIKE to hear. Feeling what I WANT to feel.

Needing more oxygen for my poor, overwrought brain cells, I lean back. But not enough. Because now Chevy and I are definitely standing closer than two friends usually stand. And yet ... neither one of us moves. Suddenly, that image from earlier of Chevy at the end of his date comes to mind. Only, now, I'm the one standing in kissing range. I'm the one he's staring at.

Why doesn't he step back?

Why don't I?

In years of crushing on this man, we've never, not one time ever, had a moment like this. One where the atmosphere between us is practically alive, where it feels like the precursor to something else. If I had the choice, this moment wouldn't be happening in CVS.

BUT I WILL TAKE WHAT I AM GIVEN, and this moment is going to fuel my daydreams for months. Maybe for life.

Or, at least, until I find a man I like more than Chevy who actually returns my feelings.

Unless ...

Unless *nothing*. Chevy doesn't feel like this about me. He's just standing here because I'm fixing up his hand. Because I'm here. Because ...

Because ...

Because ...

I swallow hard, forcing myself to focus on the conversation we're having. I grab that thread like it's a lifeline and try to hoist myself out of the quicksand. "I take care of myself."

"You sure do."

I need somewhere to look other than Chevy's blue eyes. His hand! I drop my gaze, turning his hand over in mine, examining the bandages. They look adorably ridiculous—child's bandages on his big hand.

"Tiny? Are you okay?"

I meet his gaze again, drawn by the concern in his voice. His eyes are intently focused on me, sending a ribbon of desire rippling through me. "I'm okay."

"Good. That's—good."

He licks his lips, and I am SO proud of myself for not glancing down at his mouth. But then he tucks a strand of hair behind my ear. His fingertips glide over my cheek, my ear, my jaw. I am UNDONE.

"If you need anything, anything at all, I'm here for you, Tiny. Always."

Anything like ... a marriage proposal? A kiss to ruin me for all other kisses?

It's honestly depressing how desperate this one encounter has made me. Chevy gives me a tiny shred of attention and some mild flirtation, and I'm ready to elope.

"I know. You're one of the good ones, Chev."

I swear, this moment feels like a kissing moment. Normally, I'm fully aware how one-sided the attraction is. Me—pining after Chevy. Me—thinking about what it would be like to be his. Me—wondering how soft his lips would be and if his perpetual five o'clock shadow would leave me with beard burn.

But this moment? It does NOT feel one way. Even as the thought crosses my mind, Chevy's gaze drops to my lips.

My neurons are firing with the frantic energy of children at a birthday when the piñata finally breaks.

"Val!"

Lindy's voice is more than a bucket of ice water dumped over my head. It's like being dropped into the Arctic Ocean. I jump back from Chevy, grateful it's Lindy, not Winnie, standing there impatiently.

"We're gonna be late," she says. "Come on."

I take off without looking back, not even when Chevy calls, "Thanks for fixing me up, Dr. Tiny."

His words make me think about playing doctor, which is NOT where my thoughts need to be. Especially as Lindy yanks me aside before we reach Winnie's car.

"What was *that*?" she hisses.

I can't answer, because honestly, I have NO idea.

CHAPTER 4

Chevy

"Do you think I have a weak chin?"

Patrick Graham asks this absurd question with a completely straight face, and I do my very best not to punch him right on the chin in question. I think I've done enough punching for the night.

After driving back from CVS with a lot of unanswered questions swirling in my head (Namely: who's pregnant? And: what the HECK was that moment between Val and me?), I met up with the Graham brothers to provide a much-needed distraction from the weirdness of my week.

It's mostly working. We're hanging out at Pat's newly renovated house while his daughter, Jo, sleeps upstairs. If anyone has noticed me being quieter than usual, no one has said a word.

"Your chin could launch a thousand ships, Patty," I say, and his oldest brother, James, snorts.

It's true, though. His whole jaw is, in fact, what a romance novel would describe as "able to cut glass." I know this because my sister, Winnie, left her books all around my house during the (thankfully) brief time she stayed in my guest room. I picked up one—okay, *a few*—to see what all the fuss is about.

Turns out, romance novels aren't so bad. But the heroines all have a type: a man with a good, strong jaw and muscular forearms. With zero hope of ever having a six pack and a jaw that will never cut through anything at all, I'm more side character material. The funny one. The friend.

Pat puts a hand over his heart. "Aw, Chev. I should put that on a business card. Or maybe just a t-shirt."

"I don't know." Collin, the middle brother, sets his bottle down and grabs Pat's face in his hand, turning it left and right like he's examining a horse until Pat swats him. "Some neck yoga might help."

Pat rubs a hand over his jaw. "Neck yoga?"

"Or face yoga?" Collin frowns and pulls out his phone. "I forget what it's called, but I saw it on an Instagram ad."

Not one of the Grahams needs whatever *face yoga* is. All three brothers could all be cover models or romance heroes with their deadly sharp jaws (for glass cutting), broad shoulders (the better to carry you with, my dear), and muscles that look like they were ordered straight from a catalog (in size Extra Large and Extra Cut). Even their dad, who is in his fifties, still looks this way. It's genetic superiority at its finest.

And because Tank, Collin, and Pat played pro football and were wise with their finances, they're loaded. Which is why they're here at all—Tank purchased Sheet Cake, Texas, treating the revitalization of our town like some kind of HGTV special.

If the Grahams weren't such decent guys, I'd hate them all. Instead, I decided to adopt myself into their family. If you can't beat them, better attach yourself to 'em like a tick.

"No." James scowls at Pat and Collin. "No face yoga."

"You say no to everything." Pat leans closer so he can look at Collin's phone.

"No is your favorite word," Collin adds.

Pat chuckles. "It's your theme song."

"Your brand promise."

"Your aura."

James meets my eyes, looking ninety-five percent exasperated and five percent amused.

I shrug. "I'd say it's more like the basis of your molecular composition. But it works for you, buddy."

At least, it did with my sister. And in an extreme opposites-attract bromance, James is the brother I've become closest to. Which mostly has to do with the fact he's dating Winnie. They say to keep your friends close and your enemies closer, but a more practical modern application is to keep your friends close and your sister's boyfriend closer.

At first, it was to make sure he was treating Winnie right. Then, when I realized how completely *gone* James is for her, I relaxed and began to enjoy his particular brand of grumpy. The man may be a slab of granite (both physically and in his personality), but he's a gooey, toasted marshmallow for my sister. I find it endlessly amusing.

Also, knowing Winnie was able to move past the issues I'm still stuck behind, that she's really giving this love thing a go—well, I wouldn't say it gives me hope, exactly, but it makes me feel less defeated.

"No one is buying *face yoga* from an Instagram ad." James

says this like he's talking about purchasing a vial of the Ebola virus from a back alley.

Pat's eyes take on a gleam I've come to know well. "Try and stop me."

"This article says it stimulates your lymphatic system," Collin says, continuing to scroll. "That's science, James. And it can improve the structural appearance of your face. I'll split the cost with you, Patty. We can share an account. Like Netflix."

"You're both idiots." James shakes his head and takes a sip of his beer.

I find myself trailing a finger over the bandages on my knuckles. I told Val I'd trade them out for a more masculine option, but the truth is, I kind of like them. They remind me of her.

"What happened?" James asks, nodding toward my hand.

What DID happen? To be honest, I'm not sure I could answer if I wanted to.

Ever since yesterday, Mrs. Fleming's words and Mari's words have been ringing in my ears. The comparison to my father. The question of my happiness. The accusation that I'm fighting ghosts.

I don't say any of that, though I suspect James would relate to the wall-punching.

"Occupational hazard," I tell him.

"Did you pick out the bandages yourself?"

I channel my inner hand model and twirl my wrist so he can see all the angles. "You like? I've got the box in my Mustang if you need one."

He only grunts as Pat and Collin argue loudly about which level of program they should buy. Because apparently, they're doing this.

I lean closer to James. "Do you think this is better or

worse than whatever the ladies are discussing at their book club?"

James scoffs. "I'd rather be a fly on the wall there. Because I'm pretty sure they don't discuss books."

"What do you think they *do* talk about?" I've always wondered.

Our mother was a member of the LLLS, and Winnie took her spot after Mom died. Neither one ever said a word about what happens in one of the meetings.

It's got to beat a discussion about face yoga and weak chins.

"No idea," James says. "I heard Mari whispering about some kind of big news when I was picking up lunch at the diner."

I try to keep my expression level. Big news? Like ... *pregnancy* big?

"We could crash the meeting," I suggest casually.

James raises one dark eyebrow. "Yeah?"

I tilt my head toward Pat and Collin. "It's got to be more riveting than this conversation."

Which is true. But also ... I need answers. Less about what goes on in Sheet Cake's secretive "book" club and more about Mari's big secret. Especially if it involves Val.

I also need a different kind of answer. I need to know what was up with the fireworks between Val and me that practically blew the roof off the CVS. Who even has a *moment* in CVS?

Maybe I imagined it, the harsh fluorescent lights triggering some kind of meltdown in my brain. Because I've never allowed whatever unnamed thing simmers under the surface where Val is concerned to come up for air. Not until tonight.

I haven't allowed myself to think about Val as anything

other than Winnie's friend. I don't think about how being around Val feels like being wrapped in a soft scarf made of sunshine. I don't consider how beautiful she looks when she laughs, which is often and loudly. I've barely noticed how amazing it is that she can look so good wearing paint-splattered Dickie's coveralls.

Okay, so maybe I have thought about all these things. But I have a special and impenetrable steel vault in my mind where they live.

I've certainly never stood as close to her as I did tonight, let her touch me the way she did while bandaging my hand. Not once have I been flirty or leaned close to whisper in her ear, relishing in her visible reaction to my closeness.

So ... yeah. I'm pretty desperate to see her again. Not because I plan to continue whatever THAT was. Nope. That is a Bad Idea and is Never Gonna Happen.

My brain and my body need a factory reset to my default position. They need to be reminded that I can't have those kinds of thoughts about Val. Winnie's threats aside, Val is the kind of woman who deserves a good guy willing to put a ring on it. Considering I don't plan on getting married, oh, *EVER*, thanks to my deep-seated Daddy issues, Val shouldn't be on my mind. She can't.

Especially not if there's any truth to what people keep telling me, that I'm just like my dad.

"You know," I tell James, setting down my beer, "I have a key to the back entrance of the library."

He offers me a rare grin. A wicked one. "Officer Boyd, I'm shocked. You're not so law-abiding, after all?"

I shrug. "I'm a public servant; it's a public library. Seems okay to me."

"Do we take Tweedle-dee and Tweedle-dumbbell?" James tilts his head toward his brothers, who are arguing about whether to use a credit card or PayPal to sign up for their face yoga subscription.

"Pat has to stay for Jo," I say. "Plus, you think either of them could keep their mouths shut if we snuck in there?"

James snorts in response.

I stand quietly, slowly, so as not to attract attention. "Then let's get out of here while they're still figuring out how to downward dog their faces."

CHAPTER 5

Chevy

JAMES LEANS CLOSE in the darkness and whispers, "This is it, huh?"

My thoughts exactly.

The Ladies Literary and Libation Society isn't quite what I imagined. James and I came in through the upstairs fire escape door. The alarm has been broken forever, something I'll remember to address Monday morning with the fire marshal. It's unsafe, but at least it also allowed us to creep to the top of the library's landing next to the grand, curved staircase.

We're standing in the shadows, near enough to the balcony rail to look down without being seen. James conveniently chose a spot where he can see Winnie's profile, allowing me to discreetly watch Val as well.

Which sounds creepier than it is. I'm not, like, *watching*

watching, like some kind of ghoul of the library staring down from the shadows. More like, I'm a kid with a fever and Val is the thermometer that keeps telling me my fever is still there.

The fever, of course, being these uncomfortable attraction feelings which are—yep—still here. Not just CVS-related.

Okay, time for that reset, brain. Let's get with it, body. Back to the norm of pretending Val is nothing special. That the sight of her doesn't always make your blood hum like it's been electrified. That when she touched you earlier, you didn't start to feel actual feelings and …

Hang on. This reset is WAY off-track.

"A little underwhelming if you ask me," I say, my eyes on Val's hair.

There is absolutely *nothing* underwhelming about her hair, which is long and thick and the color of a good, strong coffee. Right now, she's taken it out of her trademark messy bun and is braiding it, her slender fingers moving through the strands gracefully.

Those hands put these bandages on my knuckles, I think.

My fever is RAGING. The reset is FAILING.

James shifts quietly beside me, and I rip my gaze away from Val with no small amount of effort. And only after I've let my eyes skate over the swipe of paint I saw on her cheek earlier in CVS. It's become kind of a game for me—always looking for color on her skin. Her fingertips or nails are almost always a safe bet, but I love it when I catch a swipe of blue or green on her cheek or a streak of yellow in the tips of her hair as though she leaned too far over a cup of paint.

Focus, deputy. You're here to reset those kinds of feelings, not indulge in them. Also, you need to solve the mystery of Mari's big secret and whoever is pregnant.

"I thought it would be more … " James trails off, clearly fighting for the right description.

"Exciting? Interesting?" I offer.

"Anything other than this."

The Ladies Literary and Libation Society is *not* a book club. Not a wild party either. More like … a formal committee meeting to help plan town business. With alcohol. At least, I'm guessing, based on the wide variety of flasks. Though Ashlee Belle has a whole tea set.

Also? To my total surprise, Big Mo is here. The gentle giant and cook in Mari's diner is in a quiet corner with a six-pack of root beer. It's the hardest thing he'll drink—understandably so. His wife and daughter were killed by a drunk driver years ago when he lived in Houston. Now he's a Sheet Cake staple, and apparently, the only male allowed in the LLLS by some kind of special dispensation.

"Let's take another swig and move on to the next order of business," Lynn Louise declares, banging a gavel on the circulation desk. All the women—and Big Mo—raise their flasks, tea cups, and glasses in a toast.

I'm hit with a sudden memory of my mom just months before she died. She was too sick from the cancer and chemo combo to attend, so they held a special meeting in her bedroom. Winnie pressed her ear to the door to listen, but Dad took me out in the back and we threw the football until the ladies left.

I focus my gaze and my attention back on the conversation below. And on Val, who finished braiding her hair and is now running the tips of her braid across her cheek like a paintbrush.

Why is everything she does suddenly so … so … so …

There isn't a word for the tight spiraling of my heart as I watch Val laugh at something Lindy says.

"We've resolved the feral hog problem," Lynn Louise says, and wild hogs are enough to snap my mind off Val.

"A big thank you to Kitty Bishop," says Judge Judie—who is an actual judge, but not to be confused with the one whose name ends in a Y. All the ladies raise their glasses, flasks, and cups. Big Mo raises his can of root beer.

"So, *that's* how the feral pig problem was solved," I mutter.

"I've never seen a feral pig," James says.

"They're big, mean, ugly, and will overenthusiastically aerate your yard for you," I tell him. "Y'all didn't grow up hunting, I gather?"

"Football was our sport of choice," he says. "Only football."

Down below, Val is shaking out her braid, finger-combing the long locks out again. I've never been a hair man—is there such a thing?—but Val's long locks are simply mesmerizing.

Yep. Still popping a high fever. I'm in need of aspirin and an ice bath.

I need to put Val back where she belongs—squarely in the sister's best friend box.

Why won't she go back in the box?

"Didn't you have a date tonight?" James asks, as the women below move on to discussing the Sheet Cake Festival, which is a few short weeks away.

I don't really want to get into my date. It's pretty embarrassing.

When I saw Monika, a perfectly pretty and probably very nice girl, waiting outside the restaurant, I was struck with a feeling like motion sickness. Mrs. Fleming's and Mari's words squirmed around in my head like tiny parasites, making me think about uncomfortable subjects like if my mom would really be proud of me, if I'm actually like my father and in what ways, and if I'm really fighting with ghosts.

So, like an idiot, I blurted to Monika, "I can't go to dinner with you. I'm not the man you're looking for."

It took approximately half a second for me to recognize I basically stole the line in *Star Wars* (*A New Hope*, but let's face it, everyone always calls it just *Star Wars*) where Obi Wan says, "These aren't the droids you're looking for."

I even waved my hand through the air as I said it, and realizing this made me laugh.

At which point, Monika stepped forward and whacked me in the arm with her purse. Which I probably deserved. Though according to Texas penal code twenty-two, it was technically assault.

When she stormed off, I deleted the dating app from my phone, and wandered around Sixth Street, feeling strangely restless and way older than all the college kids stumbling around from bar to bar. I'm too old for that. Too old to keep casually dating women I'm not really interested in. Wandering too far from the man I think my mama would want me to be—and I blame this thought on Mrs. Fleming and Mari. And maybe even James and Winnie with all their in-love happiness.

Whatever the root cause, a feeling of pent-up energy built and built until I slammed my knuckle into a brick wall in an alley, needing some kind of release.

Which led me to CVS.

Which led me to Val.

Which led me to my current feverish situation, where I don't understand what's going on with me as I watch Val over the balcony railing.

I definitely can't explain any of that to James Graham.

"Let's just say ... the date ended before dinner started."

He only grunts at this, but it sure as heck sounds like a grunt of disapproval. I choose to ignore it. Did I ask *him* for dating advice? I most certainly did not. From what I understand, James didn't really have relationships before Winnie, so it's not like he's in a position to give any sort of nuggets of dating wisdom or pass moral judgment on me.

He clears his throat. "I need to talk to you."

"About my dating life?"

"No." When he frowns at me, my stomach bottoms out. Because I think I know what he's going to ask—to marry my sister.

And I know what I'll say. Yes. Obviously, yes.

But the thought of my sister getting married turns me inside out. And not for the usual reasons a brother might feel that way.

No, I've got dear old Dad to thank for my hang-ups.

See, when you're just a teenager and discover the man you've always admired, the man who appeared to love your mama selflessly while she battled cancer, who was there for you after she died—that man had a whole other family in another town, some part of you dies. The part that has faith in relationships. In other people. In the institution of marriage.

The one saving grace is that Mama never knew. She died thinking he was the man I thought him to be. I kept his secrets. Not for him. But to protect Mama and my sister. In doing so, in bottling this all up, my hope in all things pertaining to romantic love soured. And knowing that I share my father's same DNA ... I'm scared to test the limits of my own ability to commit.

The idea that Winnie, who found out about all this after our dad died, is ready to take this step—well, it's huge. I'm not sure if I'm scared for her or jealous she was able to place her trust in any person. I can't even trust myself.

Or maybe she's the one who needed the pregnancy test

and this conversation is about something other than marriage.

I'm hit with a sudden pang of longing. Mama would have wanted to be here for this. Planning a wedding for Winnie—or a baby shower, depending on where this conversation goes—would have made her whole *life*.

Only ... Mama died a decade too soon to be here for it. Loss squeezes inside me like some creeping vine.

Who will do all that for Winnie? Who will help her plan and try on dresses and all that mother-daughter stuff? Maybe Lindy and Val and Mari? Heck, I'll even go with my sister to try on dresses or look at flowers.

But no one can replace having Mama.

"I'm going to ask Winnie to marry me," James says.

Even though I was expecting them, his words leave me breathless. I blink. Swallow. Blink again. My thoughts are a file cabinet that's been upended, every folder opened and every paper scattered.

"Even if your father"—he says this word with a sneer—"were still alive, you'd be the one I asked." James's jaw clenches. He's one of the select few who know all about my dad. I knew Winnie must really love James when I found out she told him the truth.

My chest still feels tight, and I hate not having an uncomplicated response to this. Like, oh, I don't know—*happiness*.

I go for humor, always my fallback. Placing a hand over my chest, I say, "Aw, Jamie. Is this your roundabout way of asking for my blessing?"

"Yes."

Only James Graham would think *telling* me he's going to propose is *asking* me for my blessing. The man is never off-brand.

"Have you got a ring?"

The look he shoots me says I'm an idiot to think *he's* that much of an idiot. He pats the pocket of his jeans. "I've had it for weeks now. Just wanted to wait to talk to you, and for the right moment."

James is more far gone for my sister than I even realized. Winnie needs a James—the kind of man who would cross continents or fight wars for her. But a man who can also be tender with a woman who pretends like she doesn't need tenderness. James is the unlikely embodiment of both.

"Our parents didn't leave us much," I confess. "So, there's no wedding money set aside. I can always help with—"

"I've got it. I would do anything for your sister. I would give her anything she wants." He meets my gaze, eyes blazing with determination. "*Anything*. Including whatever kind of wedding she wants."

The man's intensity would give the sun's heat a run for its money. I let my gaze slide away from him, suddenly struck with a deep sadness and an itchy longing I could do without.

I can't relate to what James just said. I've never felt anything like what he does for Winnie. Never had someone I'd do *anything* for—at least not for romantic reasons. Never believed I'm the kind of man who could be steady for someone.

I hear the faint sound of Val's laughter rising up. I shift, finding her profile, noting the bit of paint on her cheek. Just seeing it there steadies me.

"Well?" James asks.

I force down another welling-up of emotion. Winnie —*married*. It means my little sister is moving on while I'm still standing still, waving as she passes me by.

My gaze finds Val again just as she laughs at something Lindy's saying. The sight only makes that emotional heartburn in my chest and throat more painful. It's on the tip of my tongue to say yes. Of course, I approve. Of course, I'll say yes. But I can't let James get off that easily.

"I'll take it under consideration," I tell him.

I expect James to protest. Or growl. But instead, he's frowning down at the women below where the room has gone silent. "Well, there's the big news," he whispers.

I totally missed it while thinking about Winnie and marriage and trying not to have a mini panic attack. I can feel the massive shift in the atmosphere downstairs. The room has gone positively still. "What is it?"

"Sounds like Mari is moving back to Costa Rica to be with a sick aunt."

Something inside me shakes loose and falls down in the vicinity of my toes.

Mari—leaving Sheet Cake? That question is only a blip, eclipsed by immediate concern for Val. I mean, sure, Val is a grown woman. But she and her aunt are more than close— Mari is really Val's only family. Not to mention the fact that Val lives in a garage apartment above her painting studio—at Mari's house.

Where will Val live? How is she feeling about this huge change? If anything like the rest of the room, not amazing.

"When do you go?" Judge Judie demands.

"What about the diner?" someone else calls.

What about Val?

I glance her way, and she's sitting unnaturally straight, like some master puppeteer has an iron grip on her strings. Even from the side profile I'm getting, Lindy and Winnie are staring with a mix of shock and outrage.

So this is news not even *they* knew. I thought the three musketeers shared everything with each other.

Like who's pregnant. I push that thought out of my mind. I can only take so much right now. This whole week feels like a fleet of Mack trucks have unloaded their shipments and left the contents strewn all over what *was* my completely neat and organized life.

"I'll be leaving next week," Mari says, and there is a gasp worthy of an afternoon soap opera. "Big Mo is taking over the diner, and the new owners will close on my house in a few days."

"What about you, Valentina?" Eula Morgan asks, her long nails looking especially witchy as they clink against her wine glass. "Are you going with her?"

Of *course* she's not going. Val—going to Costa Rica? No way.

But when Val doesn't answer right away, all the breath in my lungs evaporates. Actually, *evaporation* is too gentle of a word. It's more like a cement block dropped from the top of a building landed on my chest and crushed my lungs completely.

She wouldn't leave Sheet Cake. Would she? I mean, Costa Rica was Mari's home, so it makes sense she'd return at some point. But Val has never been there. Her friends are here. Her life is here.

I'm here, I find myself thinking desperately, like I have any right at all to consider my role in Val's choices.

"That's the plan," Val says, finally.

Pain shoots through my knuckles as I clench my fists at my sides. THAT's the plan? That's the PLAN?

That isn't a plan. It's a disaster. It's a mistake.

"Not right away," Val adds quickly. "In a month, maybe? I haven't bought my ticket yet, so …"

I'm having one of those moments where time seems to bend. Like my life is a movie where the special effects are moving things in and out of focus, speeding up and slowing down. I step back, leaning against a bookshelf, needing to feel something solid to ground me.

Tiny is moving? To *Costa Rica?* In a *month?* For how long? Why?

All the emotional things I've been trying to deal with tonight return with a vengeance. It doesn't make much sense why I'm reacting this way.

Get control of yourself. Val is a friend, I remind myself. *Friends can come and go as they please. You give your friend a handshake and a slap on their back and wish them well.*

So why isn't my body having an appropriate friend-like response?

"What are you gonna do about it?" James asks, his voice low.

I jolt. I'd forgotten he was there. "Me? Do about what?"

"Val."

"Why would I do anything?" I scoff, and when he glances over, I don't like the look on his face. It seems to indicate he sees my struggle. Like he *knows* the warring thoughts in my head right now.

But that's impossible, because I don't even know what I'm feeling or why. Not a chance James Graham knows me better than I know myself.

Unless you're drowning in a big, ol' vat of denial and James is holding out a hand to pull you out.

"You just look like you *want* to do something," he says.

"It's not my business what Val does with her life," I tell him, not knowing how much of a lie it is until I taste it on my tongue.

Without another word, I push my way through the emergency exit, not bothering to wait for James to follow.

CHAPTER 6

Val

TRUE BEST FRIENDS are your Rick Astleys—they're never gonna give you up, let you down, or desert you. (Or however the song goes.)

ANYWAY. I'm reminding myself I should be grateful for Rick Astley friendship as Winnie forcibly drags me down the small alley next to the library. The flip side of the tenacious faithfulness of true best friends is that when you keep a giant secret—like plans to leave the country, for example—real best friends aren't going to let that drop. Oh, no. They're going to be all over that. Or, in my case, they're going to drag me down an alley.

Winnie is breathing hard. So hard, in fact, that her nostrils are flaring.

Normally, angry Winnie scares me. But somehow, the flaring of her perfect little nose makes me want to smile.

51

I hold it in though. Because I might not survive if Winnie sees me smiling right now.

For the remainder of the LLLS meeting after Mari and I dropped our respective bombs, Lindy and Winnie didn't say a word about Mari's announcement. Or anything else. They didn't meet my eyes. They barely moved a muscle. Which had the effect of making me sweaty and panicked.

It was like having the *Jaws* theme song playing on repeat in my head for half an hour.

Now, though, the ominous music is reaching its crescendo, and I think I'm gonna need a bigger boat.

Winnie stops suddenly and spins to face me. But it's Lindy who speaks first, standing hip to hip with Winnie, the two of them like a furious little firing squad. I feel a chill, one much deeper than the mild January cool.

"You're moving to Costa Rica?! How? Why? When?" Lindy demands.

Winnie doesn't wait for me to respond before piling on. "And you didn't tell us?!" She glares through her glasses so hard I half expect tiny holes to burn through my shirt. "Who does that?"

I do, I guess. And I really and truly feel horrible about it but saying that now won't make my friends feel any better.

When it comes to talking about big life changes or things that scare me, I'm a cartoon ostrich. I jam my head into the sand and stay still, hoping it passes.

Which ... didn't quite work in this situation. Because ostriching is not a healthy or practical coping skill.

It's like the time as a kid we played hide and seek with a bunch of kids at a birthday party. I crammed my tiny body into the cabinet under a bathroom sink and pulled a storage basket of towels in front of me. (Hide and seek is one of the places where being petite really comes in handy.)

The nervous twisting in my belly as I waited to be found gave birth to a shaky and overpowering anxiety, and I stayed hidden for four hours. The police *might* have been called.

To be clear: I learned no lessons that day, and my current situation is a prime example of this.

"I know. I know," I finally say. "I should have told you."

They wait, but my tongue feels thick. Maybe I'm having an allergic reaction to something? But because of the last-minute trip to CVS, we skipped dinner, so it wasn't something I ate.

Is it possible to be allergic to the truth?

Winnie scoffs. "That's it? You're not even going to make excuses?"

"Would any excuses be enough?"

"No," they say in unison.

"How long have you been lying your cute little butt off to us about Mari moving back to Costa Rica?" Winnie asks.

I sigh. "First, my butt is *not* little. My butt could take either of your butts in a butt battle."

"Anytime, sister," Winnie says, looking like she'd happily take the challenge right now. "Any. Time."

"Why would we be having a butt battle?" Lindy asks. "What even *is* a butt battle?"

Winnie and I both ignore the question. "Second, I've only known for a few weeks." A month, really, but *few* is a vague term. "Mari made me promise not to tell anyone. You know how this town is."

"I'm pretty sure she assumed you'd tell the two of us," Winnie says.

She probably did. But every time I thought about telling Lindy and Winnie, every time I opened my mouth to spill, I heard a whooshing noise in my head, like ten thousand birds were taking flight at once between my ears. My pulse would race and my throat would feel like it was closing up. Not unlike how I feel now.

"But why would you go?" Winnie demands. "I understand Mari going back home, especially if her aunt is sick. But what's there for *you* in Costa Rica?"

It's a good question. But another good question is: What's there for me *here*?

Why would I *stay*?

I don't voice the questions that have been pinging around my brain for weeks like a little kid hopped up on caffeinated cupcakes. It would offend my two best friends to voice it.

Because *they're* here. *They* matter.

But *they* also have Pat and James. They have solid relationships hustling them toward the next season of life—especially if Lindy's pregnant. (She hasn't had time to take the test yet.) And even though we're still best friends, things shift when people get into serious relationships. It's the circle of life—only instead of getting trampled by wildebeests, it's the slow and steady march of time stomping on your heart as friendships shift.

No matter how many guys I've tried to give my heart to, they always give it back. Usually a little beaten up, a little more worn-down. I cannot seem to make a relationship work.

My friends are headed toward spring and summer, while I'm stuck in winter with its chill air and frozen pipes. It's a winter that is very much discontent. And I see no signs of a thaw. I need a change. Something to get me out of my rut.

"I'm going to meet family I've never met. And Mari found an artist who agreed to mentor me. Nothing here has really been working out, career-wise. This seems like a solid move, to learn from someone who's painting full-time."

My friends have no rebuttal for this one. It's no secret

that my painting career is more of a hobby at this point, at least in terms of the financial return. It's the only thing I want to do. But I wasn't quite prepared for how difficult it is to sell my work.

Painting—I can do. Marketing, selling, and promoting my paintings—not in my wheelhouse.

My work is abstract, mostly focused on color and movement. Not like one giant black dot on an otherwise white canvas that looks like a toddler could do it. There's texture and color and, because I work in acrylic, it dries quickly, layer upon layer.

My boss, Mr. Silver, on the other hand, seems to think my paintings do look like a toddler painted them. He refused to hang them in his gallery and, as a way of throwing me a bone that had been filed down to a fine point, he hired me. I was just desperate enough to say yes while waiting to have divine inspiration on how to sell my work. I mean, delivering for Door Dash wasn't taking my art career anywhere.

But I hate myself for it a little more, every time I walk into the gallery on Main Street.

Having a full-time artist mentor me is an opportunity I can't pass up. Even if it means moving temporarily to another country. Tank's offer was generous and amazing, but it's also not the kind of thing I can expect to happen again. I mean, it's not every day you happen to have a connection to a multi-millionaire who needs a bunch of paintings for his many properties. I need to learn how to do this for real. And I'm smart enough to know I need help.

"I just feel ... stuck," I confess. "I'm not doing what I want with my art. I'm not seeing anyone seriously like y'all are. I need a change or a break in my life, personally and professionally."

Lindy just blinks at me, her mouth hanging open. "You're really doing this," she whispers.

"I am."

So why does the idea of leaving fill me with dread instead of excitement?

I can't think of real, solid reasons NOT to go, so why shouldn't I take this opportunity?

Chevy's face flashes in my mind, and I refuse to acknowledge it. My giant unrequited crush on my best friend's brother is definitely *not* a reason to stay in Sheet Cake. Because, as I said, it's unrequited.

Louder for the people in back: UNREQUITED.

No matter what transpired in CVS earlier. I'm sure what felt like a MOMENT was just more one-sided hopeful pining on my part.

Only—it felt like something more.

Not enough MORE to change my plans. In fact, Chevy is all the more reason to go. Maybe all that time and distance will help me get over him. Finally.

"How long will you stay?" Lindy asks, sniffling. Winnie pulls a tissue out of her purse and hands it over.

"My visa is for a year. But I don't have to stay that long," I add quickly.

This statement is met with an eerie kind of silence. One that makes my stomach tighten into a knot.

"A year?" Winnie's voice is barely a whisper.

"I'll probably come back sooner."

Maybe? I honestly have no idea because I still can't imagine leaving. Or living in a foreign country, even if I'm with Mari, who feels more like home than anywhere I've lived.

"If Mari's leaving next week, where are you going to live?" Lindy asks.

I glance at Winnie. "I was hoping your guest room?"

Her face falls. "Kyoko's moving in tomorrow."

"We've got space," Lindy says, and Winnie and I exchange a glance.

Because their level of PDA when Jo isn't looking is disgusting. Enough to make my ovaries shrivel up and die right inside my body.

"I'll figure it out," I say. *I hope.*

Without warning, Winnie throws her arms around me. Lindy embraces me from behind, forming a friend sandwich. I sigh, snuggling into them as I reach one arm awkwardly around Lindy behind me and the other around Winnie's waist. The relief is immediate.

"I'm sorry." I wish I didn't have the wobbly, about-to-cry voice, but I totally do.

"I'm sorry too," Lindy says.

"Why are *you* sorry?" Winnie asks.

"I'm sorry because I don't want her to go—even if it's a good opportunity. I'm being selfish."

"Well, I'm not sorry. I'm mad." Winnie pauses. "And sad."

"Me too," I whisper. "Or maybe just the sad part."

I can't be angry with anyone for the state of my life. Which feels like it's the shape of a giant question mark. Or maybe one of those infinity symbols, which leaves me walking in a boring circle.

"Why are y'all hugging in a dark alley?"

It's the second time tonight the three of us have been startled by a man's voice. Right now, I don't have anything to even throw. Lindy gives a little shriek, but Winnie sighs and steps away, ending our hug sandwich.

"James—why are *you* in the alley?" she asks.

"I was walking back to the loft. Heard shouting," he says.

"It wasn't shouting," Winnie clarifies. "More of a discussion."

James raises one dark eyebrow but says nothing. I can almost hear him thinking, *A discussion … with shouting.*

"Sounded like fighting to me," another voice says, this one making the little hairs on my arms stand up and my heart falter before picking up speed. Chevy joins James at the entrance to the alley, leaning on the brick wall.

"You," Winnie says. "Now I *really* think you're following us."

"Nope," Chevy says. "Just a small world … after all."

Winnie groans, but I grin at his cheesy joke. I happen to love cheese. As a food and as a style of joking, in movies, and in emotional moments with my besties. I'm all about the Velveeta everything.

Heartstring tugging greeting cards? Here for it.

Arguably emotionally manipulative commercials with sad dogs in the pound? Weirdly, yes. I love them. (And though I don't want a dog, I donate every time I see one of these commercials.)

Ridiculously cheesy and predictable Hallmark movies where you hold your breath for the kiss in the final two minutes? Give them all to me!

Chevy's sense of humor? Absolutely.

I study his face as much as I can without looking obvious, searching for any sign that something's different. A sign that maybe I *didn't* imagine the flirtation earlier. That maybe the tension between us *wasn't* imaginary or only one way.

But Chevy only smiles the same easy smile that's made my knees weak for years. The same one he gives his sister. And Mari. And just about everyone he meets.

Disappointment sours my mood. But only a little.

Because even if it's not a special smile for only me, it's a *Chevy* smile. My very favorite in the world.

"Can we maybe exit this alley?" he asks. "Not like it's a safety concern here or anything, but it kind of smells like pee."

Now that he mentions it...

The five of us reconvene on the sidewalk not a moment before Pat's truck screeches up to the curb. He hops out, making a beeline for Lindy.

"Who's with Jo?" she asks.

"Still safely asleep. Collin's still there," Pat says before planting a non-Hallmark appropriate kiss on Lindy's mouth.

I'm grateful at least ONE of my friends isn't into PDA. Winnie and James tend to keep their kissing under wraps. Which really means in the storage closet at Dark Horse Brewery. I unfortunately discovered the hard way a few weeks ago.

"I wanted to find out where these two jokers snuck off to," Pat says, giving James and Chevy a look. Neither one offers up why they left or why they're here. "But I found something better. You ready to go home, darlin'?"

"Wait," Winnie says. "Give us a second, boys."

James and Pat retreat a few paces down the sidewalk while Winnie pulls the three of us in, our hands clasped and foreheads touching. It's something we've done forever. I like to think of it as our head huddle, but I never say that out loud because it sounds dumb.

"We're all gonna be fine," Lindy says, but she's sniffling. I feel her trembling next to me, and I give her hand an extra squeeze.

Neither Winnie nor I respond, but we don't move for a solid minute, just staying connected for a few moments longer. I try to commit it all to memory—the feel of their hands in mine, their smells, the feeling of security and safety with my best friends.

You really want to leave this? The voice in my mind sounds like Winnie.

I don't answer it. I don't argue. I just hug my friends and try not to think about saying goodbye. About next steps. About change. About being left behind, even though technically, I'm the one leaving.

And I definitely try not to think about the man a few feet away who's definitely *not* thinking about me.

Winnie lowers her voice. "Lindy, you still need to take that pregnancy test."

"Byeeee," Lindy calls, breaking out of our embrace and booking it to Pat's truck as fast as her cowboy boots will take her.

Maybe I'm not the only ostrich.

Pat must take Lindy's hurry to mean she's VERY excited to get home for reasons I'd rather not think about, because he grins and sprints around to the driver's side, calling, "See ya!"

And then there were four.

"I'll walk you home?" James asks Winnie, and it's pretty adorable to see the giant, gruff man ask such a sweet question.

Winnie's newly completed loft is a few blocks away, basically across the street from the loft James shares with his dad, who splits his time between Sheet Cake and Austin. She told me that they sometimes walk each other home, back and forth to each other's lofts, for half an hour.

They're stupidly, disgustingly, wonderfully adorable.

Is it too much to ask for a guy who will be stupidly adorable with me?

My eyes cut to Chevy because they're gluttons for punishment. I expect him to be looking at James and Winnie too, but his brown eyes are on me. He blinks like I've startled him and looks away.

Winnie pokes me in the arm, giving me a look that's less lovey-dovey and more Arnold Schwarzenegger's I'll-be-back. "As for *you*—we'll talk later."

Winnie and James are barely out of earshot when Chevy whispers. "Yikes."

Yikes is right.

"Can I walk you to your car?" Chevy asks. "After all, I've got to help maintain the safety of the town."

Sheet Cake is about the safest place you could walk to a car alone. But I'm not about to argue with the man. In fact, I'll happily pretend to be terrified of my own shadow if it means Chevy walking me to my car.

Until I remember: Winnie picked up Lindy and me and planned to take us home.

And then forgot all about me because she got distracted by her boyfriend. *Awesome.* Never mind that I didn't even remember until just now. It doesn't ease the sting of being forgotten.

"Actually ... could I trouble you for a ride home?"

"Of course," Chevy says with an easy grin.

I'm feeling suddenly and strangely shy. "You really don't mind?"

With a wink that floods my entire system with instant dopamine, Chevy's smile widens and his dang dimples appear. "I'll even let you pick the music."

CHAPTER 7

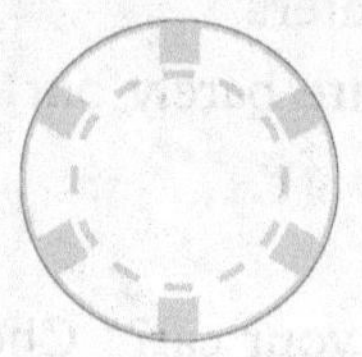

Val

In Chevy's Mustang, I opt for silence, not music. I need some quiet to settle my overwhelm. Lindy might be pregnant. My friends now know I'm leaving. And then the flirtation with Chevy at CVS.

Maybe that's why the silence between us feels loud. Not settling. Chevy keeps shifting in his seat, and every so often, I feel the heat of his gaze land on me. Meanwhile, I'm over here trying not to *audibly* sniff so he won't notice me committing the smell of his leather seats—and of *him*—to memory.

Lately, I've been adding extra emotional weight to every little thing. Making note of the last time I'll drive around that pothole on Cane Street. The last time I'll have one of Big Mo's egg sandwiches with perfectly ripened tomatoes. The last time I'll feel a flutter in my belly when Chevy aims his dimpled smile in my general vicinity.

The last time I'll ride in his passenger seat, his presence sucking up all the air between us.

"What?" I ask, when I catch Chevy sneaking another glance my way.

"I just keep waiting for you to blast some kind of terrible music to annoy me."

He's not wrong to expect this. In high school, his dad forced him to give Winnie, Lindy, and me rides to school in the old truck Chevy still sometimes drives. He'd blast country—classic country, he'd point out, like it matters— and sing along loudly and off-key. Whichever of us was closer to the radio would switch it to the pop station to get him riled up by the tinny, catchy beat from a boy band.

It's a familiar game. But I'm not in the mood for games tonight.

"I thought some quiet would be nice," I tell him.

A thoughtful hum is his only response, and I want to yank him by his shirt collar and ask him what that sound means. But I don't.

"My head is too loud lately," I say instead. Then I wish I'd kept my mouth shut because what a thing to say!

But Chevy doesn't laugh or give me a weird look at this confession. He says nothing, though his hands flex. Knowing he carefully and lovingly restored this Mustang makes his big, strong hands on the steering wheel sexier. Even with the bandages.

Especially with the bandages. I can't help smiling, which Chevy of course notices.

He wiggles the fingers on his right hand. "You know I'm gonna take these off the second I get home in favor of a more studly option?"

I laugh. "Do they make studly bandages?"

"Maybe Old Spice got into the first-aid game, and I've got a Kraken first aid kit to match my Kraken deodorant."

"You wear Kraken deodorant? What does a Kraken even smell like?"

And before I think twice about it and realize how supremely STUPID this is, I lean my face over to Chevy's armpit and take a big sniff.

Mistake. Big mistake!

Not because it smells BAD—in fact, sea monster plus Chevy is now my all-time favorite scent—but because once I realize how weird I'm being, I freeze. Right here with my nose in his armpit.

Retreat is the logical option. But I'm not always logical.

And now, knowing my cheeks are going to be a dying of embarrassment red, I can't make myself move. I am COMMITTED.

"Uh." Chevy shifts, and I know he's glancing down at me, though I don't look up. I CAN'T look up. "Are you ... sniffing my pits?"

"Pit. Singular."

Because yes—let's debate semantics rather than my ridiculous behavior.

As casually as I can, I sit up, moving back over to my side of the car. To hide my blush, I take my hair down, feigning a casual refresh of my messy bun, when what I'm really doing is using a hair curtain to hide my embarrassment. Never have I been so grateful for my long locks.

I just ... smelled Chevy's armpit.

This has to be a violation of at least nineteen friendship codes and best friend's older brother codes and not revealing your crush codes and maybe even *health* codes.

Also, now I'm going to fall asleep dreaming of his scent.

Old Spice, you've got this thing on lock. *Props to you.*

"It's been a long day, and I can't vouch for my level of freshness," Chevy says.

Oh! Maybe he's embarrassed thinking he smelled bad rather than uncomfortable because I just got all up and close with his armpit.

"You smell great. I mean, your deodorant smells great. On you," I say, wishing I could hit the restart on my brain, which has obviously forgotten how to function. But this is more like one of those fasten-your-seatbelts kind of moments, because my idiocy shows no signs of slowing. "It's no wonder Old spice has a corner on the man market."

He makes a choking sound, which turns into a laugh. "The … man market?"

"You know what I mean." Laughing, I swat Chevy's arm, not realizing how flirtatious my words and actions are coming out until he shoots me a surprised look, which quickly shifts to a smile and a wink.

I'm sure glad Chevy is driving and can't look at me for too long. A few more seconds of that smile aimed my way, and I'd be doing something even more embarrassing.

Like leaning over to kiss him.

Which would be stupid—not to mention unsafe while he's driving. Safety first!

Not like I would do it when he's *not* driving. I'm not the kiss first, ask questions later kind of person.

But I'd *think* about kissing him. I *am* thinking about it. In fact, ever since the summer I turned thirteen, I've had kissing thoughts about Chevy. Fantasy thoughts, obviously, and ones of the PG variety.

Maybe *slightly* PG-13. There's a lot of room for good kissing in the PG-13 area. But anything more and I'd spontaneously combust right on the spot, leaving nothing behind but a scorch mark to remember me by.

I jump when Chevy touches my arm. "You okay over there, Tiny? I can practically hear your thoughts whirring like helicopter blades."

He does NOT need to know about my thoughts. "Nope. All good over here. What's on *your* mind, officer?"

This earns me another grin. The kind that makes unwanted things swoop in my belly. *Die, swooping things, die!*

"Many things," he says, and is it just me, or does this sound flirty?

No—it's probably *teasing*. There is a subtle but important distinction. One I'd do well to remember.

Chevy and I tease. We do not flirt. He calls me Tiny; I joke with him. It's the quintessential little sister's best friend routine. Anything more is just a product of my poor, over-wrought brain.

"Enlighten me," I say. "What are some of the many things on your mind?"

He's quiet for a few long moments. So quiet that I turn in my seat to face him. His jaw flexes. His gaze shifts from the road to his bandaged knuckles and back to the road again. Has he already heard about Mari and me leaving? I thought it would at least take half an hour after the meeting for word to spread.

"It's not my business," he says cautiously, and NO good conversation starts this way, "but did y'all drive all the way to Austin to buy a pregnancy test?"

Ohhhhh—*that*. "You saw the box, huh?"

"Hard to miss," he says. "You threw it at my face."

I force out a laugh. "Sorry. It was a reflex."

Chevy looks my way for a quick moment. His blue eyes make me feel all giddy, despite the topic at hand. "So?" he prompts, reminding me that I didn't answer his question.

I definitely *can't* answer him. It's not my secret to tell.

And until Lindy takes the darn test, I won't know if there's a secret at all.

"You're right," I tell him, as kindly as I can. "It's not your business." I also don't want Chevy to think I'm the pregnant one, but I also don't want to drop any clues to who might be.

"You're still with mullet guy?" he asks after a long pause.

"Jaxon doesn't have a mullet." I'm not sure why I'm arguing when I know I'm wrong.

"He does."

"He's just … overdue for a trim in the back."

"Mullet," Chevy declares.

"I didn't realize you were paying such close attention to my dating life," I say. Honestly, I'm *thrilled* at the mere idea that he might be keeping tabs on me. Even if it's for protective friend-of-his-sister reasons.

"Hard not to when you're dating a guy with a mullet."

"I'm not. Dating him. I mean, technically, I broke up with him."

"Technically? But not, like, actually or officially?"

"I told him I wanted to break up. I'm just not sure he heard me. So I'm going to tell him again and make sure it sticks."

Chevy chuckles. "Make sure to use small words so he'll understand."

"How about you? Your date sure ended early tonight. What's that about? Was her skirt not short enough for you?"

Okay, that was WAY over the line. It was downright mean —to Chevy and to whatever woman I just basically slut shamed. *Sorry, lady. I'm sure your skirt was just fine.*

His eyebrows shoot up. "Wow. That's …"

"Rude." I pause. "But it's also kind of accurate."

Shut up, mouth! You have exceeded your quota of embarrassing words today!

Mouth doesn't listen. It doubles down. "It's just, you know, you have a type."

"You only *think* I have a type."

"I *know* you do." I count on my fingers as I keep saying stupid words. "Heavy makeup. Revealing clothing. Fan of giggling, wine spritzers, and puppies."

"What's wrong with puppies?"

"Nothing!" I shout. My voice is VERY loud in the fairly small interior of the car. My feelings, though, are even LOUDER. And they're getting harder to shut up or shut down.

"Maybe they're also brilliant conversationalists," Chevy says lightly, but I don't miss the way he's rubbing the back of his neck.

"Are they?"

"Nope."

"Then why? Why do you only date that kind of woman? All this casual dating just doesn't seem like you."

Now I've moved from simple stupidity to downright boldness. I'm circling very close to revealing the truth of my feelings. I best tread very carefully, unless I want to go full-on confession here. Which I don't.

"I don't think it is me," Chevy says, his voice tight. "And I don't think I'm gonna keep casually dating the kind of women I'd only ever want to casually date."

My brain backs up with a traffic jam of questions.

If it's not him, why did he do it? And if he's not going to keep dating casually, what does that mean? If the kind of woman he's always dated isn't his type what is?

Could Chevrolet Boyd actually be ready to settle down?

And would he consider doing so with me?

You're about to leave the country for the foreseeable future, I remind myself. *Don't get your hopes up.*

It's just my luck that Chevy decides to change his dating policy right when I'm set to move away in hopes of moving on.

"Tiny."

He's suddenly serious, and when he reaches across to put a hand on my knee, I freeze. Any movement might scare him off, and that's the last thing I want. I love the weight of his hand on me a little too much. Even if I know it still means nothing. The sweetness in his voice weakens any resolve I have.

"You'd tell me if you weren't okay," he says. "You know you could come to me if you needed help?"

I have to swallow past what feels like a boulder in my throat. Stupid feelings! Choking me up at an inopportune moment like always.

"I know," I say quietly. I *know* he'd be here for me. I just wish it were for the reasons I want.

Unless … something really is shifting between us. Because his hand is still on my knee. He drives the rest of the way home with his palm on my kneecap, fingers lightly curled. And I do my best not to explode with longing or wondering if it means something.

When he pulls up in front of my garage apartment at Mari's, he gives my knee a single squeeze before dropping his hand.

I hop out of his car, then turn back, leaning down to give him one last look.

"Goodnight, Tiny," he says with a slow smile, showcasing his dimples.

And I'm totally blaming those dimples for this. "I shouldn't say anything, but I know you won't stop thinking about it until you know. I wasn't the one buying the pregnancy test," I confess. "Neither was your sister. But if you mention anything to anyone, I'll ... I'll ..."

His smile melts into an earnest expression, tugging at something in my chest. "Thank you for trusting me. For what it's worth, I trust you too."

And with those words washing over me, I slam the car door and dart for my studio so I can release all my big feelings by way of paint and canvas.

CHAPTER 8

Chevy

I WISH I'd thought to take a picture of Grant's face when I walk him into Wolf's bar for the first time.

Suffice it to say, the newest deputy and recent transplant to Sheet Cake was shocked first. Thrilled second. His big brown eyes wide with wonder like a little league kid walking into a pro baseball stadium to watch their favorite team.

Backwoods Bar is little more than a metal shed in the middle of a field where Wolf Waters slings beer and Sheeters enjoy drinks, conversation, and dancing out back when it's not too cold. I can hear a little George Strait trickling in even now. The bar is Wolf's way of really leaning into the fact that he's the black sheep of the otherwise wealthy, snobby, and downright cantankerous Waters family.

"A secret bar is really a thing?" Grant asks, glancing around. "It's like a speakeasy."

I bark out a laugh, and Wolf makes a face. "Speakeasy—that's a little too fancy for me. Don't you need a password to get in or something? I'd never remember, then end up locked out of my own bar. What can I get you?"

Grant glances at me.

"Can you handle your spice?" I ask, raising an eyebrow.

"Yes ... but how is that a factor when we're drinking beer?"

I turn to Wolf. "Two of those Dark Horse jalapeños, if you've got 'em."

Wolf reaches into the cooler under the piece of plywood serving as bar, handing us each a dripping bottle with no label. Grant eyes it suspiciously, and I slap him on the back. "Come on." To Wolf, I say, "I'll settle up when we go. And I like the 'stache. It suits you."

Wolf rubs a hand over his mustache, which is bushy enough to make Tom Selleck proud. Maybe even jealous. I can't decide if it's a better look than the long beard Wolf used to sport or if he looks like a walrus.

Maybe, I decide, it's *both*.

Wolf's voice startles me back into the moment. "When the winds of change are blowing, brother, the best thing you can do is hoist your sails and let them carry you along."

I'd rather drop anchor and ride out the storm below deck, hoping for the best on the other side. But I don't argue, and Grant looks at Wolf like he's some kind of life coach.

"I'll take that advice into consideration."

Grant and I settle on two rickety stools around a table that's an old, oversized barrel. I hold out my beer, and he clinks the neck against mine.

"What are we drinking to?" he asks as I'm taking my first sip.

The jalapeño infused beer leaves my lips and tongue

stinging pleasantly. "Don't know," I answer honestly. Usually, I'm the one who'd have some kind of clever answer stored away, ready to fire off at any given moment.

This week, though, my brain feels thick and soupy. No thanks to the letter, the latest of half a dozen I've received lately from someone I definitely don't want to hear from. Each one is a reminder of my dad, and I could do with *less* of those.

"All right then." Grant takes a swallow—perhaps bigger than he should have considering this is jalapeño beer—and his eyes start to water. He gets it all down, then sets the bottle on our table, wiping his mouth with the back of his hand. "Wow," he says, coughing.

"You should try my sister's jalapeño vodka," I tell him. "Talk about a kick."

"And she's the one dating James Graham?"

Almost engaged *to James Graham*, I mentally correct. An idea that still leaves me unsettled.

"Yep."

"That's cool," Grant says, but the mix of awe and excitement tells me it's not just cool. He looks like he's about to wet himself.

I take another sip of beer to hide my smile. I highly suspect Grant accepted the position of deputy here because he heard the buzz about Sheet Cake. The famous Grahams buying the town and giving it new life. The movie studio who visited just a few weeks ago and plans to relocate here to film in the now picturesque downtown. Things are changing, but we're still, at heart, a very small town.

At least, the old part of Sheet Cake. The newer part with their strip malls and shiny buildings and planned communities and separate police force—the newbies are still just as much outsiders as they've ever been.

Anyway, as much as I love it here, I can't figure any other reason a person would move here from a real city. Then again, Grant's from Dallas, the city all other Texans love to hate.

As the doors creak open behind me, Grant's eyes widen. This time, I know it's not the beer. "Who's *that*?" he asks.

I turn on my stool, my stomach twisting with something like nerves as Val walks in. She's frowning at her phone, not looking where she's going, and runs right into me.

Her phone goes flying, and I reach out to steady her, my hand landing with far too much ease around the curve of her waist. Like it was meant to rest there. Always. I swallow hard and remove my hand as soon as she's steady.

Her brown eyes meet mine, and I try to stifle the effect she has on me. Because she shouldn't. She can't.

I'm both grateful and annoyed when Grant breaks whatever thing is stretching between us, shoving the phone practically in her face. "I'm Grant. Here's your phone, Miss uh …"

Val moves a tiny step away from me, taking her phone from Grant's outstretched hand. He smiles, all golden retriever puppy. Eager and adorable.

When Val giggles, a firestorm of an unfamiliar emotion lights inside me. It has to be jealousy. But never once in my life have I felt it before. And I shouldn't now.

"I'm Valentina," she says, setting down the phone to shake Grant's hand. For a few seconds too long if you ask me. "Most people call me Val." Her eyes cut to me. "Or Tiny."

"Tiny?" Grant says, his smile widening, and dangit if Val doesn't giggle again.

"The only one who calls her Tiny is *me*."

The words come out far too growly and much too loud. So much so that there's a brief lull in conversation in the bar.

Grant blinks at me in surprise, then glances down at his lap. That's right, buddy. I'm the alpha here. And maybe I don't have the right to and shouldn't even if I did, but this woman is off limits and so is my nickname for her.

I swing my gaze to Val's. She's blinking rapidly, her lips slightly parted. I can't tell if she's shocked in a good or bad way by my outburst. Either way, I'm not sorry. No way is baby-faced pretty boy Grant going after her. The man might be twenty-two, but he looks like he's never had to shave a day in his life.

Needing to break the tension, I nudge Val with my shoulder. "What brings you to Wolf's tonight? And where are your partners in crime?"

"Wolf asked me to come in." Did he, now? I shoot the man a look, but he's busy talking to some old timers. "And Winnie and Lindy are ..." Val trails off as her phone buzzes on the table in front of us. She frowns.

And because I'm a cop, not because I'm nosy or still feeling all kinds of unreasonably jealous, I look at the name flashing across the screen. *Jaxon.*

"He spells his name with an X? Guess we can't blame him for his parents' choice."

Distractedly, she says, "No, legally it's spelled with a -cks. He just likes the X."

More reason to dislike the man. "I thought you broke up with him."

"I did." She shakes her head, and for the first time I realize her hair is down. Most of the time Val keeps it up in some kind of messy bun or braids. Seeing it long and loose and thick around her shoulders, hanging almost to her waist,

I am overwhelmed with an urge to reach out and tangle my hand through it. Instead, I take a sip of beer.

"And he's still calling?"

Her smile is tight. "The man doesn't seem to want to let go."

I give Grant a look. "Val's ex also has a mullet."

"He does not!"

"I know you're not blind, Tiny. It's a mullet."

"He just needs a trim and—"

"Mullet."

That earns me a smile I feel all the way down in the soles of my feet. Basking in her smile is like getting drunk on sunshine. Val gives me a playful shove.

"Be nice, Chevy. Do I need to get started on your exes?"

Definitely not. "They can't be exes if we were never in a relationship. And no. I'd rather not."

I don't want to make too much of this. Nor do I want to compile a list of what I did and did not do with my dates. But I also don't like Val believing the reputation I've earned for myself. Especially since it's not altogether accurate.

"Hey," I say softly. Earnestly. "I'm not some Leonardo DiCaprio, trying to sleep my way through the world. That's not who I am. Okay?"

She nods, her features softening. "I know, Chev." There's a long pause, and Val glances at the bar. "Anyway. Better see why Wolf wanted me to come in."

Picking up her phone, Val pats my shoulder and makes her way over to Wolf. I keep one eye on the two of them but can't miss the grin on Grant's face.

"I was gonna ask for her number, but it seems like she's already been claimed," he says. "How long have you been in love with her?"

A vehement protest is rising in my throat when the

door to the bar slams open, hitting the metal wall and breaking off one hinge so it hangs crookedly. And there in the doorway stands Jaxon. Lover of mullets and the letter X.

He stumbles inside the bar, unsteady and a little bleary-eyed. In his hand is a bunch of flowers that look like he plucked them straight from the field outside. And one bunch of leaves looks a whole lot like poison ivy.

"Valllllllllllll," he croons, and if all the heads hadn't already swiveled in his direction, they would now.

"Let me guess," Grant says. "That's Jaxon? With an X?"

"Let's call him by his real name," I say. "Mullet." I stand, already moving toward Val, who's frozen at the bar.

I beat Jaxon to her, which isn't hard considering the man smells like a distillery. Val looks up at me with wide eyes. "I didn't tell him where I was," she hisses. "And I definitely didn't tell him to come."

"I've got you," I tell her, and when Mullet is only two steps away, I slide both arms around Val's waist and pull her flush against my chest. Immediately, she relaxes into me with a sigh, like this is where she's always belonged and she's been waiting her entire life for this moment. My heart thudding like a jackhammer, I lean down, my lips brushing the shell of her ear. "Just play along, sweetheart."

She shivers, and I take that as a yes.

Best or worst idea I've ever had? Unsure. Ask again later.

Mullet stops a few feet away, so fast he almost falls forward on his face. His hand falls, the flowers and poison ivy sagging. "Val," he whispers. "You moved on?"

I tighten my grip, pulling Val a fraction closer. Then I nuzzle her hair. She smells like spun sugar and summer, and I'm the one who needs a reminder to just play along. Pretend. Not real.

"I'm sorry," she says. "You always said you didn't want to be exclusive. It just kind of happened."

Mullet's eyes go wild for a moment, and I tense. Grant stands, giving me a nod, and I know he's thinking this can go a few ways. One of them might include a jealous rage and drunken attempt at a brawl. But Mullet goes the other way. His face crumples and he lets out a broken sob.

"But I only dated like three other people when we were together," he pleads, and I'd really, really hate the man if he weren't so pitiful.

Val stiffens against me, and I slide one hand up to grab her hand, twining her fingers with mine. "You were actually dating other women?"

He nods. "But it was always you. I knew it would always be you, Valentina."

Someone snorts. I think it's Wolf.

"I'm sorry, Jaxon. It's not gonna be me."

"Is it because of him?" Jaxon eyes me, sizing me up and clearly finding me lacking.

Too bad I'm the one holding her in my arms, pal.

Val tilts her face to look up at me, and I think all my body's systems shut down at the look in her eyes, which is something like pure adoration. But when she presses a kiss to the edge of my jaw, everything starts back up again in full force.

Pretend! It's just pretend! I try to reason with my poor, over-worked heart, ramming against my ribs like some caged animal. Not helping.

Val turns back to Jaxon. "I've known Chevy my whole life. We've always been friends but ..." Once again, she tilts her face to look at me, meeting my gaze head on as she says, "But I've secretly been in love with him for years."

Is that true? It can't be true. Back in the day, I knew she

had a crush. But the three-year age difference seemed like a bottomless canyon between us. And then later, she was always in a relationship with some loser like this one.

Val winks, and something in me tumbles and falls down hard.

Because, I realize, no matter how much I keep trying to shove Val back in the friend and best friend of my little sister box, she no longer fits. In fact, I think the box just crumbled to dust.

But this isn't real. So don't get your hopes up, I tell myself.

Unfortunately, I think it's too late. My brain may get it, but my body missed the memo.

"But I brought you something," Jaxon says.

"If it's the flowers, don't touch them," I murmur to Val. "Some of that's poison ivy."

But Mullet didn't mean the sad excuse for flowers. At that moment, two guys enter the bar, struggling to contain some kind of cage under a beach towel. Whatever's inside it sounds like it's struggling just as hard to escape.

"I know how much you like those magic movies," Mullet says, waving the guys over. They're making slow progress as whatever living thing they've got under there struggles.

"*Lord of the Rings?*" Val asks, just as Mullet says, "*Harry Potter.*"

With a sinking feeling, I think I know where this is headed. And I'm just about to shout not to take the towel off the cage when the two guys do exactly that.

They pull off the towel, revealing a massive owl, beating itself against a thin wire cage.

Val gasps. Mullet grins as though he's just accomplished some great feat. And the cage door springs open, freeing the owl.

It seems to be a rule of nature that when a bird of any

kind gets inside a building, it will fly anywhere *except* toward an open door or window. This proves to be true right now.

The owl flies in a frenzy through the bar, completely avoiding the open door. People scream and duck, diving to the floor. I pull Val behind me, and she presses herself against my back, her hands fisted in my shirt.

I feel bad for the owl, who has obviously been through it tonight. Mullet and his two friends—both of whom ran right out the door, leaving the cage, towel, and avenging bird behind—obviously aren't well versed in avian care. Where did they even get an owl? I'm pretty sure they're not legal to own in the state of Texas.

Mullet, obviously not a bird lover, starts swinging his sad bunch of foliage, which only draws the owl's attention. The bird snatches the whole sad bouquet from Mullet's hands, only to drop them right back on his face.

Good. I hope the man gets poison ivy on his eyeballs.

A sudden, sharp whistle pierces the air, but it's not the owl. Nope. It's Wolf Waters, still standing behind the bar but with one of those big black gloves I've seen used in nature shows by people handling birds.

The owl makes one more slow circle through the room, knocking over a few more beer bottles as it goes, then lands right on Wolf's arm like the most perfectly trained creature.

The whole room goes silent. Wolf murmurs softly to the bird, who fluffs out its feathers and settles in. Turning so the bird is facing the wall and not the room full of panicked people, Wolf speaks in a slow, careful voice. "Bar's closed, y'all. In an orderly and quiet fashion, please exit the building. I'll trust you'll settle up your tabs tomorrow."

I expect pandemonium. But surprisingly, people rise slowly and make their way out the door in near silence. Grant takes Mullet by the elbow and gives me a nod to let me know he's got this. Val and I are the only ones left when Wolf turns back around with the owl.

He smiles, and the massive bird blinks its wise eyes at us. Val peeks around me, then slowly moves to my side. As though it's an involuntary movement, my arm slides around her waist, holding her to me.

"Wolf, you just happen to have one of those bird gloves behind the bar?" I ask, keeping my voice low and steady.

Smiling, he strokes a hand down the owl's back. "I like to be prepared. Back in the day, I used to work with a rescue. My specialty was birds of prey. Haven't gotten to handle one of these in forever." His voice shifts into baby-talk. "But you're a real beauty, aren't you? Did those big meanies scare you? You don't belong in a cage, do you?"

The moment you think you know your town and its people is the moment someone shocks the heck out of you by being a bird handler and owl whisperer.

"What are you gonna do with it?" Val asks.

"You see the tag on its leg?" Wolf asked. "This is a rescue. It's why she's used to being handled like this. I'll make a few calls in the morning. I bet those guys stole this beauty. Poor girl."

I'm not going to ask how he knows the bird is a she. When I glance at Val, she's biting her lip, looking at Wolf like she's half in love with him. I move my hand to her lower back. "Shall we get out of here, Tiny?"

"Yeah. Do you need help cleaning, Wolf?" she asks.

"Naw. I'll take care of it once I get my girl settled."

"Aw, that's adorable." I try to urge Val forward, but she seems to have planted her feet. "Oh—what did you want me to stop by for?" she asks.

Still stroking the bird, Wolf grins at Val. "I heard you were in need of a place to stay. I wanted you to know I've got a spare bedroom in my bunker all fixed up. It's yours if you want it."

Val laughs. "Bunk in your bunker? I still don't know if it exists, Wolf. I thought it was more of a legend."

"Oh, it's legendary," he says, flashing a wide smile. "But very real." Wolf punctuates this with a wink. The owl on his arm makes a soft, agreeable *hoot*.

Oh no, he doesn't. Maybe it's that wink or simply residual feelings from being Val's five-minute fake boyfriend, but whatever the reason, I sling my arm over her shoulder, pulling her closer and not caring one bit how possessive I sound.

"I've got you covered, Tiny. You can stay with me."

FROM THE NEIGHBORLY APP

Subject: Wolf Waters is an owl handler?

SweatPea_43

OMG was anyone else at Backwoods Bar last night to see the OWL? It was the wildest thing I've ever seen. And I had no idea Wolf Waters could handle birds like that.

1BigBass

I'm sorry—did you say Wolf was handling an owl in the bar? That has to be against health codes.

Vanz

The whole BAR is against health codes. But the sheriff and deputies drink there all the time, so they let it slide.

Cal_45

Two of the deputies were there last night when the owl flew in. But it was Wolf Waters who took care of the problem.

BagelBytes

I'm sorry—there was an owl in the bar? Is it okay? How was Wolf Waters handling it? And did they release it? I don't think they're legal to own in Texas. Not unless you're a licensed rehabilitation specialist. And wasn't there just a ram attack at the bar too???

The_Real_Shell_E

I'm sorry but seeing the pictures of Wolf with that glove and the bird—that was HAWT. He can take me into his bunker anytime.

Chels

Ew. Also, does the bunker exist? Raise your hand if you've ever seen Wolf's bunker.

BagelBytes

Birds shouldn't be kept inside of a bunker, so I hope not. I'm going to make a call to the fish and game wardens to make sure someone follows up on this. Also, has the bar ever had a check from the Department of Health Services? Now might be a good time.

DeltaDeltaDelta

Someone said they saw some kind of brawl right before the owl showed up. Anyone know anything about a fight???

DB

All I know is the guys who brought the owl were non-Sheeters and shouldn't have been there in the first place.

HP_Fan

Was the owl carrying any letters?

CHAPTER 9

Val

You CAN STAY WITH ME.

Sure, I might have had an owl swooping down over my head. But the thing that I woke up thinking about wasn't a bird. Or the sight of Wolf Waters handling the massive owl.

Nope—it's that one simple sentence from Chevy, echoing in my head like the refrain of a Taylor Swift song that you can't—and don't want to—get out of your head. Actually, it fits right into the chorus of "You Belong with Me," so now I know what I'll be humming all day.

If I could snatch the words out of the air and have them tattooed on my skin, I would. Because Chevy invited me to stay in his guest bedroom. Which is in his house.

Where he also lives.

Oh, and don't get me started on how it felt to so very briefly pretend Chevy was mine. To lean back into his solid chest and feel his arms slide around my waist like they were made for just that purpose.

Did he feel the same way? I can't stop my mind from spinning out. He definitely didn't seem to consider it a hardship, stepping in to be my pretend beau. Does anyone still use the word beau? I know if Jaxon did, he'd add an X.

But enough about him. Between Chevy and the attack owl, I think he's gone for good.

Unfortunately, the side effect of using Chevy as my get-out-of-a-relationship-free card steered my brain in the direction of imagining it was very real. Or that maybe one day, it could be.

And now, I'm going to move in with him. Temporarily, but still. That cannot be good for my overactive imagination, which will make the leap to much more than friends or roomies. If a very brief fake dating made my brain feel like we were really a couple, what will living with him do?

Five more minutes of thinking, I tell myself. Only five more minutes of lying in bed, remembering the events of the night before. Except the part where I made my very real confession about being in love with Chevy. We'll just chalk that up to me being an undiscovered Oscar-worthy talent. Hopefully, Chevy didn't see the truth in those words.

When the door to my apartment bursts open, it's been way more than five minutes, and I'm still lying in bed, humming as I relive the moment when Chevy nuzzled my hair. I bolt upright as my two besties surge inside, followed by a hesitant Kyoko, who looks a little unsure.

I've only met her a few times, so normally I wouldn't ask her to hang out while I'm braless in bed, but I smile and wave her inside anyway.

I find myself avoiding Winnie's eyes. I'm not sure what has been posted on Neighborly about last night, but she won't be happy if she hears about me living with Chevy from anywhere but me. Not to mention the whole fake boyfriend thing, which people watching might have thought was real.

I'm banking on the fact that the owl took center stage. *Please, please, let the owl have distracted the gossips from everything else.*

"To what do I owe the honor of your presence so early in the morn?" I ask, hiding a yawn with my hand.

Winnie blinks at me from the tiny kitchen area, where dishes are stacked in the sink. Likely not clean. "We're here to deal with all this. Because obviously, you aren't."

"I was getting there," I protest, but Winnie and Kyoko are already starting in on the dishes.

Lindy plops down on the bed beside me and leans in close. "I know what you did last summer," she whispers.

I don't think *I* even remember last summer. "Last summer? Do you mean the time I tried to climb the water tower to touch up the paint?"

She snorts. "No, dummy. It was an expression. I mean, I know what you did last night."

My stomach bottoms out. I'm glad Kyoko and Winnie are arguing about something related to dishes and haven't noticed us whispering over here like co-conspirators in some kind of dangerous plot. "Does Winnie know?"

Lindy frowns. "We talked about it on the way over."

I glance at Winnie as she dries and stacks my dishes. "Was she mad?"

"Why would she be mad?" Lindy tilts her head, looking puzzled. "Wait—what are you talking about?"

I lower my voice. "Chevy offered me his guest room. To stay in."

"Ohhhhhh." Lindy's eyes go wide, then flick to Winnie.

"Is she gonna freak out?"

Lindy chews her lip. "Honestly? I have no idea."

I have a sneaking suspicion Winnie won't approve of me living with Chevy. I mean, she could have suggested his guest room as an option. We've had a few text conversations about my plans since then. It didn't come up. I have to think that there's a reason for that. And I'm pretty sure I know what it is.

The first and only rule about crushes on your best friend's brother is you don't talk about crushes on your best friend's brother. I mean, everyone *knows*. I'm better at hiding it now, but when I was younger, I think I probably followed him around with a steady stream of cartoon hearts floating above my head like a cloud. The few times we have talked about my feelings, it was usually Winnie warning me away.

The reason kept changing, though. When we were younger, it was that dating her brother would be "horrifying and disgusting" (her words) for her. Then, he was too old for me. I can't remember when Winnie last said anything about it, but she brought up his inability to commit and his "propensity toward dating vapid skanks" (also her words).

I'd like to think if something really DID ever transpire between Chevy and me, which until this week has seemed completely out of the realm of possibility, Winnie would approve. I mean, she loves her brother. She loves me. It stands to reason if we were mature adults and decided to give it a real go—again, unlikely to the nth degree—Winnie would approve.

Wouldn't she?

The fact that I'm scared to even tell her I'm going to crash in Chevy's guest bedroom does not bode well.

"I'm sure it will be fine. Just tell her," Lindy says, sounding a little more sure this time. "Do one brave thing a day. That's my new motto. This can be your brave thing."

I don't point out that Lindy, so far as I know, still hasn't done her *own* one brave thing and taken one of the pregnancy tests Winnie all but forced her to buy.

"I also have to quit tonight. That's already one brave thing."

"You hate your job. Quitting should be fun."

"Mr. Silver is almost as terrifying as Winnie," I point out. My boss has a permanent scowl affixed to his face and tosses out sharp words with the deadly force of ninja stars.

"Well, I guess you can always double up on brave today and let yourself off the hook tomorrow," Lindy says.

But tomorrow's brave thing will be moving into Chevy's house. As excited as I am, it's also slightly terrifying. How can I live with my crush without my true feelings leaking out everywhere?

When Winnie claps her hands I jump. "Out of bed, you. These boxes aren't going to pack themselves."

Lindy pats my leg before hopping out of bed and dragging me by the hand. "One brave thing," she whispers.

Maybe I should start small, like just *thinking* about one brave thing for the day. I can save all the brave things for tomorrow.

Because you know what they say about tomorrows? They never come.

———

A few hours later, my entire tiny apartment is packed up into more boxes than it seems like it should take for my few belongings. I've got a bunch of bags ready to donate, and all four of us have different kinds of mustaches drawn on our faces in permanent marker.

It feels so very *final*.

The mustaches keep it from feeling too depressing though. Because you can't take anyone seriously when they have a drawn-on handlebar mustache.

Despite Lindy's frequent pokes to my ribs and the way she keeps gesturing to Winnie and mouthing, *Tell her*, I've so far avoided any brave thing. Unless you count killing a spider I found behind a stack of books. Which totally counts. It had *hairy legs*.

"I'm sorry I stole Winnie's guest room," Kyoko says, tucking her short dark hair behind her ears. "I can totally sleep on the couch or we could share a bed? I don't snore, but I might accidentally spoon you."

"She found a place," Lindy says, throwing me under a speeding double-decker bus.

The little traitor.

"Oh, good," Winnie says, pushing one box so the corners line up more exactly with the one below it. "Where?"

She can't get upset when I've got a walrus-like mustache on my face, I think desperately. Then, infusing as much cheer and casualness into my voice as I can, I say, "Chevy offered up his guest room."

You know the expression, *it feels like someone walked over my grave?* Well, as the mood in the room takes a sudden sharp turn, it feels like someone jumped up and down on my grave, then dug up my bones and ran them over with a train.

Winnie's head turns toward me slowly. Almost unnaturally so. "You're moving in with my brother?"

"Just the guest bedroom," I say, as though there were any possible way I'd be moving into Chevy's bedroom. "I mean, obviously not his room. Or his bed. Separate rooms and separate beds! Because he has a guest bedroom. And it's empty because you moved out. Remember?" I clear my throat. "I'm sure you do."

"Shut up," Lindy hisses, and I do.

Kyoko stares between the three of us, clearly trying to discern why I'm babbling stupidly and why Winnie has an intense but unreadable expression on her face.

I mean, Winnie *can't* be mad. That would be stupid. And selfish. And—

"Okay," Winnie says, but her marker mustache seems to be twitching.

"Okay?" I ask, not sure if my ears are broken or just Winnie's brain.

She opens her mouth, but before she can speak, Lindy yanks a pregnancy test from her purse. She holds it high in the air like it's some kind of treasure.

Winnie, Kyoko, and I all gasp in unison. I could absolutely kiss Lindy for choosing this moment, providing a distraction and taking one for the team. The team, of course, being me. I'll go ahead and forget about the part where she pretty much forced me to tell Winnie.

Mostly because I can't wait to find out if she's pregnant.

"I'm ready," Lindy says. "Time to pee on a stick."

CHAPTER 10

Val

IN THE FADING EVENING LIGHT, I walk as quickly as I can in these heels to the gallery. For evening events, I usually trade my boring daytime khakis and blouse for an almost as boring black skirt or black pants and blouse. Once, I even borrowed a blazer from Mari when Mr. Silver suggested it.

A *blazer*. Even the word sets my teeth on edge. Blazers don't deserve their name—which implies fire, action, maybe passion.

Definitely not a boring, stiff, shoulder-padded jacket that made me feel like I'm sixty-five, not nearing twenty-five. I follow a few fashion influencers on Instagram who are my age and can pull off wearing blazers. But I think it must be some kind of voodoo magic. Or a filter. Like the Blazer Chic filter.

Tonight, I'm doing some blazing of my own—like the

actual meaning of the word, not the stuffy jacket. I opted to borrow a dress of Lindy's that's sleek, black, and shorter than anything I usually wear. But it looks good on me, and the little half-cape attached to the shoulders make me feel like a superhero.

It's the dress equivalent of a power pose. I feel fierce and battle ready to say those two little words: I quit.

I mean, I already talked to Winnie about living with Chevy and *that* went fine. It wasn't even *too* hard washing off my marker mustache. I am on a roll.

"Blazer this," I say, channeling Aragorn as I go to push through the double doors into the gallery.

Except—and I should know this since I use this entrance on the daily—they're *pull* doors. Not push.

Which means my *Lord of the Rings* inspired momentum sends me slamming face first into the glass.

So much for blazing. Let's hope this isn't a sign of things to come.

My eyes meet Mr. Silver's through the door. I wait for disapproval, judgment, or—this one is far-fetched and comes from a very naïve part of my brain—concern.

None of the above. Just a total blank expression, like he's a scantron test sheet without a single bubble filled in.

He does, however, hand me a bottle of glass cleaner and a microfiber rag the moment I pull the doors open.

"If you wouldn't mind removing your skin cells from the glass," he says, his tone as crisp as a winter frost.

Only once I'm done scrubbing my stupidity from the door do I approach Mr. Silver, who is straightening the already straight frames on the wall and frowning at the perfect lighting.

"Do you need something?" he asks without turning.

I wonder what happened to make him this way. Was his

personality always this way? Or did he, like a piece of fruit left on the vine, grow sour and rotten over time?

"I'm putting in my notice," I say, proud of the lack of wobble in my voice. The strength. Until it withers and dies under Mr. Silver's glare when he turns to face me. "To, um, quit."

"You're quitting." It's more statement than question, and when I nod, he just keeps on staring.

It's not surprising that Mr. Silver hasn't heard about Costa Rica. Neighborly made sure the entire town got the news about Mari and me by the morning after the LLLS meeting. But Mr. Silver isn't the type to engage in gossip—on an app or otherwise. In fact, he seems like the type to scorn the very *idea* of an app solely built for town gossip.

"How long will you continue to grace me with your presence?" he asks drily.

"I don't know exactly." When Mr. Silver continues to stare, I add, "I haven't purchased my plane ticket, so I don't know the dates. Two weeks?" Golly, that seems soon. Also, the longer I stay, the longer I get to live with Chevy. "Maybe a month?"

His frown, which I already thought had plumbed the deepest depths it could, deepens. "You're not just quitting—you're moving away?"

"I'm going to Costa Rica with the aunt I live with. Mari—you might know her? She runs the diner ..." I can see by the slight wrinkle in his nose that Mr. Silver doesn't *do* diners.

Heaving a sigh as though the very sound of my voice pains him, Mr. Silver says, "What's in Costa Rica?"

I'm shocked the man who has shown almost zero interest in me and has certainly never asked me a question is now asking more than one, all in a row.

I skip right over the more personal reasons. "I'm going to

work with an artist—Luis Henry Aguilar. Kind of an apprenticeship."

Mr. Silver only nods, his severe face hiding whatever his real reaction is to this. "And what about your family? Your friends?"

Thoughts of Chevy and the way his arms felt around my waist flash in my memory, and I do my best to shut them down.

It was PRETEND, I remind myself. But some deep part of me has latched on to those quick few minutes and is holding fast, like some kind of lovesick leech. I only hope I can keep it together the next time I see him. Which should be tomorrow morning, when he said he could help me move into his house.

I'm sure by then I'll be …

Well. Probably still reliving the moment. But maybe by tomorrow I'll be able to hide it better.

"My extended family on my mom's side is there. Mari leaves next week, and I'll join her sometime after."

I swallow down an impossibly lumpy lump in my throat. Because, despite seeing a donation truck come and haul away most of her furniture earlier today, despite starting to pack up my own things, I am ostriching SUPER hard about Mari actually leaving. And about me leaving, which is why I haven't bought my ticket yet.

"Where will you paint until you go?" Mr. Silver asks. "Isn't your studio at her house?"

I don't remember telling him where my studio is, but I must have. Some days, just to break the tension of his dark moods and the silence in here, I babble about anything and everything. I must have mentioned turning Mari's garage into my studio.

What's really funny about his question is the fact that he

isn't asking where I'm going to *live* once Mari leaves. Just where I'm going to *paint*.

"I'm not sure." Which wouldn't be a problem except for Tank's paintings. Chevy's house is small, and even if he didn't mind me trying to make space, I'm way too messy. The man keeps his house as clean and sterile as an operating room. This is one of the details on the to-do list I keep putting off for another day.

"I have a studio you could use." Mr. Silver says the words with ultimate casualness, like it's not totally bananas and completely out of character for him to offer something like this. To offer *anything*.

I stare. Then stare some more. He … has a studio? And he's offering it to *me*?

"What's the catch?"

He looks mortally offended. "Catch?"

"I assume there's a catch," I say. "You haven't wanted to sell my paintings in the gallery. You're barely civil to me. This is actually the longest two-sided conversation we've ever had. I guess I just don't understand. I thought you were run completely by AI."

Wow. I guess doing one brave thing a day makes me mouthy.

Mr. Silver doesn't argue with what I said—not even the AI part, which should have sparked some kind of response. Instead, he puts his hands on his hips. "Do you want the space or not?"

"How much would I need to pay you?"

If he looked mortally offended a moment ago, he looks *immortally* offended now. Like he was so offended he died, and now is so offended, he returned as the undead.

"You don't need to pay me. I'll text you the address and the garage door code. Move your things in whenever it's convenient for you. And if you don't want a free space to paint, that's your poor choice."

And before I can pass out in a dead faint from shock, Mr. Silver turns away. "Set up the wine table. Guests will be arriving soon."

Okay, then. THAT's more like it.

———

An hour later, I am seriously regretting my wardrobe choice. Lindy looked very dubious when I asked to borrow a dress for tonight. She has a few inches on me in height and I have more than a few on her in the hips and chest regions. When the fabric fit over my hips and backside without any tearing sounds, Lindy wanted to call Winnie to see if we were dealing with a *Sisterhood of the Traveling Pants* magical situation.

But there is nothing at all magical about the way the dress —which fit just fine when I stood still or spun in front of a mirror—tugs and pulls as I move around the gallery. The hemline goes up. The neckline goes down. It's like my belly button is some kind of vortex, sucking all the fabric toward my middle.

After one too many of the male patrons seemed more interested in gazing at me than the paintings, Mr. Silver asked—more like *commanded*—me to stand behind the reception table and pour drinks.

I'd be more frustrated if I weren't relieved to have the barrier the table provides. Also, Mr. Silver has been glaring at the men, not me, so it feels like protection, not punishment. Almost—ALMOST—like a sign of concern or care. Just like offering me the use of his studio.

If I believed in astrology, I'd be looking up what the heck

is happening to the planets and stars today. Because my boss is totally out of alignment.

A broad chest suddenly blocks my line of sight.

I give myself exactly three seconds to examine the starchy, white shirt with pearl snap buttons. My eyes snag on the badge, a brass star inside a circle on one side of a broad, broad chest. The pearl buttons and badge together make for a dead sexy set of accessories.

But it's the man wearing them who makes it hard to swallow and a little hard to breathe.

I finally let my eyes meet his, hoping I'm exuding a calm I definitely don't feel. "Hello, deputy. Fancy meeting you here."

In a room full of cocktail dresses and suits, Chevy should look out of place. Sheet Cake's police uniforms are as Texas as it gets: the aforementioned pearl snap button shirt (which also comes in khaki or blue), a pair of blue jeans, and a leather belt with a Texas-sized brass buckle. Footwear for Chevy is a worn pair of cowboy boots, and let's not forget the suede ten-gallon hat perched on his head.

The very first time I saw him in uniform, my childhood-turned-teenage crush immediately graduated into one of those sure-to-wreck-your-life infatuations.

"Evening, Tiny." He tips his cowboy hat, and be still, my stupid heart!

My cheeks heat like a convection oven. Butterflies take flight in my stomach like traffic control has ungrounded them all after a thick, morning fog and then released them all at once. It's butterfly chaos in there.

I fumble for an internal override button and am pleased enough with the response I manage. "What brings you into this fine establishment? Looking for a new piece to add to your collection?"

Look at me! Acting normal, normal, normal.

But then Chevy flashes me a smile that demolishes my manual override. The button melts right into the console. My knees tremble and knock against the table.

"I'm in the market for something," he says, rubbing his jaw. "I'm just not sure what."

Oooh! Pick me! Pick me!

But he's gazing at the paintings. Right—he's in the market for something to go on his *walls*. Because this is a gallery.

I've been in Chevy's neat-as-a-pin home enough times to know his walls are definitely in need of *something*. While the updates he did inside are impeccable with the refinished hardwoods, fresh light paint, and modern fixtures, his decor makes minimalists look like hoarders. The walls are bare, the windows have blinds but no curtains, and the only personal touches are a few throw pillows Winnie bought for him and a framed photograph of his mother in his bedroom.

Not that I've spent any significant time in his bedroom! I just happened to peek in once when Winnie was living there and Chevy was on duty. Curiosity made me do it. His room was as devoid of decor as the rest of the house—not so much as a tiny dust bunny and no frills—except for the photo. I can't decide if he's a minimalist or just needs help with the finishing details of a house he so beautifully restored himself.

Even if he *needs* art and color on his walls, I know these paintings are not exactly in sheriff salary price range.

"See anything you like?"

His gaze snaps back to me so fast I startle a little. He does a quick scan of my face, then his gaze dips for the first time. His eyes widen as he quickly glances at the rest of me.

My bare legs, hidden behind the table, erupt in goose bumps.

When his eyes return to mine, I swear, the blue of his irises has been almost swallowed up by black. But surely he's not looking at me like that because *I'm* something he likes? I am basically the equivalent of a goal post cemented into the ground of his friendzone. Always have been.

I swallow when he doesn't look away but continues to smolder. *Always will be?*

Chevy says nothing, and I don't even remember my question. Did I ask a question?

When in doubt, run your mouth—that's my motto.

"Want a drink? We don't have beer, but there's red and white wine. How cute are these little plastic wine glasses, right? I had to put all of them together earlier. The stem comes separately in the box so I had to snap them in place. Can you even drink on duty, or—"

"I just got done with work, and I'll take white." A slow smile plays on his lips. "The sweeter the better."

Why does everything he's said since walking in the door tonight seem to hold double meaning?

Oh, right—that's just my very fervent plot of wishful thinking sprouting weeds again. I better pluck them all up before they take over.

"One sweet white wine, coming right up!"

I fill one of the small plastic cups I was just babbling about with moscato and order my hands not to shake. They don't.

I am a veritable pillar of strength.

Until I hold out the plastic wine glass. And then my whole arm starts trembling so badly I nearly dump all the wine out on the table.

Chevy's hand finds my elbow, steadying me as he plucks the glass from me with his other hand. "You okay there, Tiny?"

I'm torn. I'd love nothing more than to let Chevy hold my

elbow forever, his grip warm and safe. But I can't keep fanning the flames of my feelings for Chevy with all the touching this week. The faking. The ... *flirting?*

My feelings burn hot enough on their own without extra oxygen. Or lighter fluid. Last night's five minutes of fake boyfriending has clearly thrown off my entire equilibrium.

Oh, and let's not forget I'm supposed to move into his house tomorrow. How on EARTH will I hide or stifle all this attraction under the same roof as the man?

I jerk my arm back as delicately as I can. "I am all good. Peachy."

Chevy takes a sip of wine, his eyes on me the whole time, bright with amusement. *Not attraction!* I tell myself sternly. I'm acting like a fool, and he thinks it's cute because he doesn't know WHY I'm behaving this way.

He licks his lips as he lowers the glass, and I force myself to maintain eye contact, only watching the motion with my peripheral vision. The man has perfect lips. Not too thin with a little extra plumpness on the bottom. Plus, no matter what time of day it is, he's got the right amount of stubble framing his mouth.

When I kissed his jaw last night—-a bold and stupid and amazing move—it felt exactly as I always dreamed it would. Velvety with a delicious little bite.

What I still don't know is how that stubble would feel as his soft lips press against mine.

"So, what's the deal?" Chevy asks, interrupting my kissing daydream and making me startle, knocking into the table again.

No deal. I have zero deals. Especially not one where I'm trying and failing to remember how to behave around you.

"Deal with what?" I ask.

"Usually you're out here." He gestures toward the room, where more than a few patrons are eyeing his uniform.

Whew. He's not some kind of mind-reader privy to my inappropriate thoughts.

But wait …

"Usually?" I ask. "You've never come to an event at the gallery before."

"I've watched you at a few of these events, talking up the paintings."

Chevy has … *watched me?*

I lose the ability to speak, too overcome by the weird signals I feel like I'm picking up. My radar must be broken. I'm picking up something from another channel or hearing nonexistent voices in the static.

Aren't I?

Chevy tilts his head as though confused by my uncharacteristic silence. "That's you in your element—talking about all the fancy art stuff I don't understand. Why are you playing waitress tonight?"

I'm saved from having to answer when Mr. Silver steps up to the table.

"Excuse me," he says, eyeing the wine in Chevy's hand as though considering whether or not to snatch it from him. "Is there an issue, officer?"

With slow deliberation, Chevy turns to my boss. The two men are a study in contrasts. Chevy with his stocky build and warm, playful air, and Mr. Silver as thin and sharp and cool as his name.

"No issue." Chevy takes a slow sip. "Just thought I'd stop in and check things out."

I swear I see Mr. Silver's lips twitch. *One does not simply walk into a gallery and check things out*, I imagine him saying in Boromir's voice, and wow—this is my second *Lord of the Rings* moment of the night. Clearly, I'm jonesing for a rewatch of my favorite movies.

"We have the proper licenses necessary, I assure you."

"I know. I checked." Chevy takes another sip of wine, holding up his pinky as he does. I barely manage to hold back a snort. "I was just hoping Valentina"—I cannot fight a whole body shudder when he says my full name—"could show me some of the paintings."

Mr. Silver's gaze flicks to me, then back to Chevy. "Of course."

Before my boss changes his mind, I step out from behind the table. And if I'm not mistaken, Chevy's eyes widen a little again as he takes in the full effect of the dress. Maybe it didn't end up working so well for adding bravery, but if it makes Chevy look at me like this, I'll call it a win.

Taking his arm, I tug him toward a painting at the back, away from other people. I attempt to locate words about the painting of a very angry looking man whose skin is painted in shades of green. The name on the card is "Dissonance."

"Huh," Chevy says. "I don't think I'd have chosen that name."

I grin. "I think a better title would be 'Angry Alien Loses Library Book and Must Pay Outrageous Fine.'"

Renaming paintings is a game I like to play, especially if I'm feeling resentful about my paintings NOT being good enough for the gallery. Chevy laughs so hard that I have to take his wineglass to keep him from spilling. I take a sip, wondering if this will calm my nerves or make me loopy.

"Now that's a painting I'd buy," he says. "Where would you reckon I'd hang it?"

I tilt my head. "Perhaps over the toilet in your master bathroom."

He laughs again, steering me toward the next painting. "How about this one?"

The canvas is brightly colored with various circles intersecting and overlapping. "This would work well in your dining room. I call it, 'Ordered Lobster; Got Fruit Loops Instead.'"

His laughter emboldens me—or makes me giddy and stupid—and we move from painting to painting this way. By the time we reach the last landscape, most of the other guests are gone, and Mr. Silver is packing up the wine and clearing the table. That's my job, but if he's not complaining, I'm not about to help.

In a softer voice than he's used all night, Chevy says, "I actually wanted to stop in to check on you, Tiny."

"Check on me?"

"Well, to check on *us*."

"Us?"

I really, REALLY like this two-letter word when the pronoun refers to Chevy and me. Me and Chevy. US.

"I wanted to be sure we're okay. That I didn't cross a line or anything."

How do I tell the man I want him to cross ALL the lines? I want to be one of those handwriting primers they give out in elementary school with a row full of Ts, every single one needing Chevy to cross lines all the way across the page.

"Pretending like that can be … confusing. So, I wanted to make sure we're clear. Especially with you moving in."

I was way too slow to realize what he meant. Probably because I was distracted hearing him talk about *us*. But the *us* he meant was the *friends* us. Not any other kind of us. Not the line-crossing us I was hoping for.

"So, we're good?" Chevy asks. "Still friends?"

He just *had* to go there. The most offensive F-word in the world.

"Nothing has changed," I manage to say. A painfully true statement. I dig up a meager smile from the trenches of my very soul and plaster it on my face.

"Good," Chevy says. "That's good. I don't want things to be weird while you're living with me." He clears his throat. "Staying with me."

Things *weren't* weird. Now, though, they are. We stand there, not touching and no longer talking, staring at this ugly painted field until Mr. Silver graciously interrupts, asking me to clean up. I've never been so grateful for menial, minimum wage tasks in my whole life.

CHAPTER 11

Chevy

Normally, on a rare morning off, I'd be relaxing with a cup of coffee and Ray LaMontagne music. Reading a book, bingeing a show, or doing Sudoku.

Today, I am on my hands and knees, stress-cleaning the grout in my shower with an old toothbrush. Penny tile is not for the faint of heart. I do have coffee on the counter and Ray is crooning, but I am nowhere near relaxed.

In an hour, I'm meeting Val at her place to help her move in. And I'm not sure how I'm going to manage sharing 1500 square feet with her.

I swear, it's like ever since Val bandaged me up in CVS, whatever fraying moral strength I've been using to ignore my attraction to her—which *must* be ignored because Winnie will kill me and because I'm not relationship material—finally snapped. Getting to claim her, even in a pretend sense, at the bar did nothing but give me a taste of what could be. And despite what I told her last night in the gallery, friendship is *not* what I want.

I could barely keep my eyes from roving over her in that dress. Don't get me wrong—to me, Val looks best in one of her many pairs of paint splattered coveralls because they're just so *her*, but getting a glimpse of Val's bare legs and her curves...

I scrub a little harder, really putting all my weight into it. My back is going to feel this tomorrow. So are my knees. But what really and truly hurts is the organ beating in my chest, the one I like to pretend is only good for circulating blood through my body and absolutely *nothing else*.

Why now? Why am I suddenly feeling all these ... feels?

My sister started it with her stupid pinky promise in the cemetery. If I could pass out two pieces of advice to seniors on their graduation, it would be one: don't install penny tile unless you really love scrubbing grout, and two: never make promises in a cemetery.

It happened on our annual visit to our parents' graves, only this time, Winnie and I both confessed the same secret we'd kept without knowing it: that we both knew about our father's other family. I knew longer than Winnie, who didn't find out until after he died. Not sure which is worse—me knowing and having to look at his lying face for years or Winnie not knowing until it was too late to confront him.

And Winnie would have confronted him. Which is something I didn't ever do after accidentally finding his second phone and reading through his texts to Amelia—his other wife.

Like a coward—like *him*—I pretended everything was

totally normal and fine. For years. Meanwhile, a part of me shriveled up and died at the realization that my father was never the man I thought.

He died not knowing I knew. Not knowing how much his actions, which he probably never thought would impact us, changed things for us both.

And it was in that emotional graveside moment that Winnie made me promise we wouldn't let our father's choices ruin our relationships. At least one of us has held to that promise. Me? I'm still pretty convinced I can't risk a relationship at all. Not when I'm terrified the rotten apple might not have fallen far from the tree.

But now, I'm haunted by the stupid promise I made to my sister.

"Grown men shouldn't make pinky promises," I mutter. "And they definitely shouldn't choose penny tile for a shower floor."

When there's a knock at the door, I'm relieved for a reason to get off my knees. Even if it's just someone soliciting. Eight o'clock is a little early for people selling magazines or solar panels or whatever the latest door-to-door thing is, but these people don't seem to care for boundaries. I opt not to put a shirt on, since strangers tend to be more than a little uncomfortable with random shirtless dudes answering the door.

What better way to scare off a guy selling solar panels than with my nipples?

For good measure, I casually dip my hand into the front of my sweatpants. Not so far as to be obscene—just enough to cause a great deal of awkward discomfort. For them, not me. Because I'm totally fine shirtless with my hand halfway in my pants.

But when I pull open the door, it's not a salesman or saleswoman I'm scandalizing.

It's Val. And by her wide, brown eyes I can see she is *definitely* scandalized. Maybe even scarred.

I yank my hand out of my pants so fast it probably set a world record.

"Tiny?"

She is frozen, mouth half open, and I'm not sure if it's my bare chest still on display or the whole hand-in-pants situation, but she looks like a newborn baby deer caught in the headlights of a Mack truck. Meanwhile, I'm blushing furiously—something I haven't done since I was probably in junior high.

What self-respecting adult male blushes?

The kind who answers the door with his hand in his pants, apparently.

"I thought I was meeting you at your place in an hour," I say.

"That was the plan. I just couldn't sleep and figured I'd load my car and make the first trip." She starts to slowly back away, not meeting my eyes. "I'm sorry. I shouldn't have come early without calling or texting. I probably woke you up and—"

I step over the threshold and take her by the elbow, steering her back toward the house. Even though this also steers her toward me and my bare chest. For a brief second, she makes eye contact with my pectorals before jerking her gaze away.

I will *never* open my door shirtless again.

"Hey, now," I say. Gently, like I'm trying to coax a scared kitten out from under a crawl space. "I'm up. I've been up. Get in here."

"Are you sure?"

I take the box from her hands. "Come on, Tiny."

She's still hanging back, and I can see, not for the first time recently, how lost she looks. How small. Protectiveness wells up in me once again, warm and solid. *Protectiveness is fine. You feel this for Winnie. For Lindy. It's just the same.*

It is not even a tiny bit the same, but I shift the box to one hip and wrap an arm around Val's shoulders. "I've got coffee, but I don't know if I have enough cream for you. You take one ounce of coffee for every six ounces of cream, right?"

This makes her smile, and it's a better feeling than a winning lotto number.

"No," she says. A pause. "*Half* an ounce of coffee per six ounces of cream."

"Well, in that case, I *definitely* need to run to the store."

"I'll buy my own cream," Val says. "In fact, as a thank you, we can go to the store together and I'll stock up. Things for me and some things for you. Maybe I can make you dinner?"

Val buying groceries. Val in my kitchen. Val making me dinner.

The thoughts are flying at me like one of those baseball pitching machines has gone haywire, sending balls at full speed right at my head.

"One thing at a time—let's get you settled."

The hallway leading back to the two bedrooms has never felt as small as it does right now, walking with Val under my arm. This house—a modest two-bedroom craftsman bungalow—has also never felt so cramped. Not even with my sister living here and sucking up all the oxygen in the place. Leaving her romance novels all over the place. Buying me throw pillows. Having lovey-dovey phone conversations with James.

Val's presence has a whole different impact. It's one I feel deep down in my bones. The air is charged, almost like the house itself is waking up, taking notice, watching to see what will happen next. I would not be shocked if the tea kettle jumped up and started singing for Val to be our guest.

"You'll be in here," I say, leading Val into the guest room.

Not like she doesn't already know where my guest room is. But she allows me to steer her anyway. I drop my hand from her shoulder as she looks around like she's never set foot inside before. I'm grateful I washed the sheets and cleaned up after Winnie, who left books, hair ties, and a pair of blue underwear I picked up with a coat hanger and flung directly into the trash.

I set Val's box down on the dresser. "Make yourself at home. I've got a few extra things stored in the closet or dresser, but I can move them if you need more room. As you know, my room's just right across the hall."

Something I suspect I'm going to deeply regret. If only I had a two-story house and could be separated by a floor and some stairs. Knowing there's only about twenty actual feet between our beds—that's going to keep me up at night.

Val still isn't speaking, a fact which worries me. She's *always* speaking. Smiling, chattering, *emoting*. I learned that word from Winnie, who claims that James has a lot of feelings but isn't good at *emoting* them. Val is normally an Olympic-level emoter, and right now, she's locked down tight around whatever she's feeling.

"Are you okay?" I ask.

Val walks around the small room with her back to me, taking in the blank walls and the empty closet. I don't do clutter or fuss. Bare, clean spaces calm the noise that stays like static in my head, especially after a long day on shift.

Val leans her hips back on the bed, finally turning back to

offer me a shy smile. I'm suddenly aware of the fact that we are in a bedroom. Alone. I'm also still shirtless, which I'd forgotten until Val's eyes briefly dip down.

I'm not a particularly shy man. Even without the six- or eight-pack of abs that the Grahams come equipped with in all standard models, I'm broad and solid. Strong and capable. Never shy.

But with Val just a few steps away, I feel exposed. It takes effort not to swipe the white duvet off the bed and wrap it around myself like a poofy toga. I swear I hear an echo of my mama's voice, scolding me not to entertain girls in my bedroom, most especially not with the door closed. *Never* with my shirt off.

With sudden and striking clarity, I can picture Mama right here, wagging her finger at me and reminding me about house rules while apologizing to Val for me being an oaf. In my mind, Mama's face is as it was before she got sick, pink cheeks and bright blue eyes colored with happiness and a little bit of mischief.

It almost takes my breath away.

"Are *you* okay?" Val turns the question right back on me, and I realize I'm swaying where I stand.

I turn on my heel and force myself to walk—not bolt—out of the room. *Her* room.

Val has a room now. In my house. Mi casa is her casa and all that. No biggie. It'll be just like having Winnie—

NO IT WON'T.

Because there is nothing remotely sisterly or even friendly about the feelings that keep bubbling over, no matter how forcefully I slam the lid on the pot.

Friend, friend, friend, I chant.

Nope, nope, nope, some devilishly delighted voice in my head sing-songs.

And then I picture Winnie standing there, all smug, holding up that stupid pinky, reminding me of my promise to *try*.

Surely, though, Winnie didn't mean for me to try with *Val*. Not after her threats about my manhood.

I realize I'm standing in the middle of my own hallway, one foot in the air because apparently all these voices in my head are enough to halt my gross motor functions and make me freeze mid-step.

Now is not the time to examine my feelings or remember why Val and I *cannot* be a thing.

Because from where I stand—one foot still mid-air like some kind of shirtless man imitating a flamingo—the reasons are starting to seem awfully flimsy. Except when I remember how many people keep telling me I'm just like my dad. That's why—*he's* why.

"Chevy? Are you—"

"I'm just dandy."

Just DANDY?

Who talks like this? I force my feet to keep walking and flash Val a smile over my shoulder.

"Lemme get dressed and we'll head back over to get the rest of your stuff in my truck. Does that sound good?"

I make it to my room before she answers, slamming the door closed and leaning against it, my breath coming fast. No sense in pretending I'm cool. If freezing in the middle of my hallway didn't clue Val in, saying I'm *just dandy* had to do the trick.

But her voice is soft and sweet as she says, "Thanks, Chevy."

I hear Val's reply through the door like she's right next to me, practically whispering in my ear. This house is the opposite of soundproof. Noises travel from end to end like a game of telephone between two cans and a string. Recently, I bought a sound machine just so I wouldn't have to hear Winnie's hushed, flirty phone conversations with James late at night.

Now, I'll be using it to cover up any sound reminding me that a woman I definitely have feelings for—feelings I will absolutely NOT act on—is sleeping right across the hall.

CHAPTER 12

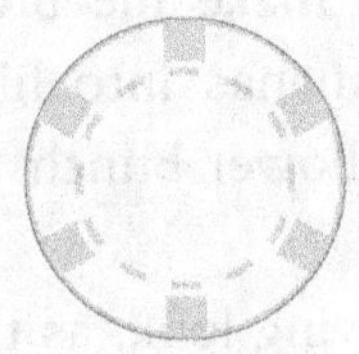

Val

I AM HAVING A MOMENT. A moment of total domestic bliss. If I tilt my head, squint my eyes, and do a little bit of pretending, I can pretend that Chevy and I are a real couple, doing our weekly grocery shopping together.

"What do you normally eat for breakfast?" I ask Chevy, leaning on the handles of the grocery cart as I try to catch his gaze.

At his insistence (which only bursts my domestic bliss bubble a little), Chevy and I are navigating two separate carts through the produce area of Sheet Cake's itty bitty grocery store. Like true Sheeters, we avoid the Walmart Supercenter in the newer section of town. With a sign that reads *Groceries and Goods*, this store is small, clean, and run by a very grumpy man named Frederick. It's more expensive than Walmart with less selection. But Frederick is the kind of man who

115

knows if you ever shop anywhere but here and gives you judgy eyes.

Actually, Frederick *always* gives the judgy eyes. They're just worse if you walk in with the stench of Wally World anywhere on your person.

"You don't need to make me breakfast." Chevy puts a bunch of still-green bananas into his cart. I reach around him to grab a much yellower bunch. "Or anything else," he adds.

He gives me a reproving look, as though he thinks I have secret plans to construct him a tree fort in the backyard or wallpaper his living room. As if.

I love his neat and tidy house, though it definitely needs some artwork on the walls and some pops of color. We made quick work of moving my stuff into his house, though I haven't unpacked the first thing. All my boxes are in the guest room closet, which makes my life feel strangely small. Because it can fit in a CLOSET.

After we got everything but the art stuff, which I left to move another day, our stomachs were rumbling, so we made and ate the plainest, most boring sandwiches ever because Chevy has no food in his house. I insisted we come here to stock up after seeing the scrubbed clean but very empty fridge. Food first. Unpacking later.

And if I'm imagining us as a couple, doing our weekly grocery shopping for home, is that so wrong? Except in my imaginary scenario, we'd have one cart, not two, and we'd be flirting, not arguing about whether or not I'm allowed to make him breakfast. We'd also be doing more touching. A *whole lot* more touching.

"My schedule is really unpredictable," he continues. "When Winnie lived with me, we just got our own stuff and ate separately."

In my imaginary scenario, there's also a whole lot less mentioning of Chevy's sister.

I'm not Winnie, I want to insist, not for the first time today.

All morning as we moved my things from the garage apartment to his house, Chevy seemed intent on dropping reminders about our *friendship* like breadcrumbs. Only instead of using them to mark out a trail back home as we walk deeper into the forest, it's like he's using them to lead me out of the forest and back toward the friend- and little-sister's-friend zone.

Every time he makes a comment lumping me in with Winnie, I deflate a bit more. I'm practically a flat tire at this point, thwapping and bumping my way along the road.

Honestly, I'm fixing to scream. Or maybe I'll just ram Chevy's cart with mine. It would be a whole lot more satisfying.

No matter what people say, violence sometimes IS the answer.

"How do you feel about stuffed French toast?" I ask instead. Because I am nothing if not tenacious. I am like a little, yappy dog who's latched onto Chevy's pant leg by my tiny teeth. And I'm not letting go until he REALLY shakes me off.

"What's stuffed French toast?"

I almost do a little dance in place, because I *knew* this would get him. "Only the best thing you'll ever eat. Once you try it, you'll be ruined for all other breakfasts forever. You think you can handle that?"

"Sounds like a challenge," Chevy says, knocking his shoulder into mine as he herds me toward the deli area. "I do like a challenge."

Noted. "Do you work tomorrow?"

"I go in at noon," he says.

"Perfect. You'll have time to eat, recover by way of a brief food coma, then be all ready for a hard day's work keeping law and order."

"Sounds like a da—"

He stops himself from saying *date*—but only just barely. I'd like to reach inside him, yank the word *date* right out of his body, and stick it in my pocket for safekeeping.

Clearing his throat, Chevy amends, "Sounds like a *plan*."

Thwap goes my poor, deflated flat-tire heart.

Is the idea of dating me *really* so horrible? I'm not sure whether I want to give my crush a Viking burial complete with a flaming funeral pyre or double down and decide that I, too, like challenges.

I swear, lately I've seen evidence of something here. Not a friendly something. And if that's true, why does Chevy seem so intent on redrawing these lines?

More importantly, how desperate does it make me if I keep erasing the lines in favor of new ones? I've never wanted to chase a guy or be the one to initiate. I may not need grand gestures, but give me romantic pursuit!

With Chevy ... I don't know. Maybe it's the knowledge that I'm leaving making me more risky. (Or desperate?) Perhaps it's all the little moments lately where I swear there's something more. Even our five minutes of fake dating felt very, very real. So, am I dangling a carrot—or stuffed French toast—in front of Chevy, just *hoping* he'll give chase? You could say that.

"Great!" I force a cheery smile as I try to move past Chevy.

He stops my cart with one strong hand, holding my gaze. "You don't owe me anything, Tiny. Friends do each other favors. It's a thing."

Gah! That word again! *Friendsssss…* In my head, it sounds like the hissing of a snake.

I glare. "I don't feel like I *owe* you, stubborn man."

Even though I really kind of do.

"You don't need to earn your keep," he insists.

I huff. "If you're not going to let me pay you rent—"

"I'm not."

"—then you're going to let me cook for you. At least a few times a week."

I can see the resistance in his face, but Chevy does not yet know the depths of my resolve. He's about to learn. Because I AM going to cook for him.

I'm not Winnie, who's all force and no nuance when she wants to get her way. I have my own bag of tricks, and I reach down deep to pull out one that will work on Chevy.

Biting my lip, I drop my gaze and soften my tone. "Unless you don't *want* me to. If you don't think you'd *like* my cooking, I understand. If you don't want me *bothering* you …" I trail off, letting my voice wobble just the tiniest bit at the end.

A dirty, dirty trick. One hundred percent manipulation.

But also one hundred percent effective.

Chevy reaches out, squeezing my shoulder as he steps closer. "Aw, that's not it, Tiny. You can cook for me."

Winner, winner, I'm making Chevy dinner!

Er—breakfast.

I drop the act and grin, catching the expression on Chevy's face shift the moment he realizes he's been played. It is glorious.

"Glad we got that settled," I say cheerfully. "Now tell me what you like to eat."

His mouth drops open. "You fight dirty, Tiny."

"You'll thank me once I start making you meals."

He chuckles, looking like he's going to protest again, but as our gazes lock and hold, his laughter fades. As does the humor in his eyes, replaced by something a little more intense.

The air between us shifts, the way it keeps doing lately, and my skin prickles with awareness of how close we're standing.

Am I swaying toward him? Or is he swaying toward me?

Please, please, PLEASE—let it be both.

Chevy draws in a quick and audible breath, sliding his hand from my shoulder up my neck, leaving a trail of tingling skin in its wake. I catch and hold my breath as his eyes drop to my lips.

This is happening! This. Is. Happening!!!

Near the deli counter with all those sliced meats staring, but who cares because CHEVY IS ABOUT TO KISS ME!

His hand brushes my cheek and my eyes flutter closed as he …

He …

He …

Ruffles my hair.

Nothing says *friend of my little sister* quite like a noogie. And just like that, I've been punted back toward the friend zone.

CHAPTER 13

Val

CHEVY DISAPPEARED the minute we finished unloading the groceries, and I'm pretty sure it's because he's avoiding me. Which I REFUSE to take personally. Living with people and sharing spaces can be weird. He and I spent most of the day together, which is more time than we've ever hung out. Maybe he just needed a break.

I mean, to ME, it felt like something I could very much get behind. Together in the kitchen, we fell into an easy rhythm, moving around each other without needing to even communicate in words. I tossed the bread; he caught it and put it away with a wink. He handed me frozen pizza and our fingers touched; I cleared space for it in the freezer while my hot cheeks cooled. And when he brushed against my back while passing me, goose bumps appeared all the way up my arms like they were super eager fans doing the wave in a sold-out stadium.

We talked about nothing and everything—laughing and teasing the way we normally do. For a little while at least, he stopped dropping those *we're just friends!* bread crumbs. It made me happy. It made me feel—for the first time since Mari told me she was leaving—*safe*. Like I have a home. The ache in my chest was both pain and pleasure.

Until Chevy put the last box in the pantry and then bolted out the front door, calling out, "Make yourself at home and don't wait up!"

It stung. Like, an angry beehive swarming on you kind of sting.

The last part is what really got me. He doesn't want me to wait up. Does that mean he'll be home late? Or … not at all? Does he have a date? Will he bring someone back with him?

There is no way I can live here if it's going to be a front-row seat to Chevy's dating life. Wolf's bunker—here I come!

To distract myself from thoughts of Chevy out with someone else right now, I put on a show with absolutely zero (or maybe point one percent) romance—*Criminal Minds*—and eat ice cream straight from the carton. Have I been simmering in jealousy like it's a slow cooker recipe? Perhaps.

A knock on the door makes me jump. Because who would be knocking on Chevy's door after nine o'clock at night?

Possibly a serial killer who knows I'm home alone, ditched by the man who clearly had enough of me today.

Unlikely. This is Sheet Cake. If there were a serial killer, he picked the wrong town. Nosy people on Neighborly would have him caught *before* he even attempted murder.

Another thought strikes fear straight into my heart like a bolt of lightning. Maybe it's a woman here to see Chevy. I swallow, frozen in place by this MUCH more terrifying thought.

Give me a serial killer! Please!

But it's Winnie's voice I hear along with another, harder knock. "Little pig, little pig, let me come in!"

The moment I unlock the door, Winnie practically dives inside. I hadn't realized the temperature drastically dropped since this afternoon—the mild winter days we've had lately were swallowed up by a bitter, frosty chill. I guess the wind I heard whistling against the eaves earlier was a cold front moving in.

"Sorry. I couldn't find my key," Winnie says, striding through the room with the comfort of someone who used to live here.

I sink back down into my spot on the couch, waiting for the inevitable inquisition. I've known Winnie would want to talk ever since I saw the look on her face when I said I was moving in with Chevy. I don't know exactly what this conversation will be like, considering the last time she warned me away from him we were both in high school.

"Did you turn this up?" Winnie's peering at the smart thermostat on the wall. She taps it, giving me an accusing look.

"I don't even know how to work the thing."

"Interesting," Winnie says.

Is it?

Winnie tosses her leather jacket on the back of an armchair, then turns all her attention to me. Leaning forward, hands clasped. Eyes narrowed. As always, she's impeccably dressed with her blond hair in a high ponytail, a black pencil skirt, tights, and motorcycle boots that somehow work for her mix of modern and 1930s fashion icon.

Me? I put on pajamas at five o'clock.

"So, you moved in with my brother," she says.

"I did. Yes."

We stare at each other for an uncomfortably long time. And then I throw a pillow at her face. She's too startled to even catch it, and it falls to the floor, pulling a few flyaway hairs out of her ponytail.

"You obviously have things to say," I tell her. "So, go on. Say the things. I'm listening."

Winnie smooths her hair back and tightens her ponytail. "I just ... I'm worried."

"About?"

"You. And Chevy."

"There is no me and Chevy," I tell her, the words landing somewhere between truth and a lie. "He spent all day making 3D models of our *friendship* to remind me where I stand with him."

"And yet he turned up the heat for you."

I throw my hands up. "He's been gone for hours. Long before the temperature dropped. He didn't touch it, and neither did I."

"He has an app," Winnie says. "He installed this last month and was all giddy about being able to adjust it from his phone. But he's a total cheapskate when it comes to paying for utilities. Whenever I tried to stealthily adjust it, Chevy turned it right back down with his app. Now? It's on seventy-nine. Practically scorching."

I shrug. "So, he adjusted the heat. I don't get it."

Unless ... is this a tiny gesture like the ones I've always hoped for from a guy?

"Here's the thing about my brother." Winnie's expression shifts. A subtle thing, but I see it in her distant eyes and the tightness around her mouth. "Chevy knew about our dad way before I found out. Since he was in high school, apparently. He just bottled it up and kept quiet about it, the same as me. For years."

I search for something to say. Anything at all. But what Winnie and Chevy's dad did was so horrible. So strange and unbelievable that I'm as speechless as I was when she first told Lindy and me. He seemed, from the outside, like a typical dad. A *good* dad, even. Worked a lot and took trips, sure, but after their mom died, he raised them on his own.

I know it had to have wrecked Winnie, and she found out after he died. I try to imagine Chevy, carrying this truth around for so many years. He's always seemed so bright and sunny, playful and optimistic. Steady and sure.

But he's known about his dad all along?

The familiar prickle of impending tears starts in my nose and eyes. My tender baby heart is ready to go full-on mush. "Winnie—I'm still just so sorry."

She waves a hand carelessly, though I know her feelings about it aren't careless at all. "I don't think Chevy has fully processed his hurt and grief. I'm not sure he knows how to process."

Sounds familiar. But I'm not going to make a comment about it *now*.

"I'm also not sure," she says, pausing to make sure she catches my eye, "if my brother knows how to process good feelings either. If he knows what to do with feelings at all. Chevy is about as emotionally available as an old boot stuck in mud at the bottom of a lake."

"That's vivid imagery," I say drily.

Winnie ignores this. "I love you both. And I don't want to see either of you getting hurt."

"Would you be so against it?" I blurt, and once again, my mouth is about five steps ahead of my brain. Winnie goes completely still at the question. But I press on, pushing my finger against what feels like a marrow deep bruise. "If Chevy felt something for me, and if he weren't an emotionally unavailable old boot—would you be happy for us?"

I try to keep my tone light, adding humor to the question, but it's the heaviest, weightiest thing I've ever said out loud. And I'm terrified of the answer.

Winnie crosses the room before I can blink and sits so close, she's practically in my lap. Taking my hand, she gives me eye contact so intense I almost wither under the force of it.

"I want so much for your happiness. And for Chevy's. If that happiness were together? Best news ever." She shakes her head, smiling. "I am all for two people I love times a billion being in love with each other."

Relief fills me, making my limbs feel suddenly lighter. "Really?"

Winnie squeezes my hand, and I swear I feel my bones crunching. "Unless the two people I love times a billion broke each other's hearts. And then, I can't think of anything worse."

I swallow hard, staring at the person whose friendship has lasted just about as long as my crush on her brother. And as my temporary relief ebbs, my limbs now feel heavy and waterlogged. Because in truth, I can't think of anything worse either.

"Well, now that we've resolved that issue, which may only be a hypothetical, what are we going to do?" I ask, desperately hoping for something to give me a break from thinking Chevy-related thoughts.

"Netflix and chill?" she asks, then laughs. "The literal kind. Do you have ice cream?"

"Do I have a pulse?"

Winnie slides her fingers to my wrist for a moment. "Congratulations! You are not a zombie. Yet. Let's raid your freezer, eat on the couch because Chevy never wanted me to, and then watch something a little less murdery than *Criminal Minds*."

CHAPTER 14

Chevy

I BARELY YANK my hand away as Pat leans across the pile of poker chips, trying to grab my phone. "No texting at the table, deputy," he says.

"Sorry."

I drop my phone in my lap and check the smart home app *one more time* before clicking the phone off. I think it should be warm enough in the house. If it's working. It *has* to be—it's a smart home. Fancy high tech stuff. It worked last month, but the weather has been so mild lately, I haven't had to adjust it.

I picture Val shivering on my couch, and I open the app again and turn the heat up another degree.

"It's your bid," Collin says, giving me a pointed look.

"Right," I say, picking up my cards while trying to

remember what game we're playing. Hold 'em? Omaha? Five-card stud?

I move the cards around in my hand like I know what I'm doing. Usually, that would be true. Tonight, however, at the Graham Fam poker night at Pat and Lindy's new place, I'm totally useless. I might as well be trying to read tea leaves. "I'll check."

James clears his throat next to me, a low rumble that's almost a laugh. "I already bet twenty-five."

"In that case, I fold." I shove my cards toward the center of the kitchen table, relieved to be out of this hand.

Big Mo tosses a chip in the center to call James's bet and Collin does the same. But just as Collin adds his chip to the center, his phone lights up in the front pocket of his dress shirt.

"I said no phones!" Pat moves quicker this time and plucks Collin's cell right from his pocket. Pat makes a face when he sees the face on the screen. "Oh. It's your girlfriend. Or ex-girlfriend?" he adds hopefully, but Collin shakes his head, glaring as he tries to grab his phone.

"*Girlfriend*—current. Give it back, Patty." There's a warning in Collin's tone, but Pat ignores it, moving the phone out of reach.

"Well, I can fix that for you in a jiffy. Let me just shoot her a quick text ..."

"Don't you dare send Liza a message." Chairs scrape across the floor as Pat's fingers fly across the phone screen and Collin grabs for it.

"Boys," James says in a warning tone, but he's completely ignored.

Even if Tank were here, he'd have no better luck trying to head off this fight.

Pat jumps up, tipping his chair over. Collin's cards scatter as he begins chasing Pat around the table. Beast, the half-blind Pekingese, continues snoring on the sofa in the family room, but Amber jumps up, tail wagging in typical yellow lab fashion as she trots behind Pat and Collin.

I, for one, don't mind the distraction because it gives me a chance to check my phone. The app *says* my house is heating nicely. So why can't I stop obsessively checking?

"Do you have a problem with your thermostat?" James asks, peeking into my lap where I've opened up the smart home app again.

I notch the heat up another degree before clicking off the phone again. "It's just a new system. I put in one of those smart homes with an app. And this is the first really cold day since that freak snow."

Sheet Cake has what I'd call balmy cold winters. We get freezing days, sure, but a lot of sunny days too where it might creep into the sixties. We had some flurries the week before Christmas, the first sight of snow here in six years. I got my smart home set up the next week, just in time for the weather to warm up. We spent Christmas in short sleeves with sun on our faces. Because that's how life works.

"You're not home, but you're turning up the heat?" James asks.

"I just want to make sure it's functional in case I need to return it." The return date has long passed. But James doesn't need to know that. Or anything else.

"So, it's the *smart home* you're concerned about?" James takes a slow sip of beer, watching me carefully.

It's hard not to crumple like a house of cards under his gaze. "Yep."

"You're not worried about whether or not the *person* in your home is warm enough?"

Am I really THAT obvious? I stop just short of asking, *What person?*

"Nope."

He grins, and that's when Collin and Pat hit the floor, rolling through the kitchen with Amber bounding after them. Collin's phone goes flying, sliding across the tile floor and coming to rest by Big Mo's boot.

He shakes his head, picking up the phone and setting it on the table. "You wanna cash me out, James? I best be heading on if I'm gonna get up to cook in the morning."

"No problem," James says, starting to count out chips and cash.

The buy-ins are low at poker night, much lower than one might think for a family who probably all have six to seven figures in the bank. Then again, not wasting money on things like poker is probably why the Grahams still have loads of money. Their fiscal responsibility is a thing to be admired. Or resented, depending on my mood.

"Are you gonna be okay when Mari leaves?" I ask Mo.

"It'll be like losing a limb," he says with a soft, sad smile. Thinking of Val leaving, I really get that. "I'm hiring someone to run the business side. I just want to cook."

"That's good. Because I might starve without your cooking," I tell him.

He eyes me, a small smile playing on his lips. "Sounds like you've got your own chef under your roof now, one who learned from Mari herself."

I open my mouth to argue that Val is a temporary roommate, not my personal chef, but then remember her promise to make me stuffed French toast in the morning. My stomach rumbles a little at the thought, though I still don't know what stuffed French toast is.

Big Mo stands, taking what's left of his root beer and his

winnings from James. Then he steps right over Collin and Pat, who are still writhing around. Thankfully, they're too out of breath to keep insulting each other. It's mostly a lot of grunts, thuds, and heavy breathing.

"Night ... Mo!" Pat wheezes as Collin rolls them until he's on top.

"Don't get blood on these nice, new floors," Mo calls, and then the front door closes behind him.

"Collin," James says, "your phone's right here if you want to stop beating up on Patty."

"I'm the one ... winning!" Pat insists, right as Collin pins his arms with a triumphant whoop.

Collin rolls to the side just enough to let Amber get to Pat's face. He tries to wiggle away, but Collin holds him down fast. Amber puts two paws on his chest as she keeps on with her tongue assault.

"Uncle! Uncle!" Pat cries between giggles, but Collin doesn't move for another few seconds.

"Don't take my phone again," Collin says, getting to his feet and swiping the phone from the table. "And definitely don't text Liza for me."

"No promises," Pat says.

"I don't understand why y'all can't be supportive." Collin straightens up the chairs tipped over in the chase, grumbling as he goes. "You're both in serious relationships."

"Yeah, but your girlfriend is the worst," James says.

"Amen," says Pat from the floor. Amber's now stretched out beside him on her back, with Pat scratching her belly.

Collin glares at James. "Not you too!"

I've never met Collin's girlfriend, but I've heard all about her. Mostly about how she's terrible and everyone in the family hates her for reasons that Collin seems hellbent on ignoring. I start stacking chips back in the box, wondering if Val is still up.

I stack a little faster.

"She's not good for you," Pat says. "And she's gotten all up in your business. Like, your *actual* business. What trainer asks for access to your finances?"

Collin huffs and drops into a seat, crossing his arms. "Harper doesn't have time to help with the bookkeeping anymore. Liza offered. What's the difference?"

"The difference is Harper's our sister. We trust her. Not just to balance a spreadsheet. But to have access to your *financials*."

"I trust Liza." Collin pauses, frowning down at his phone. "And I'm just so tired of the dating game, you know? I want to be *done*."

The room goes quiet as Pat shuts off the sink and turns, looking for once like he can't find a single word to say. But then, because it's Pat, he finds some words anyway.

"Why don't you let us help you find someone? Someone we actually *like* for you. Someone who would be good for you."

"Liza is good for me," Collin says. But he sounds more stubborn than sure.

"What about Val?" James asks this question in the kind of voice that's TOO innocent. It's the voice kids use when they're trying to kick over a hornet's nest worth of trouble. "She's single."

I drop a handful of chips on the table with a clatter but refuse to look up. I'm too busy grinding my molars into dust.

Pat claps his hands. "Well, then, there you go! Can you imagine? Three brothers dating women who are best friends? Epic."

I *can* imagine. And I don't like it even a little bit.

"Val's pretty," Collin says thoughtfully, and I just barely manage to keep from starting the second physical fight of the night. "But I don't know her well."

"Then break up with Liza and ask Val out. *Get* to know her," Pat urges, and the urge I had to punch him the other night comes back even stronger than before.

I wonder if I could possibly take on both Collin and Pat at the same time.

"Unless," James says thoughtfully, drawing out the word, and now I'm wondering about a three on one. "Unless anyone here can think of a reason he shouldn't."

Collin and Pat just give him looks like he suddenly sprouted a tree branch from the middle of his chest. I'm glaring when James's gaze pins me with a deadly look.

"Anyone at all."

"She's moving to Costa Rica," I say, trying to sound casual and not like I'm over here trying to prevent an aneurysm.

James waves a hand. "Temporarily. She'll be back."

"You could write letters," Pat says, eyes bright. "Women *love* that kind of thing. You were always the Shakespeare out of all of us."

Collin snorts. "Just because I wrote one poem that made it into the high school itinerary magazine—"

"A sonnet," James corrects. "You wrote a sonnet."

A freaking sonnet? Do the Grahams really have to do everything well?

"Women swoon for sonnets." Pat wiggles in his seat, resembling a giant, overgrown, annoying puppy. "So, don't worry about the distance."

"Any other objections?" James asks, still looking right at me.

I say nothing at all. I'm too busy picturing Val with

Collin, holding hands. Val, opening letters full of *sonnets* from Collin, a beaming smile on her face.

Val, coming home to Sheet Cake and running right into Collin's arms.

"Should you be thinking about this when you currently have a girlfriend?" If I sound a little rude, well—too bad.

Pat looks smug when he points at Collin. "He's right! And the fact that you're even entertaining the idea of someone else should tell you everything you need to know, brother. If you really wanted to be with Liza, we wouldn't be having this conversation."

James says nothing, but I can almost hear him telling me we *also* wouldn't be having this conversation if I spoke up and said … what? What would I say?

It's not like I'm going to throw my hat in the ring or stake some claim on Val.

If Collin were to ask Val out—after breaking up with his current girlfriend, of course—she'd be a fool to turn him down. The Grahams are like the gold standard of men.

While I am … I'm just …

I'm …

NOT IN THE RUNNING. Because I'm not going to date Val. I don't do serious. I *can't* do serious. I *won't* do serious— same difference. Period. The end.

But I *should* get home to make absolutely sure the smart thermostat is working. I wouldn't want Val to freeze to death her very first night in my house. I can't act on any feelings I may or may not be having, but I can at least commit to keeping Val safe and warm.

CHAPTER 15

Val

WHEN I HEAR keys in the door, I wake up groggy and foggy on the couch. *Criminal Minds* is paused on the screen, covered by a message from Netflix asking me if I want to keep watching. For once, I really don't. I've had enough serial murders to last me a lifetime. After Winnie left, I put it back on.

What time *is* it?

Chevy gives me a soft smile as he walks in, locking the door behind him. I hope the relief isn't super evident on my face that he's alone.

"I thought I told you not to wait up," he says.

His voice is gentle, wrapping around me warmer and softer than the throw blanket I pulled over my legs earlier. It's one I brought from my place because Chevy doesn't believe in throw blankets. He has exactly two pillows on the

136

couch Winnie bought for him. One of which is still on the floor from where I threw it at her head earlier.

"Mmm," is the only answer I can manage as I burrow deeper into the couch cushions. "I didn't wait up. I was sleeping. I like your couch."

Chevy sits down on the other end of the couch. I try not to faint with shock as he lifts my legs and settles underneath them, putting my feet into his lap. This is like every Christmas present and birthday gift I've ever wished for all rolled up into one.

Especially when he starts lightly rubbing my feet.

I try not to react in any way, afraid any movement or the sound of contentment I REALLY have to work to hold back would scare him into stopping. Or declaring this a *friendly* foot massage.

Then I think about Winnie's worries, which I can't help but share. Chevy has reminded me multiple times this week about friendship.

But he's also rubbing my feet. And Winnie made such a point about him adjusting the thermostat for me. His thumb brushes over my ankle and I shiver. *Don't read into it*, I tell myself, like I don't already have a wall set up in my mind with all the clues thumbtacked up and connected by red string, trying to solve this mystery of how he *really* feels about me.

"How was your night?" he asks.

Now, THAT'S a loaded question considering the conversation I had with his sister.

I stick with the facts. "I binged *Criminal Minds* and ate ice cream out of the carton. Pretty lame," I add.

"Sounds better than my night."

Which was spent ... *how?* I can't ask. I won't ask. I guess I can console myself with the fact that if it was a date, it doesn't sound like it went well. And now he's here, rubbing my feet, not with someone else.

Chevy gives my feet a squeeze and I swear, I feel it in my heart. "I should have stayed home with you."

"Yeah?"

He keeps his gaze on my feet, resuming the massage. "I wanted to give you space. To unpack or just feel at home."

You make me feel at home. I'm glad I at least have the where-withal to keep that confession inside.

I shift so I'm on my back, looking up at his face. "I don't need space."

I definitely don't WANT space. What's the opposite of space? Industrial strength super glue? *That's* what I want.

"Good to know," Chevy says with a chuckle. He clears his throat and gives my toes a squeeze. "We should get you to bed."

Yes. WE should.

But with his big hands gently massaging my feet and his presence warming me, I don't want to move. "I'm not tired," I mumble, my voice the very *definition* of tired.

"I call poppycock."

"Poppycock?"

He grins, and my heart feels like it was just given a hug by two defibrillator paddles. "It's what my mama always said instead of BS. She said even saying the initials were like cussing."

Neither Winnie nor Chevy talk much about their mom. I don't say much about mine either, but that's because she's not worth a single-syllable word. But Mrs. Boyd was the best kind of mother. Sweet and tender, yet full of vibrant life. Fun. Dependable.

Losing her hurt more than having my own mom walk out. I can only imagine how it felt for Chevy and Winnie. And I *have* to imagine because, again, neither one ever said much, grieving in their own very different, but both private, ways.

Just like they both stuffed their feelings about their father down deep. I study Chevy, wondering what it would be like to find out your seemingly loving parent had a whole other family. It makes me want to head over to the cemetery and stomp right on Mr. Boyd's grave. Or maybe leave a bag of coal in lieu of flowers.

How did Chevy turn out to be such a good, trustworthy man after that trauma?

He stands up, dropping my feet back to the couch. Disappointment hits me like a cinder block.

That is, until Chevy bends down and scoops me up in his arms, the blanket still tucked around my body like I'm a burrito. I let out a surprised squeak and wiggle, trying to free my arms from the blanket.

Chevy tightens his grip, grinning down at me. "Nope. You're not escaping, Tiny."

I'm not trying to escape, dummy. I wanted to wrap my arms around you like a clinging vine to a tree so you can never let me go.

"Is there an extra charge for bedtime delivery services at this hotel?" I tease.

"This is a home, not a hotel. But I do accept tips. Not the monetary kind."

"Tips like … don't eat yellow snow?"

He chuckles. "Why is that always the one people start with? Who's eating all this yellow snow anyway?"

"A very good question."

When we get to my door, I am SO tempted to wedge my legs against the door jamb so Chevy can't walk me inside. I am NOT ready to stop being cradled to his chest like a human burrito. Instead, I try to surreptitiously burrow in a little deeper, relishing every moment.

"And here we are," Chevy says, trying and failing to maintain a believable British accent.

"Are you trying to be a butler?"

"Alfred has always been my favorite character in any Batman movie."

I cackle at this, which means I'm wholly unprepared when Chevy tosses me on the bed.

I'm sure Chevy didn't mean to do so with such force. He was being playful. I KNOW he didn't intend for me to bounce once, then roll right off the side and hit the floor.

Because I'm still burritoed in the blanket, I can't catch myself, which means my face whacks right into the hardwood floor. Inexplicably, my elbow jabs my stomach, knocking the wind right out of me.

"Tiny!"

Chevy is kneeling beside me in an instant, turning me over. He yanks the blanket off, examining me for injuries. Despite the ache in my head and my inability to breathe, I love being the object of his full attention.

Worth it!

"I'm so sorry," he says. "Are you okay? Val? Val!"

My breath returns with a gasp. It's been years since I've had the wind knocked out of me, and I'd forgotten the panic that comes while waiting for my lungs to resume their full function.

Chevy picks me up again—*hallelujah!*—and this time sets me carefully on the bed.

"Sorry," I gasp. "I knocked the wind out of myself."

"I'm the one who's sorry."

His face is a giant letter of apology, and his eyes snag on my forehead. Everything happened so fast, but based on the throbbing ache, I whacked it pretty good. Chevy winces.

"Let me get you some ice. You're getting quite the goose egg."

When he disappears, I skim my fingertips over my forehead. Yep—there is a sizable knot swelling right in the center.

Fantastic. Just what every woman wants when trying to relocate out of the friendzone. A giant, sexy knot on the forehead. Sooooo attractive!

Chevy returns with a baggy filled with crushed ice.

"You don't need to—"

I stop talking when his hand slides into my hair, cupping the back of my head as he tenderly presses the ice to my forehead.

I rescind my earlier statement: Bumps on the head are the best! Five out of five stars. Would definitely recommend.

"I'm so sorry," Chevy says again, shaking his head. "I didn't think the bed would act like a trampoline."

"It's okay."

It really is. Because anything that buys me a little more time with Chevy is all good with me. Especially when he's cupping my head and leaning close. The ice—I could do without. It's freakishly cold. But I will suffer facial frostbite to have Chevy holding me like this.

"I can't believe I did that," he says.

"No one tosses a dwarf." I did NOT mean to say that out loud. I hazard a glance at Chevy, who looks understandably confused. "Sorry. *Lord of the Rings* quote," I explain.

"Is that still your favorite movie?" he asks, smiling. "I should really get around to watching."

"*Movies.* Plural. It's a trilogy. And have you really not seen them?"

He shakes his head. "Nope."

"We need to remedy this fact. Otherwise, you're really not fit to be a member of society."

"Is that so?"

"Totally so. Plus, you'll never understand half my quotes. It's like I'll be speaking another language."

"Then I definitely need to see them."

Our faces are close. His blue eyes search mine, and his hand flexes on the back of my head.

Darcy hand flex! I think, because even though I've never seen any of the movies or read the book, EVERYONE knows about the Darcy hand flex.

Before I can read too much into the movement or the way his pupils have dilated into inky black pools, Chevy presses the bag of ice into my hand and backs quickly toward the door.

"Sorry again about that whole thing. I'm just gonna head to bed. You know."

"Okay?" What hurts more than the bump on my head is the continual case of Chevy-induced whiplash I'm suffering from.

"Cool deal."

And then, while I watch, Chevy shoots me a pair of finger guns then disappears, slamming the door behind him.

CHAPTER 16

Chevy

Finger guns.

I, a grown man, a homeowner, a responsible citizen and officer of the law, practically bolted from Val's room last night after giving her ... finger guns. And that was after doing my best impression of a caber toss with her body and leaving her with a knot on her forehead.

Let's not forget giving her a noogie in the grocery store.

Who even am I?

The only thing that's clear this morning is that I am a man running on not enough sleep. I spent most of the night tossing and turning and trying *not* to think about Val. Trying not to replay all the stupid things I did yesterday. Like tossing her, which I feel horrible about. Then there's the moment when I thought about kissing her. Followed by my hasty exit and ... the finger guns.

"You are a fool," I tell myself, dipping my face under the showerhead. "An idiot."

Here's the thing: I don't understand why I'm struggling so hard to quell an attraction that didn't exist—or maybe I *pretended* didn't exist—for years. Years!

Val has been living here less than twenty-four hours and already, she's under my skin like the sexiest kind of splinter. It felt so normal, so RIGHT to grocery shop with her and then put things away in my kitchen. To come home after a long and lonely night to rub her feet on the couch.

Despite what impression I've given publicly by my penchant for dating, I've never brought a woman I'm dating back here. There's no one I'd want to have in my home. But Val ... she feels like she belongs.

The second we were done putting away groceries yesterday, I had to leave my house for fear of doing or saying something I shouldn't.

Like, for example: telling her not to go to Costa Rica. Asking her to stay here with me—indefinitely.

Or: kissing her while she has a loaf of bread in her hands.

Nothing says romance like making out while holding sandwich bread!

Maybe I should establish a no kissing policy in my house. Except that would let her know I'm *thinking* about kissing her.

But a policy or a set of rules might actually be a good idea. Just like in my freshman dorm, we had to sign a roommate contract with expectations and rules for the room. Things like what time you could play music, who cleaned up what, and also ... what to do if one of us brought a woman back to the room.

I swallow. Surely that won't be an issue, will it? There's no way I can stomach seeing Val with another guy *in my own house*. Yep—we definitely need to establish rules. And that for SURE will be on there.

I hear Val moving around in the kitchen and remember her promise to make me stuffed French toast. My stomach growls at the thought, even though I've never heard of stuffed French toast, nor do I know what it's stuffed *with*.

I only know that I can't seem to get into the kitchen fast enough.

The sweet smell of vanilla hangs in the air as Val moves around my small island with confident grace. She looks good in a way I'm not prepared for with her messy bun, pajama pants and T-shirt, all topped with an apron of mine double knotted around her waist.

I suddenly understand the appeal of a football player seeing his woman in his jersey. Not that I wear my apron enough to make it any kind of equivalent. I actually can't remember the last time I put it on. But seeing Val wear *anything* of mine gives me a warm rush of a feeling, along with one word, echoing like a drumbeat in my head: *Mine. Mine. Mine.*

Trying to ignore my caveman tendencies, I take a seat on a stool across from where she's whisking something. "Morning."

"Hey!"

Her smile is wide as she glances up at me. She's got a white streak of flour on her cheek that's downright adorable and a prominent bump on her head, which is not, especially considering I was the cause.

She must see me looking because she reaches up to touch the knot. She grins. "You like my horn?"

"Your horn?"

"Yep. Now I'm a unicorn."

I just stare. Because what can I say to THAT? "I just feel

bad. I'm not sure what I was thinking, throwing you like that."

What I was thinking at the time was what a bad idea it was to carry Val to bed. Or to be anywhere *near* a bed with her. When I tossed her, I was thinking: *Abandon ship! Run for your life! Mayday!*

"Few people in the world could pull off a horn, Tiny. But you manage to do it. You truly *are* a unicorn."

Too far? The way her cheeks pinken as she glances away assure me that I REALLY need to find the medium setting. I'm running hot then running cold. I need to locate a solid lukewarm for our interactions.

"I don't know how you like your coffee." She fills a mug and slides it my way. "I *should* since you know how I take mine. Is that part of your police training—paying attention to details like that?"

Yes … but that's not why I know the way Val pours a vat of cream into her coffee. I choose to skip right over the question rather than incriminate myself with just how many details I know about her.

"I take it black," I tell her. "Like my heart."

She scoffs, and I watch her delicate fingers dredge a thick slice of bread in egg. "Psh. You've got one of the biggest hearts of any man I know, Chevy Boyd."

Her compliment makes warmth spread through my chest and fan out to my limbs. I'm not sure I deserve it, but I like knowing Val thinks of me that way. I carefully steer us away from this conversation—which is awfully close to talking about feelings—and toward something safer instead.

"Tell me about stuffed French toast. What is it stuffed with? Where'd you get the recipe? How many miles will I need to run if I want to offset my caloric intake?"

Val giggles and proceeds to talk my ear off while I watch

her like this is the best cooking show I've ever seen. Which it is. And not just because I don't watch cooking shows.

It's Val. The way she lights up when she talks about things she likes. How she gestures wildly with her hands (which I find adorable even though I can't stop thinking about the big mess I'll have to clean up later). I love her expressive brown eyes and the flash of her smile as she talks. The giggles that punctuate her sentences. The way she's so comfortable letting her emotions hang out while I keep a tight, tight lid on mine.

Again, there's the sense that she just *belongs* here. In my kitchen. In my house. With me.

I don't realize how caught up in my thoughts I've been until she pushes a plate my way.

"It's done?" I ask.

She laughs, coming around the island with a plate of her own. She plops down on the stool next to me. Our fingers brush as she hands me a fork.

"I've been talking your ear off the whole time I was making it. Did you not notice me cooking?"

I was too caught up watching YOU.

"Guess I was just listening to you talk."

Sitting like this at my small counter, it's impossible not to touch. My kitchen is updated, but still one of the smallest rooms in the house. The island can only hold two stools. Barely. Right now, I wish I'd knocked out a wall and gone for a full kitchen renovation so I wouldn't keep brushing up against Val every time we move. Or smelling the way sweet vanilla sugar seems to waft off her every time she shifts or so much as takes a breath.

"Dig in," she tells me.

I do, cutting off a corner to take my first bite. I barely hold back an embarrassing sound of appreciation. Stuffed French toast is more like a French toast sandwich. Two slices of French toast surround a cream cheese and powdered sugar filling. The top is dusted with more powdered sugar—no syrup required, though Val drowns hers anyway, taking a big second bite before I've finished chewing my first.

"What?" she asks, a blush finding its way to her cheeks as she covers her mouth.

"Nothing. I just like a woman who enjoys eating."

There's no excuse for that sentence coming out of my mouth. Because A, I'm confessing I *like* Val. And B, what kind of man calls himself a man but *doesn't* want a woman to enjoy eating? It shouldn't *need* to be said.

"That came out wrong," I say, wishing I could backpedal, but feeling like a car spinning its tires in thick mud. "I only meant ... well ..."

"Chevy," Val says, wiping her smirking mouth with a napkin. "Don't take this the wrong way, but shut up and eat."

"Yes, ma'am."

And for the next few minutes, I don't say a word. Not because Val told me to shut up, but because stuffed French toast demands my full attention.

"What do you think?" Val asks, nudging my shoulder with hers when my plate is clear.

I tilt my head, meeting her gaze. "There aren't words for how good that was. Thank you."

Before I can respond, Val lifts a hand and brushes her fingertips across my cheek. I swallow as the air between us turns electric, crackling and charged. I wouldn't be shocked if it singed my eyebrows right off my face.

"Powdered sugar," she explains, holding up her fingers so I can see the dusting of white.

And then, while I'm already teetering dangerously close

to any number of bad decisions, Val licks the powdered sugar right off her fingers.

If it were any other woman, I'd know the move was calculated. Flirtatious. Seductive.

But Val is such an open book that I know she's not *trying* to tempt me. Even though the way she's looking at me makes it clear I'm not imagining this thing between us. Whatever I keep feeling and keep trying to stifle—well, she's feeling it too. Big time.

While I'm still trying to force myself to look away and return to normal baseline functions like breathing and swallowing and NOT staring hungrily at Val, she whispers, "Told you it would ruin you for all breakfasts forever."

It's true—her stuffed French toast legitimately might have ruined me for all other breakfast foods. But that's not all I'm starting to feel ruined for. Not even close.

"You cooked; I'll clean," I tell her.

"If you insist," she says. "Oh, I moved a few letters I found on the counter," she says, making my heart stop for a full beat.

The latest letter arrived just a few days ago, and I'd forgotten all about it. Probably because I don't want to think about the person writing them. I definitely don't want Val getting curious about them.

"They were addressed to you, but I saw 'Return to Sender' written on them," Val says. "Want me to drop them by the post office?"

I shove my stool back. "Nope. I'll take care of them."

Snatching her empty plate and mine, I'm very careful not to so much as brush my arm against any part of her. My whole focus is on those letters. I find them next to the sink, where I stack the dishes. As casually as I can, I grab the letters, resisting the urge to ball them up in my trembling hands.

On the plus side, they are a great reminder of why I need to put a stop to all this flirtation and chemistry and whatever. Val wants marriage, kids, and the whole thing. While I don't ever want to get married. I don't ever want to give myself a chance to fail someone so epically the way my dad failed us.

The letters—the latest ones sent from my father's *other* son—were exactly what I needed to get my head on straight.

"Thanks again for breakfast, Val. It's so nice to have a roommate."

I can't quite bring myself to say anything about her being a *friend*, but I think *roommate* sufficiently gets the point across. Her open expression closes like the hatch of a submarine, and then she sinks.

While I watch, the joy and ease she had while moving around my kitchen slide right down under the waves. Gone.

I did that. I ruined her good mood and crushed her spirit.

See? This is why you can't have relationships. You'll always be a disappointment.

"Right," Val says flatly. "Roommates."

With a quick nod, she exits the kitchen, leaving me holding the unopened letters from my half-brother and a whole belly full of regret.

FROM THE NEIGHBORLY APP

Subject: Casting calls?

The_Real_Shell_E

Anyone know when that movie studio is going to start doing casting calls? Or filming???

BagelBytes

I think they're looking for office space, so I'm not sure if it will be anytime soon. Maybe summer?

Vanz

Anyone know who does headshots? I need to get mine ready. I've been an extra in several movies while living in California. But the last photos were taken when I still had hair.

Cal_45

What movie studio?

BobToo

Brightmark Studios. They sent an exec and some scout to Sheet Cake over Christmas. Maybe they'll do a documentary on the Sheet Cake High football program!

JB

Doubtful. Not interesting.

Bob1

Don't even start, JB.

BagelBytes

Brightmark makes Hallmark-style films, not documentaries.

1BigBass

This is the last thing we need for Sheet Cake. Think of all the people. The traffic. This is going to bring all sorts of unsavory characters to town.

Vanz

The town is already filled with unsavory characters.

Cal_45

Like you

Vanz

Thank you. At least I know how to use punctuation.

MegaB

Okay Boomer

Vanz

I'm GenX, thank you very much, millennial.

Cesar

I'm happy to do headshots! My company is CesarsShotz and you can find me on Yelp. The website is under construction but I've got photos on my Facebook page!

Danielle_L

Do you do animals? I'd love to bring my kitty in. Her name is Possum Boots.

Vanz

Don't do it, Cesar! That cat has no hair. It's unnatural. Looks like an alien.

Cesar

I will do headshots for anyone—animal or human.

SlimShabby

What about mounted heads? I've got a trophy wall I'd really like to get some photos of.

Cesar

Give me a call and we can talk details!

Chels

Back to the movie studio thing—I heard they're going to start filming before they've fully moved the offices out here. Someone please post if you hear about a casting call!

CHAPTER 17

Val

THE DISTANCE CAN'T BE MORE than ten feet. A few hops, a skip, and a jump. Five seconds there, five back.

Okay, I'm a horrible estimator. But it can't be more than twenty feet from my bedroom door to the laundry room. Just down the short hall, through the kitchen, and bam! Laundry room.

It's not like you're naked, I tell myself, though the tank top and boy shorts underwear I've got on are pretty dang close. And socks! Let's not forget my fuzzy, knee-high socks. These are the only clean clothes I have after I dumped everything else in the wash.

Which was before Chevy came home.

I don't know his schedule, but had I known he'd be home so soon, I wouldn't have thrown basically all my clothes in the wash at once, leaving me in only this. How long are his shifts? He left after breakfast, but now it's only three. Shouldn't he still be at work?

His door is shut when I peek into the hallway. No movement underneath that I can see. No sound.

Maybe he's taking a nap break, and that's why he's in his room. Twenty feet—I can make it there and back. Then, I remember Chevy said he had a few clothes in my room. I yank open a dresser drawer, finding a row of neatly folded T-shirts. Who folds T-shirts? And is there an online course in folding that Chevy took? Or did he have a college job working at the GAP? Either way, the man knows how to fold clothes with military precision.

Plucking a big blue T-shirt from the drawer, I pull it over my head. It lands a little above mid-thigh but covers up my undies. It also smells heavenly and is really, really soft.

And it's Chevy's. Which makes me feel all kinds of things I shouldn't be feeling.

Focus! Laundry! Before Chevy comes back out of his room!

Before I can rethink it, I open my door all the way and sprint for the laundry room. Chevy's door is still shut when I make it in there. I toss all my clothes from the dryer into my basket as quickly as I can.

I'm feeling totally BOSS as I start running for my room again, which is a little awkward with the heavy basket. Twenty feet—a little slower now that I'm hefting this basket. Nineteen. Eighteen.

Seventee—

Chevy's door opens. I try to stop running and turn back. And, like a cartoon character, my socked feet slide and shimmy on the hardwoods and then—oh no, *oh NO*—they fly out from under me.

The basket goes up. I go down. Right on my butt, which thankfully, was built to withstand just such an impact. Then flat on my back.

Just before the basket rains laundry down all over me.

I've braced myself to be hit right in the face by the basket, but a big hand knocks it away before it hits me. I watch him with one eye from between a pair of jeans and another pair of boy shorts. Which are on my face.

Chevy chuckles. "Are you under there somewhere, Tiny?"

"Yep. I'm here."

Totally buried under the weight of so much cotton and humiliation.

"Can I help?" he asks, and then I feel him starting to pull clothes off of me.

"No!" I shout, sitting up and grabbing his hand before he reveals more of me than he means to. Or touches any of my underwear.

"Are you wearing my shirt?" he asks, and I nod slowly as he reaches out, running a thumb over the collar.

"I borrowed it from your dresser," I whisper, trying not to react to the brush of his thumb at the base of my throat. "Hope you don't mind."

His eyes flash with something like ... appreciation. Perhaps approval. *Desire?*

Don't fall for it! I tell myself. *Remember the whiplash feeling whenever he calls you friend or roommate or compares you to his sister!*

But it's too late. The avalanche and I are one, tumbling down the steep slope together, picking up speed and accumulating mass as we go.

"I don't mind," Chevy says, and the low rasp of his voice scrapes against my heart.

Chevy's thumb is still on the collar of his shirt I'm wearing, brushing over my collar bone. Tiny pinpricks of electric heat singe my skin and spark through my bloodstream, traveling all the way down to my toes. I'm gripping Chevy's other hand still like I'll never give it back.

Wouldn't that be nice? Just to keep hold of this man forever?

Yeah, if he weren't as emotionally unavailable as an old boot.

Winnie's voice in my head is just the reminder I need.

"Good." I clear my throat and let go of Chevy's hand. He drops his other hand to his knee. "That's good," I say. "And now you need to cover your eyes and go back into your room."

"Let me help you," he says, his eyes skating down my body, mostly buried in coveralls, T-shirts, and panties. Not all of which are the boy short variety. I *really* hope the few lacy thongs I own are buried under a top layer of less embarrassing clothing items.

"That's okay." When he leans down and grabs a pair of pants, I blurt, "I'm not wearing pants."

THAT gets him moving. He drops the pants. Turns and bolts for his room. His door slams. I'm not sure I've ever seen Chevy move so fast. And of course he didn't slip and fall down.

I try not to let his rapid exit bruise my ego. Is the idea of me pantsless truly *so* horrifying?

I quickly stuff all my clean clothes back in the hamper. As I'm almost in my room, Chevy's voice comes through his closed door.

"Tiny?"

I pause in my doorway. "Yeah?"

In the few beats of silence, I imagine him apologizing. Or telling me he ran away so fast to give me privacy. Or because he likes the idea of me with no pants a little *too* much, not that the thought disgusted him.

Instead, he says, "You really should separate your lights and darks."

I kick the door closed with a slam that rattles the windows.

Aside from pantsless apocalypse—which sounds like the next big hit brought to you by the studio who made *Sharknado*—Chevy and I settle into a rhythm that feels comfortable and has no more embarrassing moments. It also has no more charged moments that feel like precursors to a kiss, which I find highly disappointing.

We both work kind of odd hours, so I haven't seen him much in the last two days. But he promised he'd be home for dinner, so I'm making gallo pinto, which is Costa Rica's version of beans and rice. It's one of Mari's favorite dishes to make at home, though it's never been served at the diner. "Too simple," she always says. But sometimes simple is the best. Especially when I like to add bacon and sauté the onions and peppers in bacon fat.

"Smells like a police joke come to life," Chevy says when he walks in the kitchen, looking good enough to eat, still in his uniform. Today, it's the blue shirt with pearl snaps and darker blue denim, worn almost white at the knees. He sets his cowboy hat on a stool and roughs a hand through his hair.

And I look down at the pot so if he sees me drooling, he'll think it's about the food. "A police joke?"

"The bacon." He steals a corner of a piece from the paper towel where I have it draining.

I swat him with the wooden spoon. "No bacon thievery, please! And do people really make those kinds of jokes?"

"Let's put it this way: I have been gifted donuts more times than I can count and heard about every variety of pig joke."

"That's disappointing," I say.

He shrugs and settles in on a stool across from me. "I'm used to it."

"No—I mean, it's disappointing they don't gift you bacon. Between donuts and bacon, I'd go bacon every time."

Chevy grins, and the sight of his dimples make my stomach do some kind of anti-gravity maneuver. I focus on crumbling the bacon and adding it to the pot with the beans and rice. "I hope you're hungry," I say, still not looking up.

"Always. Especially for anything involving bacon."

"Good. This will be ready in about five minutes if you need to change or anything. Not that you have to change. I like you in your uniform—I mean, I like your uniform, but if you—"

"I'll change really quick," Chevy says. But instead of leaving the room, he starts undoing his shirt, right there at the island.

Snap! Snap! Snap! go the pearl buttons.

Thump! Thump! Thump! goes my heart.

The only thing saving me from falling into a full-on swoon is the fact that Chevy has on a T-shirt underneath. But it's tight and white and stretches across his broad body. Look—I can't deny the Grahams have got it going on with all those muscles on muscles on muscles. But Chevy is perfection to me. He's big and strong, but also soft in just the right ways. You can keep your six-pack abs and let me have a man who's strong and yet huggably soft.

Or ... just *this* man.

All the snaps are undone, and I try to remember what I'm doing—turning off the stove before I burn the rice at the bottom. Still, I can multitask. Right?

I can watch Chevy peeling off his shirt from under my lashes while also dishing up the gallo pinto. Easy. It's hard, however, not to dump it everywhere when he hangs his shirt off the back of his chair, then stretches his arms overhead. The fabric of his fitted shirt goes taut across his broad chest.

The spoon in my hand falls and clatters to the floor.

"Five second rule!" I declare, sounding slightly manic. I bend down and hold up the spoon triumphantly.

Chevy's lips quirk. "I think that's usually with food. I'll take a clean spoon, if you don't mind."

"Of course.." I toss the spoon in the sink, then grab another and walk around with our bowls.

"You know you don't have to make me food," Chevy says, but I can see the way he's eyeing the bowl appreciatively.

I nudge him with my elbow. "I want to."

"Well, I want to tell you to stop, but this looks delicious, so I won't. Is this beans and rice?"

"The Costa Rican version. It's called gallo pinto," I tell him. "I guess every culture has their own version of beans and rice. According to Mari, Nicaragua and Costa Rica are locked in a death match trying to claim gallo pinto as their own. You need this on top."

I hand him the Salsa Lizano, which is a must for this dish. Before it was available on Amazon, Mari had her cousins send her packages of the hot sauce, and I can still remember her squeals of glee when they'd arrive.

"Are you excited about going to Costa Rica?" Chevy's question is careful, and it makes me feel a little like I'm in an interrogation room.

"Yes?"

"Try to sound a little more sure," he teases, tapping his spoon with mine. "Also, this is amazing."

"Thank you." I take another bite, thinking while evaluating my cooking. Maybe a little more spice or sweetness next time—roasting the red peppers first might do the trick. "I'm excited about going, but nervous too."

"Want to talk about it?"

I appreciate that he's asking about Costa Rica, and appreciate even more that he's asking if I want to talk about it. Which ... I really haven't. Not to anyone. I didn't go deeper with my friends than cursory answers. And I absolutely haven't told anyone why I'm scared to death of such a big change.

Setting my spoon down, I swivel on the stool to face Chevy. We're way closer than I realized at the small counter, and I can see the way darker blue and gray fleck his eyes.

"I feel like I should go. Like I *have* to. And I do want to, at least a little. My family has been ..." I search for a word, getting distracted for a moment watching Chevy's jaw flex as he chews. "Pretty nonexistent. Other than Mari. My mom—gone. My sisters—gone as fast as they could. Last I heard, they were both living somewhere in the Midwest? I tried to keep up with them, but they just don't care."

I can see Chevy wanting to say something, wanting to offer comfort in some way. But I've cried enough tears over my messed-up family. Now, I have Mari. And, maybe soon, some other aunts and uncles and distant second cousins.

And one day, I hope a husband and a family of my own that I will love fiercely and never, ever think about leaving. I glance at Chevy, then away.

"I've never met my family in Costa Rica before, but Mari insists they've always wanted to meet me. They just don't travel. It will be good to connect with family, to see where my family came from. I'd love to pick up some Spanish, since I barely know more than any kid in Sheet Cake who had Mrs. Thomas in high school."

"I had her!" Chevy says. "And I know how to say *hello* and *it's hot.*"

"Exactly." I pick up my spoon again, playing with the food in my bowl rather than eating it. "I also know it will help to have a mentorship like this with a real, working artist. I need some help figuring out what that looks like."

"Tank bought a bunch of your paintings, right?"

"He did." And I'm antsy to move my stuff into Mr. Silver's studio so I can work on finishing them. I think Chevy's helping me in a few days, right before Mari leaves, something I'm trying not to think about. "But it's not like that's a solid strategy, just hoping some rich guy will buy a dozen paintings at once without even seeing them." I sigh, staring down into my bowl. "I'm just struggling to see where I belong in the world, in my life. So, this seems like a good plan for me. For now."

"And after?" That careful tone is back in his voice.

I shrug. "I'll come back. And then … I don't know."

Give me a reason, Chevy. Come on. Ask me to stay. Or to come back for you. To you.

"Well, you've got a place here if you need it," he says, and it's close to what I really want, but still so far away.

I want begging, passionate pleading, can't live without you kind of stuff. Not a general invite to crash in his guest bedroom. *Sigh*.

He pushes away his empty bowl. "Which reminds me—while I've got you sitting here, I want to do something."

Chevy disappears from the kitchen, only to return a moment later with a notebook and a pencil. He flips the notebook until he finds a blank page. I try not to be too nosy, reading through what looks very much like a daily bullet journal. Chevy, journaling? Interesting.

"Roommate rules," he says, and while I'm processing this statement, I watch him write those same words along the top of the page in messy, blocky letters.

I shift on my stool. "Have I already done something wrong?"

"No," he says a little too quickly, and then I remember me running pantsless through the house. At the very least, THAT. I've tried to keep my things picked up, but where Chevy is almost clinically neat and tidy, I'm more of the Peanuts' Pigpen, only I leave a trail of my stuff instead of dust. Chevy brought me a sock the other day he said he found in the pantry. I have no idea how it got there, but also wasn't at all surprised.

"So what are the rules for, exactly?"

"My freshman year of college, my RA had us all do this with our roommates. It's more like expectations about things like watching TV at different times, quiet hours, cleaning up after yourself, and, um, having people over. Stuff like that. Didn't you have to do that?"

I shake my head, but my brain tripped over the last option Chevy mentioned. *Having people over.* Of course—Chevy wants to talk about rules so he can have a woman here. Now, I'm not shifting on my stool but squirming. I barely touched my food, but I wish I'd eaten even less as my stomach churns.

"Makes sense," I say, hoping Chevy can't sense how close I am to needing a paper bag to breathe into.

"We can start with the easy stuff," he says. "Can we agree on no wild parties? Or loud gatherings past midnight without asking the other person first?"

"Sure." Like I'm going to have a wild party. Even in college, I wasn't a party girl. But I'll take this softball.

Chevy continues with the soft pitches—things like if one person cooks for both, the other does the dishes, and if we're eating alone, we clean up after ourselves—long enough to lull me into false comfort. So, when he suddenly switches gears, I nearly topple off my stool.

"How about … no nudity in the common areas," he says, already writing it down. "Pants and shirts required outside of bedrooms and bathrooms."

This one is totally aimed at me and my pantsless laundry dash the other day. But I'm not the only one who's broken this rule lately.

"Fine. Let's add this one—no answering the front door shirtless and with your hand in your pants," I say, blinking innocently like this is some total hypothetical.

"Okay." He clears his throat, then eyes me sideways. "And no running through the house without pants on."

I glare. "You weren't home when I threw all my clothes in the wash."

"But you knew I was home when you came out to get them," he points out.

"I tried to hurry! That's why I fell over. Because I was trying to get back to my room."

Chevy taps his pen on the page. "Noted. But from here on out, pants are non-optional."

"Fine," I say.

"Good."

He taps his pencil on the paper, and I tilt my head, reading down the list. Everything but the clothing-required portion is pretty tame, and not really a big deal. But he still hasn't said anything about bringing over guests. As in, *dates*. I know it's coming since he mentioned it, but the idea makes my whole head ache. But I'd rather hit this head-on than listen to Chevy dance around it.

"How about sleepovers?" I ask.

He clears his throat again, then switches from tapping the pen to drawing violent little circles that look like they'll rip right through the page. "Like ... you having Winnie and Lindy sleep over?"

"Nope. Like one of us bringing someone home after a date."

Not like I make a habit of this. Chevy and I are opposites in this—I'm the serial monogamist while he's the casual dater. But if he wants to make rules, we're gonna MAKE RULES.

Let's see how long it takes you to sweat, Chevy.

"I don't think that will be an issue for me," he says slowly.

"It might be an issue for me."

The point of the pencil breaks off on the page, and his eyes snap to mine. "You're planning to bring guys home with you?"

I shrug. "Maybe. Is that a problem?"

His nostrils flare the slightest bit, and it reminds me so much of Winnie when she's mad. "No," he says, but the words sound like they're being forcibly yanked out of him. "That's fine. Just have your guests follow these same rules."

"I'll make sure they're fully dressed—at least outside the bedroom. Same for you?"

Can Chevy tell this is all just talk? That I would *never* bring some guy back over here, even if that was something typical for me. Which it absolutely is not.

But he doesn't seem to realize I'm just messing with him. Trying to push him toward some edge of something. Jealousy, maybe? Okay, yeah. I'd like to see him jealous, the way I feel imagining him even on a date, much less bringing someone else home.

He shakes his head. "Getting that specific about overnight guests isn't necessary."

"I think it is."

"It's not for me."

"Why not, Chevy?"

He sets the broken pencil down, then closes the notebook before catching and holding my gaze again. "Because you are the only woman other than my sister who has ever slept in this house."

Oh. *Oh.*

This knowledge is almost too much for me. I shouldn't take this to mean I'm something special, because it's not like I'm sharing his bed. Just the friend in the guest room.

And yet ... this knowledge does something to me.

Knowing Chevy hasn't ever brought a woman back here makes my jealousy disappear like fog in the bright light of his confession.

"I'm not going to bring anyone home either," I whisper. Opening the notebook, I pick up the pencil and erase the last rule he wrote about guests. "So, no need for a rule at all."

"Are you sure?" His question sounds like a challenge.

I set down the pencil, briefly running my fingertips over his knuckles, already healed with new, pink skin in place of the cuts and scabs. "There's no one I want to bring home," I tell him, feeling the uncomfortable itch of vulnerability.

Because the only man I want is already here, I think but don't say.

Can he read it in my eyes? My skin feels as thin and transparent as a piece of plastic wrap.

"Then I guess we're settled," he says.

"I guess we are."

"If anything changes ..." He trails off, and I know there's

only one rule he's talking about. Or, rather, a non-rule, since we took it off the list.

"It won't," I promise.

When he smiles at me this time, slow and soft like we're sharing a secret, I have to clutch the edge of the counter to stay upright.

"Same," he says.

CHAPTER 18

Val

"Please explain to me what's happening here," I say.

"Which part?" Lindy asks with a chuckle, glancing beyond her fence where Pat and Jo are standing in the yard. Pat has a backwards spoon in his mouth and Jo is tossing pieces of chicken nugget into the grass.

"All of it, please."

Lindy and I are rocking gently on the back porch swing of her newly finished house, snuggled into a fuzzy blanket. A far cry from the falling-apart home that used to exist on this same spot, the new house is perfect—thanks to Patrick Graham, who wouldn't be satisfied unless the place was straight out of Lindy's Pinterest board dreams. That man seems to be in a constant battle of one-upmanship with himself to spoil Lindy and Jo.

When Lindy called and begged me to be here for moral

support when she tells Pat and Jo about the baby, I practically sprinted to my car. Chevy is helping me move my paintings to the studio a little later, so I had a tiny window of time. I wouldn't want to miss this.

"Jo read some article about how crows are super smart and will keep coming back if you feed them. Sometimes they bring people gifts. Shiny things. I think she's hoping for an entire charm bracelet."

This is so perfectly Jo that I can't help but grin. It's also perfectly Pat. "A noble dream. Wait—crows eat chicken nuggets? Seems a little cannibalistic."

"I know, right? They also eat peanuts, fruit, crackers, and, of all things, meatballs. Our grocery bill is going to get nuts."

"And what's Pat doing with the spoon?"

Lindy chuckles. "My dear, sweet husband is doing face yoga. He and Collin got some app that's supposed to help with the elasticity in your face and prevent wrinkles."

"Because that's something Pat and Collin are worried about?"

"Apparently."

"The crows make a lot more sense. Should *we* be doing face yoga?"

"Absolutely not," Lindy says.

As we watch, Pat flexes his jaw, making the spoon bob up and down in his mouth. Lindy and I dissolve into a fit of giggles, and I pull the fuzzy blanket tighter around me. The sun is warm on my face and the temperatures have warmed slightly after the front blew in a few days ago, but I am ready for spring.

As if summoned by our conversation, three crows appear, swooping down into nearby trees. Jo throws the last few bits of food, and then she and Pat back away toward the house.

After a moment, the birds hop forward, picking up pieces of nugget from the grass.

"Wow. They're bigger than I expected."

"Louder too," Lindy says. "It's such a total Jo and Pat thing."

Pat slings an arm around Jo, and the movement scares the crows. They flap a little ways off, cawing in a way that sounds a whole lot like yelling. Pat backs up a few more feet, tugging Jo with him, and the birds cautiously return.

I bump Lindy's shoulder with mine. "You know they're going to lose their minds with happiness when you tell them, right?"

Lindy's quiet for a moment. "It's so weird. For years, I felt trapped—here in this house, this town, this life I didn't choose. Even in small ways. Like, if I wanted ice cream in the middle of the night, I couldn't just get in my car and go to the store. I had a little person who couldn't be left alone. I mean, we're talking pre-Door Dash days. Do you know what that's like?"

I don't. I mean, I do remember the pre-Door-Dash days. But I have absolutely no idea how it feels to suddenly be in charge of a whole other person, whether you can get ice cream delivered in the middle of the night or not.

I still feel kind of like a baby in comparison. I've had Mari to lean on rather than having to provide for myself. Much less providing for myself *and* a child.

"You're kind of my hero, Linds."

"Don't get all mushy on me, Valley Girl."

"You started it!"

She laughs, though her wet sniffle in the middle tells me she's still feeling all the feelings. *Me too, sister. Me too.*

"No one tells you how being a mom is like attaching a tether to your body, to your soul. It's physical, like me not being able to leave the house at night. But it's also *emotional*. I have all this worry, all the time. Jo's smarter than the other kids. Different. Will she be okay? Will she be bullied? I'm not sure I can do this with one kid. How can I do it all over again with another?"

All I know is that listening to her talk, I ache so badly for this life. I want to be an artist, yes. But even more than that, I want to build my own little family. I've always wanted that. It's why I always throw myself into every relationship I have. I want this so badly it physically makes my chest tight.

And yet, I'm still so very happy for my friends to have found this.

I lean my shoulder into Lindy's. She leans into me right back and sighs. "You've done so good," I tell her.

"Have I?"

The wavering in her voice has my tear ducts going into high alert.

"*Yes.*"

Her eyes brim, and I burrow into her shoulder. She leans her head on mine. "This will change everything," Lindy says.

"But a good change," I say. "A great one. A beautiful one."

"Speaking of changes—how's it going living with Chevy?"

I groan. "Let's talk more about you and the baby. Please?"

Lindy gives the end of my braid a tug. "Come on—three-sentence update. Winnie's not here. You can tell me anything."

"There's nothing to tell."

Pulling away enough to shoot me an assessing (and disbelieving) gaze, Lindy says, "Nothing?"

I blow out a breath and look back to the yard, where the crows seem to have finished their nuggets and are cawing loudly at Pat and Jo. "Fine. I like him. He doesn't like me. The end." I make a face. "He made up rules for us."

"What kind of rules?" Lindy asks.

"Roommate rules. I think because he happened to catch me running through the house pantsless." When Lindy's mouth drops open, I quickly add, "He didn't see anything! I dropped laundry all over myself. The point is that if he were interested, he wouldn't make rules."

"I made rules for Pat when we got fake-married." Lindy sounds smug. "And look where that got me."

"Yeah, well. Chevy and Pat aren't the same. I bet you made the rules and Pat spent all his time trying to break them. Whereas, we aren't married, Chevy made these rules, and I don't foresee him trying to break them. Even if we've had a few … moments."

"Moments?" Of course, Lindy zooms right in on that. "Details, please. The juicier the better."

I wish I had juicy things to tell her. But as I quickly recount the little moments where we had some kind of connection, they all sound so thin. Not like bricks building something solid, but more like playing cards precariously stacked into a house that will blow over at the first tiny breeze.

"I always suspected Chevy might have feelings for you."

I almost fall off the swing. "You did? You've never said anything!" When Lindy doesn't answer in less than one point five seconds, I grab her arm and shake her. "Why? Tell me!"

"Don't shake the baby!"

"You can't use the baby for excuses yet. It's too tiny to be bothered by shaking. Answer me, woman!"

"Stop manhandling me first," Lindy says. And like the very calm and mature person I am, I shake her once more, then let her go. "There's nothing definitive I can point to. Just small things. He gave you a nickname. Only you. No one else. And I know for a fact Winnie never had to warn him away from me."

I feel a shiver worthy of a whole battalion of people walking over my grave. "Winnie did what?"

Lindy makes a face. "I don't think she knows I know. But I overheard her threatening Chevy if he ever hurt you. Maybe I shouldn't have mentioned it."

This information is taking a while to process. Like I've tried to upload some fancy software to an early 2000s Windows system with seventy-five open programs. I never even considered that while Winnie was warning me away from Chevy, she might be doing the same to him. I can't decide if I'm upset with her for telling Chevy to stay away or honored she cares so much she threatened her own brother for me.

"Was this recently?"

"Years ago. Don't be mad, okay? We were in high school. My point, though, is that Winnie didn't warn Chevy away from *me*. She was only concerned about you, Val. You've got to ask yourself—why?"

Oh, believe me—I'm asking myself why. I also want to ask Winnie, which might be tricky because that means telling Winnie that Lindy told me after overhearing it years ago. Is this why he keeps pushing me away when it seems like something might be shifting between us? Or is it something else?

For now, I'm going to chew on this.

The crows fly off, still making a lot of racket and, so far as I can see, leaving no charm bracelets behind. Jo runs back toward the porch, Pat trailing behind, still making the spoon bob up and down. But as he approaches, he slides it into his back pocket, beaming at Lindy like she's his universe's only sun.

I want someone to look at me like that. So badly it's almost a visceral throb in my whole body. And deep down, it's not just a general someone I want. It's Chevy. It's only ever been Chevy.

"On another topic," Lindy says. "Are you going to be okay when Mari leaves?"

I squeeze my eyes closed. "Do you have to bring up every single thing I don't want to talk about today?"

"That's what friends are for," Lindy says.

"Well, in that case, no. I don't think I'm going to be okay. I'll cry like a whole room full of babies and—"

Lindy suddenly sits straight up, her face ashen. "Speaking of babies ..."

And that's all the warning she gives before jumping up and vomiting over the porch railing into the bushes.

"Mom!" Jo says, freezing at the bottom of the stairs.

I'm on my feet in a second, rubbing Lindy's back while trying not to look at the puke. She heaves another few times, and then Pat's there, ripping off his shirt—of course, because it wouldn't be a complete day without Pat taking his shirt off —to tenderly wipe the tears from her cheeks.

"Hey, darlin, what gives? You okay?"

Lindy shoots me a panicked look. I know she had a whole speech prepared, but I think that ship has sailed. I shrug and give her shoulder an encouraging squeeze.

She takes a deep breath and turns to Pat. But she doesn't need to say a word. He takes one look at her expression, and a smile brighter than the sun breaks over his face.

"Really? For real?"

Lindy sniffs, smiling through a fresh round of tears. "Not how I wanted to tell you but ..."

"Tell you what?" Jo makes it to the top porch step, hesitating as her gaze swings from Lindy to Pat. "Are you sick?"

After Lindy took the test, she told Winnie and me she never wanted Jo to feel self-conscious or weird about Pat and Lindy having a biological child. It's been one of her biggest worries about having kids—how Jo might react.

"She won't feel left out or unloved," I assured her then. "Y'all just keep loving her the way you do, and it will be fine."

Not that I have any experience. I only know what it looks like to NOT be on the receiving end of great parenting. But as I step back now, giving the little family some space, I see proof I was right not to be worried.

Pat gives Lindy a quick hug and then, grasping her hand, he drops to his knees before Jo. "Jojo," he says. "We're going to need your help with something really important. It's a job only for you, and I know that you're going to be so great. Think you can handle some extra responsibility?"

Jo gives him her most serious expression. "I swear it."

Pat grins up at Lindy, who nods. "How would you feel about being a big sister?"

With eyes as big as serving platters, Jo shrieks, trying to jump up and down while trying to hug Pat and Lindy both at the same time. All the jostling must upset Lindy's stomach again, because she goes back to heaving over the railing, this time with Pat and Jo both whispering soothing words and rubbing Lindy's back.

I don't realize I'm full-on crying with the snot and every-thing until I've quietly slipped away to my car. None of them noticed I left, which is fine, really. It's their big, sweet moment, and I want them to have it alone. It's also almost time to meet Chevy to move my studio, which means I need to pull it together.

But the whole drive back to his house, I feel like I'm on

the verge of collapsing in on myself. There is a black hole of longing in my chest for that. For family of my own.

I've never felt so lonely.

When I park in front of Chevy's house, he's just pulling his cruiser into the driveway, grinning as he hops out. The sight of him in his uniform, looking so happy and so handsome starts a fresh round of tears. I lean my head on the steering wheel and sob, refusing to look up when there's a soft knock on the window.

"Tiny," Chevy says in a soft, crooning voice. He tries the handle but it's still locked. "Open up."

"No," I say through a hiccupping sob.

"Don't make me get out my slim jim."

"I love Slim Jims."

He chuckles. "I don't mean the food. I mean the tool to open locked car doors."

"Oh." I laugh a little and click the button to unlock the doors. Even so, I let out a squeak of surprise when Chevy leans in, his Kraken scent filling my nose as he unlocks my seatbelt and hauls me out of the car, crushing me into a hug.

We stand like that for a few minutes, my body limp like an unstuffed rag doll, my toes barely dragging along the ground. Chevy just holds me, his body so warm and strong as his breath tickles my cheek. Eventually, I find the ability to move and wrap my arms around his neck.

"You know I'm here," he says, his voice a soft murmur.

"I know."

"I hate to see you sad, Tiny,"

"I'm not sad."

He pulls me tighter, and when he makes a humming sound, the vibration moves from his chest to mine. "Are you telling me these are happy tears?"

"Mostly. I *am* happy." I'm also desperately sad.

Chevy doesn't say anything for a few beats, he just holds me. And I try—a very valiant and totally unsuccessful effort—not to wish for something more than just friendly comfort. Finally, Chevy tips his head back, still keeping me tight against him but now searching my face, which I'm sure is a red, puffy, tear-streaked mess.

Chevy yanks me back against his chest with a groan. "You're killing me, Tiny."

As I settle in, squeezing him tight as I breathe in his Kraken scent, I think, *You have no idea.*

CHAPTER 19

Chevy

THE SMILE on Mari's face is the kind that gave birth to the phrase sly as a fox. I'm instantly on alert.

"So, how's it going with your new roomie?" She leans on the broom handle, standing in the middle of her empty living room and looking at me like she knows *exactly* how it's going.

I cross my arms and raise my brows. "Fine. Normal. Roommate-y."

Val and I are here to pack up her art studio, but I stopped in Mari's house first to see if she needs any help. Or, really, just to see Mari. She leaves tomorrow, and it still hasn't sunk in. The house is nearly empty—no help needed here—and she's doing some last-minute cleaning, a bandana tied around her white hair and broom in hand. The whole house smells like lemon cleaner.

"Is that so?" she asks.

"It is."

"Interesting." With a hum and another sly smile, she goes back to sweeping.

I should head out to the studio to help Val load the truck. I shouldn't respond to what seems like bait, dangling in front of my nose. "What's so interesting about it?"

Mari doesn't look up, continuing to sweep what already looks like a clean floor. "Oh, I just thought maybe living with her would finally wake you up to how you feel."

"How I feel about having a roommate?" I ask, hoping I can keep playing dumb. No such luck.

Mari stops sweeping. She also stops smiling. "You're a good man, Chevy. And you're your *own* man. You. I hope you know that."

A prickling, itching sensation claws its way up my spine. Because what Mari's saying and yet *not* saying sounds a whole lot like she knows the deepest reason I have for making roommate rules with Val. For trying to keep her at arm's length, at *friend* length, even if it's getting harder and harder.

Which would mean ... Mari knows about my dad.

Everything about my dad.

I can't ask, because that would mean talking about it—about him. And I don't want to ruin a perfectly nice day.

"Do you know that, Chevy?" she continues. "Do you know that you're a good man? That no one else's mistakes have to be yours?"

"Yes," I whisper, working as hard as I can to keep my voice from wavering. It's difficult when my heart is flailing around like a fish on land. I'm also not entirely sure I believe that single syllable I just uttered.

But I want to.

Her eyes narrow. "You'd better know it." And then, like we didn't just have an unexpectedly vulnerable moment, she goes back to sweeping. "Better get out there and help Val."

I practically bolt from her house. And on the short walk to the detached garage, I do my level best to push the entire conversation from my mind. I keep trying to forget about my dad. And people keep bringing it up. Or my half-brother sends *another* letter like he did today. I can't seem to escape him, and every reminder cuts me a little deeper. Mari may have been trying to reassure me—and she may have a point —but it was just one more reminder of my dad and of why I'm *not* pursuing Val.

Because, ultimately, I'm not concerned about my sister's warning. She'd get over it. Maybe even learn to like it.

And I'm not worried about risking my friendship with Val. Or, anyway, I think it would be a worthy risk.

It all comes down to me feeling like my father's actions have stained me somehow. That his unfaithfulness hums in my blood.

Pausing just outside the open doors, I lean my head against the siding and try to just breathe. It's funny how all those involuntary things your body does on its own all the time without you thinking about it can suddenly become ALL you think about. And then, they're no longer involuntary. If I were to stop focusing on taking deep breaths right now, I'm pretty sure my lungs wouldn't be doing their thing. Which only makes breathing harder.

You're fine. Everything is fine. And in a few weeks, Val will be gone. You won't have to worry about who you are or aren't or whether it was the best or worst idea in the world to have her come live with you. BREATHE.

I'm not sure how long I stand there, forcing oxygen in

and out slowly, but the sound of Val singing to herself as she moves around inside the building brings the world back into focus. I don't think I realized it was out of focus. But the sound of her voice—which is slightly off-key and of course, she's singing some horrible pop song—has my heartbeat steadying and my breathing returning to something I don't need to regulate myself.

By the time I walk into Val's studio to find her taping boxes shut, still singing her bubblegum pop, I'm smiling. I'd bet it almost looks normal. And I've locked up all thoughts I can't handle right now in the dark recesses of my brain.

"Is that a Justin Bieber song?" I ask.

Val startles, whirling to face me and tipping over a box of brushes in the process. "Jeez, Chev. Give a girl a heart attack!"

I quickly bend and pick up the scattered brushes, shooing her away with my hand when she tries to help. "I've got it. Sorry I scared you."

"I thought you were still inside with Mari. I didn't expect you to creep up on me like some kind of silent ninja."

"Do you need me to wear bells?" I ask. "I feel like that's one of those things people in books are always suggesting."

Val gives me a funny look. "What kind of books are you reading?"

Romance novels, though I'm not admitting that out loud. What can I say? Winnie got me hooked. And rather than checking them out at the library, where someone's liable to post on Neighborly about a town deputy reading bodice rippers, I've been reading with the Kindle app on my phone. Nice and discrete. No drama here. Also, it means I don't have to answer to my sister, who would find some way to turn this back around on me.

Before I can make up an answer, Val tips the brim of my

cowboy hat. "Yeah, maybe you should sew some bells on here. It would be like a cowboy Christmas all year round."

We both realize at the same time how close we're standing. Val drops her hand from my hat but doesn't step back. Neither do I. And there goes my heart again—doubling its speed as I stand here, my gaze locked with Val's big brown eyes.

No one else's mistakes have to be yours.

Mari's words linger in my mind like wisps of smoke. I want to shove that thought away, but is it possible that she's right?

Val blinks, and I take a step back. A big one. "I'll get right on the bells," I tell her. "Right after we finish this." I glance around, forcing myself not to look at Val. "Where can I start? And is there a particular way to handle the paintings? The last thing I want to do is ruin something you made."

"Boxes on the bottom. We can secure the paintings on top." Val starts to lift the box in front of her, and I snatch it.

"Nope. I'm the muscle today. You're the mouth. Tell me what to do, and I'll do it."

Grinning, she points to the door. "Then, load up the truck, Muscle. If you're quick enough, I'll buy you dinner."

"And if I'm slow?"

"I'll still buy you dinner. But I get to choose the place."

"How about if I'm quick enough you *make* me dinner."

I really, really like Val in my kitchen. We've had opposite schedules the last few days, which has been highly disappointing. But when she's cooking, I can watch her without feeling guilty or obvious about it. Plus, I've been existing on frozen dinners for years. Home cooked food of any kind is a luxury.

Meals home-cooked by Val? They're better than any exclusive dining experience.

"Deal," Val says. "Now, mush, Muscle. Mush!"

I start for the door with the box, then realize all her paintings—which I've been dying to see—are wrapped up in something like butcher paper. "Aw, you already packed up your paintings."

Val brushes past me, her fingertips skating over my forearm and making my stomach dip. "Maybe, if you're a good boy, I'll let you take a peek later."

I swallow—HARD—and I swear, I can almost hear Mari cackling from inside the house.

—————

All in all, it only takes an hour or so to pack up and get the entirety of Val's studio over to Mr. Silver's place. The light's just starting to fade, taking any warmth from the sun with it. I'm not sure which of us is more surprised that Mr. Silver's house is in the new section of town, a brick home like every other home in a planned community.

"Huh," she says.

I turn off the engine and stare at the house numbers by the door. "Planned community living is not what I would picture for your uptight, fancy pants boss."

"Same. I would have guessed he lives in some kind of modern monstrosity. A glass and metal loft where every piece of furniture looks like it could double as a torture device."

"Or maybe a mid-century modern place," I suggest.

Val giggles. "Instead, we have the 'burbs. There's even a basketball hoop!"

That there is. As I'm peering out at it, the garage door opens. And like something out of a horror movie, Mr. Silver stands there, backlit and unmoving as the door rises.

"Does that man terrify you as much as he terrifies me?" I ask.

"Don't worry Chev, I'll protect you from the big, mean art gallery owner." She pats my knee and hops out of my truck.

I wait for a beat, climbing out of my truck slowly. By the time I do, three other figures have joined Val and Mr. Silver in the garage. Three teen boys, I realize as I get closer. That's … also unexpected. Two are white, tall and lanky with shaggy brown hair, and the third is Black and a little shorter than Mr. Silver.

Mr. Silver is making introductions as I reach them. The taller boys I already know, and not in the way you want to know a cop when you're a teenager. They duck their heads a little when they see me.

"This is Valentina," Mr. Silver says.

All three boys shake Val's hand, meeting her eyes and saying, "Nice to meet you, ma'am." And not in the mumbly teenage boy way, but with actual whole syllables. The picture of politeness.

Not what I remember from my other encounter with the two boys.

Val grins. "No ma'ams. *Please*. Just Val."

"Yes, ma'am—I mean, Val," the shortest one says. His grip is strong as he shakes my hand. "I'm John."

"Good to meet you, John. I'm Chevy—Deputy Boyd, if we're being formal. And you are?"

I raise my brows at the other two, who are hanging back. They look up in surprise, then exchange a glance. The last time I saw them, they had cans of spray paint in hand and I was putting them in the back of my squad car. They were also part of the crew that first started stuffing things into Mrs. Fleming's cannons. But not anymore. I borrowed doorbell cam footage from a neighbor and these two definitely weren't there.

The first boy shakes my hand fast, darting back like he expects me to yell, "Gotcha!" and pull out my cuffs. "Bryan," he mumbles. "Good to … meet you."

The other steps forward, his expression looking like some kind of dare. I give him one right back.

"Brady," he says, his handshake a little more firm than it needs to be. Another challenge. I also don't miss the way he keeps positioning himself between me and Bryan. Brothers, from what I recall.

"It's nice to meet y'all," I say, making sure to meet Brady's then Bryan's eyes as I do.

That's right, boys. Sometimes you do get a fresh start. I won't tell if you don't.

Mr. Silver likely knows their story already, or a good part of it. A social worker picked up the boys after the arrest last year. I'm thinking this is a foster situation.

And as Mr. Silver asks the boys to listen to Val and help unpack her things, they nod quickly and eagerly. This is one of the good foster situations, then. *Really* good. No way would the Bryan and Brady I met last year be helping unload paintings for someone else.

It's blowing my mind more than a little bit.

With their help, we're done in ten minutes, setting up Val's easel and stacking canvases against the wall in a room attached to the back of the garage. The sun's gone down now, but I can tell the big windows in this room will let in a lot of light.

That's good for painting—right? I don't know the first thing about what Val does, but I feel like people always talk about artists needing good light.

"You boys play ball?" I ask as I bring in the last box. "I saw the hoop out there."

John nods eagerly, running a hand over his short curls. Brady and Bryan give more subtle nods, still looking about as wary of me as they were when I arrived.

"How about a little two on two?" I ask, then look at Val. "That is, unless you and Mr. Silver want to make it three on three."

Val laughs. "I'd rather watch. In fact, I'd pay to see this. Is there any popcorn?"

Mr. Silver, the kind of man I can't picture having or making popcorn, tips his head toward the house. "I think we can rummage something up."

They head inside, the boys grab the ball, and I park my truck on the street to give us room. By the time Val and Mr. Silver return with a tray filled with popcorn bowls and cups of water, Bryan and I are losing. Badly.

More like, *embarrassingly*. I know the nineties song says age ain't nothing but a number, but I'm feeling every number between me and these teens with their boundless energy. They're also *good*—whereas pickup games in a driveway like this are the extent of my experience.

I'm a panting, sweaty mess, and have yet to make a shot. I wish I could say having Val watch makes me more confident, but instead, her presence makes me significantly worse. Which I didn't think possible.

Bryan groans when I attempt a pass, almost trip over my own feet, and manage to practically gift the ball to Brady, who sinks it without so much as touching the rim. I bend over, resting my hands on my knees and trying to decide if I should worry about how out of breath I am.

"Sorry, man. You got the raw end of this deal," I tell Bryan, but he grins and gives my back a slap.

"Come on. You're not dead yet, old man."

I wheeze out a laugh and decide not to comment on being called *old man*. "Close. You have no idea how close," I mutter.

And because Mr. Silver and Val seem to be in deep discussion, I catch Brady's eye. "I'm gonna be cleaning out Mrs. Fleming's cannon in a few days. I'd love some help. Interested?"

Bryan's head snaps toward his brother, and I don't let my gaze stray from Brady's. He looks like he's trying to read into my offer.

"No tricks," I tell him quietly with a quick shake of my head. "And it's not required. Just an opportunity to right an old wrong."

"We'll be there," he says, and then Brady manages to get by me and Bryan to score again.

Four more points for them and I'm wondering if it's possible for someone my age to suffer cardiac arrest during a pickup basketball game. I'm leaning toward yes.

There's a tap on my shoulder. This time, it's Val. Her look is all smug amusement. "I'm tapping in," she says, tipping her head toward the lawn chairs where Mr. Silver is watching.

"You sure you want to take my place, Tiny?"

She rolls her eyes. "Don't look so shocked. I might get offended."

"It's just that you said earlier—"

"I said I wanted to *watch*. Not that I *couldn't* play. And now that I've watched, I think it's time you step aside." Her grin is fast and fierce, and all three boys whoop and holler insults.

But I don't mind being the one watching. Also, I'm not sure if my lungs are functioning properly.

"Fine. Don't go too hard on these guys." I give her ponytail a little tug before collapsing into the seat she vacated.

Mr. Silver holds out a big plastic cup, the kind you usually get from a sports game. "Water?"

"Don't mind if I do."

I take a long swallow, angling the cup so I don't miss a thing. The boys are looking about as doubtful as I did a moment ago. Val steals the ball from one of them and casually dribbles. All three tower over her, but hesitate to move closer.

"Don't tell me you boys don't think I can play because I'm a girl," she says.

"No, ma'am," all three say in unison. But their shifty gazes belie the quick response.

Val narrows her eyes and takes a lower stance, dancing back a little with the ball. "Well, come on then."

Before any of them can respond, she darts around Brady, does a neat bounce pass to Bryan, and sinks a glorious shot when he passes it back. Brady and John just stand there, looking a little stupefied.

"Life lesson, boys," she says, bouncing the ball to Brady. "Never underestimate women. Especially the short ones. And don't you *dare* hold back."

Val's swagger right now is skyscraper tall, and I stop just short of saying, "that's my girl" out loud.

Because she's not my girl. Even if a part of me is warming more and more to the idea.

And after her warning, they *don't* hold back. Mostly. I can tell all three are careful not to hurt Val, but within minutes, it's obvious she can hold her own and give back just as good.

How did I not know Val could play basketball? I feel like the room in my head where my Val knowledge lives has been undergoing a massive reno.

I've just opened my mouth to cheer for Val when John

goes in a little too hard, knocking her flat on the concrete, the back of her head taking a direct hit.

I'm there before she can move, the boys and Mr. Silver right behind. "Are you okay, Tiny?" I have a quick flashback to just days ago when I was kneeling by her after throwing her on the bed. Maybe I need to roll her up in bubble wrap.

But I breathe a little easier when she grins up at me with those big, brown eyes, proud as can be. "I *told* them not to hold back."

CHAPTER 20

Val

I'VE NEVER BEEN MUCH for diets. My short, curvy body is what it is. But there was one time I *really* wanted this dress for Homecoming. And the store only had it in a size too small. I bought it anyway and for a month tried to shed five pounds to be able to zip it up.

Spoiler alert: it never did fit.

What I remember is how I kept cheating on my diet. *Tomorrow, I'll be better,* I'd tell myself, eating a third slice of pizza. *Tomorrow, I'll start fresh. But for right now, I'm gonna enjoy this*—fill in the blank with all the foods I kept eating.

That feeling of relishing a moment I might regret tomorrow is PRECISELY how I feel with Chevy.

Tomorrow, I'll do better. Tomorrow I'll remember he's not into me.

But tomorrow exists in a separate dimension as Chevy

carries me to his truck and manages to open my door, all while cradling me against his chest.

Dear teen boys, I think as I lean my head against him with a sigh. *Thank you for not holding back in basketball. (At least not fully holding back.) Thank you, John, for the hip check that knocked me over and gave me the gift of this moment.*

After shining a phone light in my eyes to check dilation, Chevy and Mr. Silver decided I don't have a concussion. If anything, maybe a mild one.

Either way—they didn't think I needed a hospital or urgent care visit. I hate doctors, so I wouldn't have gone anyway. Not for a bump on the head incurred during driveway basketball.

I don't even remember hitting the back of my head when I fell, but there is a growing lump there—a strange counterpart to the horn that just disappeared from my forehead. Being around Chevy doesn't seem to be doing any favors for my heart OR my head.

Right now, though, despite the aching throb in the back of my skull, my head feels nice. All fuzzy and floaty, my thoughts like bubbles rising slowly to the surface before they pop—forgotten a second later.

Maybe that concussion conversation wasn't just nonsense.

But it got me here. And right now in Chevy's arms, I'm alllllll good.

"You need to unhand me, woman," Chevy says lightly, and I realize he's trying to settle me in the seat while I'm trying to set a world record for how tightly someone can cling to another person.

I giggle and let go of the death grip I have on his neck. "Fine."

"Are you in pain?" he asks as he tucks my legs into the truck and settles me on the seat.

"Nah. Mostly I'm sleepy. And my butt hurts. Can you have a butt concussion?" I ask.

"No."

"You sure? Buttcussion sounds totally legit."

"No," Chevy mutters, as he leans over me, trying to fasten my seatbelt. I am no help, limp and boneless and with what I'm going to insist is a buttcussion. "But I'm starting to think we should go to the hospital to have your head checked."

I grab his forearm. "No hospital. No doctors. Promise?"

He sighs, not pausing in his search for the buckle. "We'll see. I'm gonna have to keep a close eye on you."

I like the sound of that! I grin, barely stopping myself from nuzzling his cheek. I mean, it's *right there!*

Instead, I just study his handsome profile. "You take good care of me, Chevrolet Boyd."

The click of my belt is loud in the silence that follows my statement. Chevy freezes in place, only his eyes flicking my way. They're so big and blue. So warm. So *close.*

If I just lean forward …

In a flash, Chevy's gone. My door closes practically in my face—*rude!*—and then he's climbing into his side of the truck.

"Boo," I say, but he ignores me.

"Let's get you home."

"Home." I sigh, happy again at the sound of that. Home with Chevy. Yes. I lean against the door. I like the way the cold window feels when I press my face to it. Cold is nice.

I must fall asleep because the next thing I know, my door opens and my top half practically tumbles out into Chevy's arms.

"Whoa, now," he says, like I'm a spooked horse, not a woman with what's likely a mild concussion who was just startled awake. One of his big hands grips my shoulder gently as the other unbuckles my seat belt. Then Chevy's picking me up again. I wrap my arms around his neck and close my eyes, listening for the thud of his heartbeat.

"You okay, Tiny?" Chevy asks as he climbs the front porch steps. "Or maybe after that basketball game, I should start calling you Scrappy."

"I like when you call me Tiny."

My thoughts meander over to what Lindy said about me being the only one Chevy graced with a nickname.

I wonder about the *other* things she said too. Could Chevy have feelings for me? Ones he's been burying or denying for ... reasons?

Lindy said Winnie warned him off. Maybe she and I need to talk so she can *un*warn him. Or warn him ON.

But if that's not the reason ... do I want to know why he's resisting?

Thinking makes my brain throb, so I tell my thoughts to take a hike.

I keep my eyes closed as Chevy walks us to the house. This allows me to maintain the dreamlike feeling of this moment, where I can pretend that Chevy isn't carrying me just because he's concerned I'm injured. Or that this isn't his house, it's *our* house, and we're coming home for the night.

Not to separate bedrooms. But to a single bedroom, a single bed, and a whole night of me getting to cuddle into his chest, wearing his ring and having his last name.

Maybe *after* a shower, because neither one of us is very fresh from playing basketball. Somehow, as men tend to do, Chevy still smells great. *Like Kraken*, I think, smiling to myself.

"You like it when I call you Tiny, huh?" he asks. "I always thought I was teasing you."

"Maybe I like when you tease me."

Chevy pauses and fumbles with his keys, hopefully NOT because he realized at the same time I did how what I said could be misinterpreted. My head is way too fuzzy to explain.

Somehow he manages to unlock the door while holding me up with one hand. I'm contributing to the cause by keeping my hands wrapped around his neck like I'm a barnacle that has no intention of being scraped off Chevy's hull. Ever.

He walks us inside, kicking the door closed with the back of his boot as he does. Why do I find that such a sexy move?

"To the bed or to the couch?" he asks, and again—I long for this question in a different reality.

"Couch, I guess."

Bed means Chevy won't stay with me. Couch means I might have a fighting chance of staying right where I am, nestled against his chest.

But instead of sitting down and keeping me close, Chevy gently lowers me to the couch and tries to let me go. I make a sound of protest and tighten my grip around his neck like the stubborn barnacle I am.

He chuckles. "Val, you gotta let go, sweetheart."

Forget Tiny. *I want to hear Chevy call me* sweetheart *again and again.*

"Why? Why can't I just stay here?" I ask, knowing how needy I sound. Needy and whiny. But my eyes are still closed. This is my happy dream.

"I want to get you water and some ibuprofen," he says. "I think you're gonna have a stunner of a headache soon. Let me take care of you."

Well, when he puts it THAT way...

I sigh but remove my hands from his neck. So much for being a stubborn barnacle on the *SS Chevy*.

But I'm rewarded when he lifts my head with care and places a pillow under it. Then he grabs my soft blue throw blanket and, starting at my feet, tucks it tightly underneath me. As he moves up my legs, goose bumps break out over every part of me. He pauses at my upper thighs—which are really, really excited about being tucked in by Chevy—and his gaze flicks up to mine.

"Too much?" he asks, and I barely resist shouting, *More! More! More!*

I slide my arms flat against my body. "Cocoon me," I say.

He chuckles and continues tucking me in, making a big, dramatic show of it. When he reaches my shoulders, he pulls the blanket up to my chin. "There. How's that, future butterfly?"

His face is inches from mine, close enough for me to see navy flecks in his blue eyes. Close enough to feel his breath on my cheek. I'm honestly glad he did such a good job wrapping the blanket around me. It's the only thing keeping me from losing all control and pulling his mouth down to mine.

Would Chevy resist?

Would he pull back and remind me that I'm his *friend*, his little *sister's* friend, his *roommate*?

Am I imagining the way the air charges between us like an electrical storm on performance enhancing drugs whenever we get close?

Are the feelings I have *really* unrequited?

He hesitates, probably waiting for me to answer, but I've forgotten the question. DID he ask a question? Do we really need to use words?

Or ... maybe we could put our mouths to use in *another* way?

I swear it's not just wishful thinking. It's not the lump on the back of my head making me see things. I'm not imagining the way his pupils dilate, darkening those gray-blue eyes. I'm not making up the way his breath hitches, or the way his eyes trace a path down my cheeks, stopping at my lips. I've been kissed enough times to sense when one is imminent. And right now is one of those moments.

My heart kicks up into a wild rhythm, fueled by anticipation and desire.

Kissing shall commence in three … two …

Chevy practically leaps back, knocking into the coffee table with a grunt. I do my best not to scream with frustration.

He moves away—more like *runs* away—before I can think about trying to wiggle out of the blanket to grab him. "I'll be right back with water and drugs."

And you. But maybe come back this time without whatever reservations hold you back just when things are getting good.

I hear cabinet doors opening and shutting in the kitchen, and Chevy returns a moment later, turning on the overhead light. I groan, squeezing my eyes shut. I can tell even through my closed lids that he turns it back off.

"Too much?" he asks, but I don't answer.

Because it's not enough. All of this is suddenly *not enough*. The friendship. The roommate thing. The close-but-not-too-closeness. The flirting, the touching, the zip in the air between us and the way he keeps trying to run away, building walls between us. The pretending I don't feel things and pretending I don't notice when we tiptoe close to a line and then Chevy jerks away.

My feelings for him have always been inconvenient and impossible. Chevy never gave off anything but friend vibes, which created a hard stop between us. A period on the end of a sentence.

But that solid punctuation feels a little more like an ellipses every day. Maybe even a question mark.

At least, until every time he pulls away. And I can't decide if he's putting the period back on the sentence or just sticking things in parenthesis now. Or maybe this whole analogy doesn't work, and my head injury means I shouldn't be attempting analogies at all.

"Here you go."

Chevy sits on the coffee table, handing me a tablet and a glass of water. After I've swallowed the pill and taken a drink, he sets my glass on the table. I expect him to take a seat in one of the armchairs, or maybe to hand me the remote and leave the room. Instead, he shocks me by lifting my feet and sitting down, putting them in his lap like he did the other night. One at a time, he carefully slides off my shoes and starts rubbing my feet. It's heaven.

But I can't help but wonder if it's intentional that he's keeping his face away from my face. His lips away from my lips.

Chevy asks, "Want to watch a movie or something?"

Or *something*. I'd really, REALLY like to *or something* with him.

"What do you have in mind?" I ask.

His thumbs dig into my arches and I swallow down a groan. The man knows how to rub feet.

"Didn't you tell me I needed to watch *Lord of the Rings*? Something about being a functional member of society."

Be still, my heart! "You want to watch those movies with me? That's quite a commitment."

Chevy winks. "I can commit when I want to commit."

Can you, though? Even with my mildly concussed brain, I manage to bite back the question.

"What about dinner?" I ask. "I'm supposed to make something."

"You are not making anything. You are going to sit there and be pampered while we watch a movie. I'll order takeout. Pizza or Chinese or something else?"

"Chevy, you don't need to do all this. I fell down. I'm fine."

He frowns, sliding his hands down to my heels. It doesn't tickle—not the way it did a moment before—but the slide of his fingers on my skin makes me shiver.

"Please just relax and let me take care of you. I feel like I owe you. Since you moved in, you've gotten a goose egg—"

"I prefer horn."

He snorts. "Fine—a *horn* and now a big lump on the back of your head."

"Let's not forget the buttcussion," I say.

"Yes. Okay—the buttcussion. The point is: I'm not doing so hot as far as your health and safety. And it matters. *You* matter."

The concern in his voice makes emotion swell and flood my chest. Because I *want* his concern. But not the friend's older brother kind of concern. Not just friend concern.

No—I'd like stake-your-claim, possessive and proprietary kind of concern. The all-consuming, never-ending kind. I'd like the kind of concern that has him growling *Mine* when anyone else comes near.

Chevy leaves my feet long enough to grab a few takeout menus from the kitchen. We decide on Chinese. With the order placed, Chevy starts *The Fellowship of the Ring*, then settles back down with my feet in his lap, now softly rubbing rather than a full massage. By the time Frodo and Sam are setting off on their journey with the ring, the food has arrived, and Chevy has set up plates on the coffee table.

"Did you know Mr. Silver fostered kids?" Chevy asks, taking a bite of orange chicken.

"Definitely not. I never in a million years would have imagined him doing something like that." I shake my head, remembering the way he spoke to the boys firmly but with kindness, and how they all responded with respect. "But he sure seems to be doing a good job. Also shocking."

"Yeah." He's quiet for a minute. "But he's not very nice to you."

I consider this as I take a bite of my egg roll. Up until this week, I would have quickly agreed. No question. No thinking about it. But ever since he offered up his studio space, I've been seeing our interactions through a different lens, wondering if I've been reading things wrong all this time. Reading *him* wrong.

On the surface, Mr. Silver is brusque and yeah, maybe even rude. Underneath that though, I've started to see little signs of a gruff kindness now that I'm looking for them. Seeing him with the boys only solidified my suspicion that he's a grump with a heart somewhere under the surface.

"He's not so bad," I say.

"I think you could see the good in anyone, Tiny. And I think you also bring out the goodness in them."

His compliments make me too choked up to even thank him.

"So, is art what drives you? That's what you want to do with your life?" he asks.

Big conversation to have when my head feels soft and spongy, but I'm not going to say no. "One of the things. But even more than being an artist, I want to be a mom."

I glance at Chevy warily, half-expecting him to be tensed and ready to run. Instead, he just watches me carefully.

"I love art and will always paint, but I want to build a family—the kind I wanted and never had. Not to say that Mari didn't do an amazing job," I add quickly.

"She really did," Chevy says quietly. "For me and Winnie too."

I know he's thinking about his mom, and I lean over and pat his knee, giving him an encouraging smile.

"Anyway, that's what I want. Art and family. How about you?"

Chevy wipes his mouth with a napkin and takes a long sip of water. "I'm not sure," he says. "I love my job, but outside of work … I'm still figuring things out."

I try not to be disappointed by his answer, and I think he can tell that I am, because he offers me a typical Chevy smile, dimples on display, and then carries my empty plate to the kitchen. *He's figuring things out*, I tell myself. *That's a good thing. That's a step.*

Toward what, I don't know. But I can *hope* it's toward me. Toward us.

I can hear him washing plates and putting them in the dishwasher. He's not the kind of person who can just let dirty dishes sit out. I've always known Chevy was clean, but living with him has only emphasized his tidy tendencies. I appreciate the care and concern he takes for his things—and for his people.

When he returns, he settles back on the couch next to me. Now that I'm sitting up instead of lying down, there's no excuse for us to touch. Well, guess what? I'm not waiting for an excuse. Grabbing the blanket, I scooch closer and, like some kind of stray cat looking for a new home, snuggle right up against Chevy until he's basically forced to put his arm around me.

I regret nothing.

As he presses play and we continue watching the hobbits' journey, I'm more focused on the steady thump of Chevy's heart and the weight of his arm over my shoulders. After a few minutes, he relaxes a bit, letting his hand trail up and down my arm over the blanket.

"Who's going with you to take Mari to the airport?" he asks.

The question comes out of nowhere, and considering my intense denial regarding this particular topic, it's like Chevy's opened up the door of an Alaskan cabin, letting frigid winds blow inside. Way to kill the mood, man.

"Just me."

"Remind me of the day and time?"

He says this like we've discussed it already, which we definitely haven't. See again: me trying to avoid thinking or talking about Mari actually leaving. I've been stopping in the diner sometimes three times a day just to see her, to commit the sight of her behind the counter to memory. I'm not sure I'll be able to eat there again after she goes. But of course, I'll have to support Big Mo, so I know I will.

"Her flight is in two days. The same day as Winnie's party." Winnie decided to throw a party as a way of welcoming Kyoko to Sheet Cake. I think she planned it for the day Mari leaves for me, to keep me from crying in bed.

"I'm not working. I'll go with you."

"You don't need to do that, Chevy."

But I really, REALLY want him to. Not that I particularly want to cry in front of him—and I WILL cry—but I don't want to be alone.

And it's not like he hasn't already seen me cry—today

wasn't the first time. Anyone who's known me for more than a few weeks gets that privilege. Lindy likes to say that she's the middle ground, while my emotions all live right up on the surface and Winnie keeps hers locked in a vault.

"We'll go to the airport and then to Winnie's party. I'm not letting you go alone, Tiny."

His arm tightens around me, and if I were a cat, I'd be purring. Did his lips just brush my hair, or was that just my wishful thinking?

"You're not alone," he continues. "I hope you know that. You've got people here who love you. You've got me."

His words are a balm. But they also make me restless because he's not saying exactly what I want him to say.

Closing my eyes, I imagine moving the words around like Scrabble tiles, rearranging them into what I really WISH Chevy would say: "You're not alone. You've got people here. You've got me. I love you."

That's not what he said. But for now, I'll take what I can get, which is Chevy's sweet words and his arm around me while we watch one of my favorite movies together.

At least until he decides—again—to push me away once more.

FROM THE NEIGHBORLY APP

Subject: Goodbye, Mari!

Bob1

I can't believe the day has come. Mari will be leaving Sheet Cake tomorrow. If you haven't stopped by to see her in the diner, this is your last day! What will everyone miss most?

TheRealBob

I'll miss her smile. And the way she never minded how long we stayed in the diner, even if we were just drinking coffee.

Vanz

You really shouldn't take up space in an eating establishment if you're only drinking coffee.

Chels

Everyone knows the Bobs were big tippers. Leave it alone,

Vanz. I'm going to miss seeing what flower Mari wears in her hair.

1BigBass

I'm going to miss always being greeted with a smile. Sometimes I went in just to see her smile.

DeltaDeltaDelta

I don't eat diner food, so I don't get the big deal

Cal_45

Can we have DDD removed from the app? Or at least this thread?

DeltaDeltaDelta

It's a free country. Removing me would be a violation of my First Amendment rights.

Neighborly Mod

The First Amendment refers specifically to the scope of government over free speech. Because this app is privately owned, this does not apply. Users will only be suspended when the terms and conditions have been violated. That said, any users speaking ill of Mari will not only be suspended but banned. Please remember to be kind and above all, Neighborly!

1BigBass

Winnie told you, DDD!

SweatPea23

I remember once I had a really bad day at work and stopped in the diner because nothing else was open. Mari fed me and listened to me vent about my work situation. I'll never forget that. Or her cheese grits.

Vanz

Isn't all the food really Big Mo's food? Since he's the chef...

WayneNGarthBrooks

I thought Big Mo used Mari's recipes and that she taught him to cook

BagelBytes

I'm sad even just thinking about Mari not being in Sheet Cake. I'll continue to support the diner and Big Mo, but Mari will be sorely missed. We love you, Mari!

BobToo

Thank you, Mari. For giving us all a place to go. And for being the only business that stayed open in downtown until Tank Graham started working his magic! You were the last woman standing and you should be proud. Please come back and visit!

The_Real_Shell_E

I'm going to miss Mari's laugh. And the way she really seemed to care about every person who walked through her doors.

LindyLouWho

Mari was like a second mother to me. Selfishly, I want her to stay. But I can only imagine how happy her other family will be to have her home. Love you, Mari!

DeltaDeltaDelta

This is ridiculous. She's just an old lady running a greasy diner. Get over it.

Neighborly Mod

User DeltaDeltaDelta has been suspended and, upon further review, may be banned permanently from the app. Please remember to be kind and above all, Neighborly!

CHAPTER 21

Chevy

I'M SITTING in my cruiser, radar pointed out the window watching for the speed demons who sometimes blow through the school zone. Passing out tickets is one of my least favorite tasks on the job. But I never mind ticketing people who can't pay attention or don't care about little kids. I'll happily pass out tickets like tossing candy from a parade float.

It's also a great distraction from thinking about certain people who have become a little too distracting. A huge yawn overtakes me, and I take a sip of the large coffee in my cup holder.

Last night, I definitely didn't get enough sleep. Not even close.

First, it's really hard to stop watching a movie when you get hooked, and despite avoiding all things hobbit and

Middle Earth my whole life until now, I am totally invested. Once Val fell asleep on me, I watched until the end of the first movie. I might have even gasped at the end.

Where is my closure? What's going to happen to those little hobbits as they travel to Mordor? I will not admit to getting choked up over Boromir. And because Val was asleep in my arms at the time, no one can prove anything.

And sure—holding Val in my arms played a part in me staying up too late. It wasn't just the movie. The soft weight of her against my chest, the tiny sounds she made while sleeping, the tickle of her long hair against my arms. Even thinking about it now makes my insides feel all gooey and warm.

I'd like to tell myself it's because I wanted to make sure she was okay after getting hurt again on my watch. This time, I wasn't the one who caused her head injury. But two in one week? I have *got* to do a better job taking care of her.

But taking care of Val isn't your job, I try to tell myself.

Unless you want it to be, myself responds.

And just maybe, for the first time in my life since finding out about my father's infidelity, I'm actually considering monogamy. Commitment. My own ability to uphold vows. Like Mari said, someone else's mistakes aren't mine.

I can't let myself think about any of this too much or too hard or the idea disintegrates. It's almost like one of those optical illusion pictures—if I try to picture it, I can't. But when I let my gaze go a little hazy and unfocused, there it is.

Suddenly, the radar gun lights up, flashing numbers much too high for this street. It's a car coming from a side street, not passing the school. Still—it's almost double the limit.

"This isn't the Autobahn, buddy." I shift in my seat, setting the radar gun down and buckling my seat belt.

But before I can even start my engine, the car whips

around the corner and makes an illegal U-turn, pulling up right behind me. I consider banging my head on the steering wheel when I recognize both the car and the driver, who's headed my way, stomping her high heels.

"Step out of the car, deputy," my sister says, stopping by my window, her hands on her hips.

"You stole my line," I drawl.

"*Now.*"

With a sigh, I climb out. Winnie may be my younger sister, but I know not to trifle with her when the tone of her voice sounds like *that*. And I'm pretty sure I know what this is about. Or, at least, *who* it's about.

"What did I tell you years ago about hurting Val?" she demands.

I sigh, lifting my hat to run a hand through my hair. "That you'd end my ability to bear children."

"Gold star for you. And yet … you don't seem worried."

"Because I haven't hurt Val."

Winnie's expression doesn't change. "So you didn't throw her off a bed and give her a goose egg?"

"Oh, well that—"

"And she didn't get a mild concussion on your watch?"

"She was playing basketball with her boss's teenage boys! I was just there! And I took care of her afterward."

Her eyes narrow into terrifying slits. "How?"

"I carried her to the car and then in the house. I stayed with her and watched a movie. I ordered her dinner. And she doesn't know it, but I monitored her through the night."

Yep—I did that. Sneaking into her room to check her breathing. I even checked her pulse.

Is that good enough for my sister? Based on her face, apparently not. I tense, ready to defend myself in case of sibling attack.

But I almost trip and fall over my boots when her judgy expression releases into something totally unexpected: a smile.

No, a *grin*.

The kind of smile that tells me I'm in more trouble than I originally thought. Just like the one Mari gave me the other day when she asked about my roommate situation.

When she reaches out, I flinch. I can't help it. I may be a strong, confident man. One with a badge and a gun and a pair of handcuffs at my disposal. But I'd challenge any man not to do the same in my position.

Winnie doesn't hit me. She grabs my shoulder, squeezing. "That's the brother I know."

"Huh?"

She gives me a last few painful smacks before stepping back, crossing her arms over her chest and looking at me with the strangely unexpected look of pride. Almost like she's a dance mom and I just accomplished some kind of complicated tap routine, earning perfect scores from the judges.

"I knew you could get over yourself and be a decent guy. The kind of guy Val needs."

I glance away, where some fool in a sports car is taking advantage of my distraction to go faster than he should be through the school zone. "Winnie, it's not like that. We're not—she's not—I'm not—"

I can't quite get myself to define what Val and I are or aren't. The reality is—I'm not sure.

Val and I aren't *something*.

We're also not *nothing*.

"I'm not sure I can be what Val needs," I say finally, feeling, even as I say the words, like maybe, just maybe, I can. Maybe I could try.

Maybe, like Mari told me just days ago, I could stop fighting ghosts.

I'm not prepared when Winnie shoves me.

I stumble back, and then she's got me by the shirt collar, holding it tight in her fist as she pushes me back up against my own squad car. I forget sometimes how freakishly strong she is for her size.

Mentally, I start counting up all the infractions she's incurring, starting with the speeding, moving to the parking the wrong way on the shoulder, and now assaulting an offi-cer. I wonder what would happen if I threw her in jail. The idea of Winnie staring at me through the bars down at the station gives me a little too much glee.

"You," she says, keeping hold of my shirt with one hand while letting go with the other to stick a finger in my face. "You are going to *try*. Right? Because you pinky promised. But more than upholding your promise to *me*, this is about *you*. Not me. It's about you and it's about Val. Not about me or Dad or losing Mom. And don't discount your fear of loss, Chevy. I have it too."

The mere mention of Mom sears through me. I'd clutch my chest, but Winnie's already clutching my shirt, so I simply try to keep from doubling over.

Am I afraid of loss because of Mom?

I've never thought about it. Never processed through any of this stuff, honestly. And yeah, I know all about therapy and how mental health is as important as physical health and all that. I've just never felt like I was someone who needed help. Maybe I should have considered it more.

But these thoughts make me feel twitchy and breathless and a little nauseated. Who wouldn't want to avoid that?

"I have the same struggles, but I'm trying," Winnie says,

her voice softer now, sounding a lot less homicidal. "And if I can, I know you can. I believe in you, Chevy. I do."

That makes one of us. Or, because at least *some* part of me is starting to believe, it makes one and a half of us.

"Need I remind you of the castration threat?" I ask. "That kind of thing tends to stick with a man."

"I never said not to date her, you big dummy. Just not to *hurt* her."

Here's the thing, though—I don't know if I can date Val with*out* hurting her. And therein lies my problem. The thing that kept me up last night long after I almost kissed her. The thing that has me out here just hoping for the distraction of giving someone a speeding ticket.

Winnie lets go of my shirt and straightens my collar before stepping back. "My promise stands. If you hurt Val, I will make you sorry. And James will help."

Is it weird that I'm more afraid of my sister? Also, I highly doubt that James, who's still waiting for my blessing to propose to Winnie, would *really* hurt me. Not if he wants me to say yes.

I stare at my sister for a few seconds, studying her familiar face. Her eyes, the same color as mine, behind her black-framed glasses. She's actually doing this. She's moving past the hurt from knowing what our father did and from the loss of our mom. Winnie's being brave. She's going all-in, and what's more—I'd put money on her and James.

Would I bet that same money on me? On Val and me?

"Do we have an understanding?" Winnie asks.

"We do. Now, if we're done here, daylight's wasting and guys like that are blowing through school zones on my watch."

"We're done," she says. "For now."

I climb back in my car and fumble around for my clipboard in the passenger seat while Winnie leans on my open window. "You're a good guy, Chev. You aren't him. You're nothing like him."

"Everyone in town loves to tell me that I am," I say, slightly distracted.

"Yeah, well. That's because they didn't know him. And they don't know your big, soft, marshmallow heart either."

Winnie doesn't seem to notice me writing while she speaks, and when I hold out a ticket, she gapes at me. "What is this?"

"That's for going fifty-five in a thirty. You can make a copy and frame it up on the wall next to the one I gave your boyfriend last month."

And while Winnie's still standing there, shocked into uncharacteristic silence, I take off. Leaving her and her nosy questions that force me to think too hard behind.

CHAPTER 22

Val

IT'S OFFICIAL. I hate airports. Sure, I've only set foot inside an airport twice, but that's enough to form a very solid opinion. *Hate*.

Overhead, the speakers crackle to life paging some passenger who hasn't made it to their gate. A woman sprinting for the ticket counter almost takes me out with her rolling bag. Chevy makes a rough sound, glaring at the woman's back as he takes me by the shoulders and steers me out of the middle of the concourse.

It's all I can do not to melt into his touch, into the feel of those big hands splayed protectively over my shoulders. And it's impossible not to add this gesture of protectiveness to the mounting list of evidence that Chevy and I are heading toward something new. Something bigger. Something I've almost not even allowed myself to dream about. The protectiveness. The chivalry. The flirting. The cessation of constant *friend* reminders. The almost kisses.

The problem, though, with loving small gestures is that I start to see them everywhere. And right now—they're all just that. Tiny actions that might mean something, but I won't know what until there are words to define them.

Or, you know—a kiss. That could certainly tell me something.

Chevy steps back, dropping his hands, and I sigh.

"Val? Are you still with me?" Mari's voice cuts into my thoughts.

"I'm here." Sort of. Marginally. And this makes a fresh wave of grief now mixed with guilt flood my system. "Sorry."

"It's time," Mari says.

"Is it?" I ask weakly. "Because I think I just heard them announce a delay and—"

Mari pulls me into a hug, the kind that feels like a real, forever goodbye embrace. But this is NOT a forever goodbye. I'll see Mari again. Soon.

But this is big. It's one of those moments that you know draws a solid line in your life between before and after. I'm still not fully able to grasp the concept of Mari living anywhere but in Sheet Cake. Or maybe I don't want to.

"You'll see me soon," Mari says, laughing, when I refuse to let her go.

"Yeah." I squeeze her harder, trying to picture us hugging like this in a rainforest with monkeys chittering away—which is how I always picture Costa Rica.

I suddenly feel like I cannot possibly let her go. Would Chevy arrest me if I tried to kidnap Mari and keep her here? Or would he help me get her back in his car and stuff her in the trunk?

I hope Mari doesn't notice the way I'm starting to shake.

"Valentina," she warns. "I still have to get through security."

"I know."

"I haven't even gotten my hug yet," Chevy says from behind me.

One of Mari's hands lifts from my back. I know without looking that she's probably waving him over.

"Come, come. Might as well make it a group hug."

And then Chevy's arms come around us both, making me feel small and protected. Cherished. Safe.

Making me feel all sorts of other things too. Non airport-appropriate kinds of things.

Non-*friend* things.

Mari kisses my cheek. "I love you, princesa."

"I love you more," I choke out.

I know I'm going to cry. Now, later, forever. It's why I planned to bring her alone, knowing full well I'd need to take frequent stops on the drive back. It's hard to drive when you're bawling your eyes out, and that is exactly what I'll be doing.

And now I'll be doing so in front of Chevy. Not good.

I am not a soft, pretty crier. There is splotchy skin involved. And noises. The sniffly, snotty kind. When I blow my nose, it sounds like a foghorn. I could direct traffic or help ships get into port. If I'm hoping to win Chevy over, this is not the way.

"I can't believe you're really going," Chevy says, and am I imagining the way his fingertips brush my neck? I don't have time to really wonder, because then he says, "Sheet Cake won't be Sheet Cake without you, Mari."

Oh no! The burning in the top of my nose and stinging in my eyes is starting! I cannot fall apart here. Must. Hold. Tears. In.

It takes the kind of superhuman strength to keep the tears

at bay. I know it won't last. But for this second, I'm okay. Semi-okay. More like an active volcano someone has stuck a giant cork in. The clock is ticking on how long the cork can withstand the mounting pressure.

"Don't get too skinny," Mari says, reaching behind me to pat Chevy's cheek.

Chevy chuckles. "That's never been an issue."

"Valentina can cook. Make her take care of you! Won't you feed this man, Val?"

Subtle, Mari. Subtle.

Knowing Chevy can't see me, I grin. "I've been trying. The man is stubborn."

"Don't I know it," Mari says.

"Hey—I'm standing right here," Chevy says.

He sure is. Standing *right here*, with one of his arms slung around my shoulder and his chest pressed to my back. His fingertips are *definitely* moving on my neck—small strokes of his that are making me positively shiver.

I'm suddenly much too hot for this kind of closeness and disentangle myself from the three-way hug as quickly as I'm able. Chevy steps back, tucking his hands into his pockets. His gaze slides over me like he's checking to see if I'm okay or still have all my limbs.

Mari points a scolding finger at his chest. "I'll say it right to your face, young man. You're stubborn. Let my Val take care of you." Then she turns the finger on me. "You'll take care of him?"

Like she needs to ask. I find his eyes, hoping he'll see the challenge in mine. "I'd like nothing more."

Before I can fully decide if Chevy's cheeks are suddenly pinker than a moment ago, Mari grabs both of our hands in hers, then basically forces us to hold hands before stepping back.

Obvious much?

I could protest or make a joke, brushing off her blatant matchmaking. Instead, I link our fingers together like it's the most natural thing in the world to hold Chevy's hand.

It's a bold move. *Look at me—bold Val's come to town, y'all!*

Meanwhile, under the calm exterior of bold Val is a tiny band of minions screaming wildly and babbling their enthusiastic nonsense. Because *I'm holding Chevy's hand.*

"And you will take care of my Val," Mari says.

"I will."

"You make sure she is good until she safely gets to me. And after?" Mari lifts a shoulder and grins. "Maybe you'll keep taking care of her."

I might roll my eyes while Chevy chuckles beside me, but I'm smiling. And I don't miss the way he squeezes my fingers, instead of letting me go.

With a last quick kiss on my cheek and a wink for Chevy, Mari takes her carry-on bags and marches to the security line. The urge to chase her down and tackle her to the floor, holding her until she's missed her flight is strong.

This is happening. She's really leaving. And I'm supposed to follow her soon.

Can I? Do I really even want to go?

I've thought about these questions a lot lately. I've flipped coins and made a dandelion wish for clarity when I found an early blooming weed. Once, I even called one of those hotline psychics, who told me nothing about whether or not I should move to Costa Rica but *did* say it was my lucky week to play the lotto.

Just in case, I did play. Not even a single number matched.

The point being: I'm as unsure now, watching Mari go, as I've ever been.

I want to go and meet the family I've never met. I want to learn from a real, working artist. I want to get out of Texas—*don't take it personally, greatest state in the country*—for the first time in my life. I *need* to go. For me.

I know this, even as Chevy's hand holding mine feels like an anchor that could tempt me to stay.

And I'll come back! It's not like Chevy couldn't wait. People do long distance all the time. IF—and in my mind, it's still very much an if—something happens here.

Then, I remember the years of watching or hearing about Chevy's revolving door of women who couldn't be more opposite than me. Can Chevy do long distance? Can he even do commitment?

"That's some grip you've got there," Chevy says.

I NEED to get a grip. I'm totally spiraling into a panic tornado. But he means my hand, which is practically crushing his bones.

"Sorry."

"Don't be," he says, his blue eyes sharp and intent on mine. "I've got you."

You have no idea how you've got me.

I suck in a breath as Mari blows us a kiss, then turns away. Chevy unlinks our fingers. I don't have time for disappointment because he puts his arm around me, pulling me in close to his side.

"You okay, Tiny?"

I lean against his chest, needing his steadiness as Mari's white hair moves further and further away.

"I will be," I say, hoping it's true.

CHAPTER 23

Val

WHEN WINNIE PULLS open the door to her loft, her gaze first goes to Chevy's arm, curled protectively around my shoulder. She smiles. Then she sees my face. The smile disappears.

"You look … *wow*."

I mean, it's to be expected when I spent literally all but ten minutes of the drive back home sobbing. The only plus side is that Chevy held my hand the whole way and hasn't stopped touching me since the airport. Later, when I'm not so sad about Mari leaving, I'll be giddy about the subtle but not-so subtle shift that's taken place between us today.

For now, I'm still a mess.

Kyoko takes one look with wide eyes and pulls me from Chevy, tossing her arms around me. "Come to my bosom," she says, clutching at me like we've known each other for years. Not like she's a relatively new friend.

"Your ... bosom?"

"She doesn't mean literally. It's a figurative bosom."

"It's both. Now, shhh," Kyoko says, squeezing me tighter against what I guess, technically, is her bosom.

Winnie swats at us both. "You're blocking the doorway. Move."

Kyoko doesn't loosen her grip on me, sort of shuffling us to the side so Chevy can walk in behind us.

"Did you do this to her?" Winnie demands.

"Chill, Winchester. We just dropped Mari at the airport," Chevy explains.

"Ohhhh," Winnie says. "Got it. So, Mari left, huh?"

Even though I'm practically in need of an IV to replace my fluids, they just keep coming. You could pick me up and plant me in some drought-addled country and my tears would replenish their crops.

"I ... hate ... being sad," I sob, squeezing my eyes shut so I don't have to see anyone staring.

"Take her to my room," Winnie says to Kyoko. "We'll fix her up."

That sounds as ominous as it does comforting, but I don't fight Kyoko as she guides us to Winnie's bedroom and then kicks the door closed with a hard slam.

"Get it out, honey. It's okay."

This makes me laugh somehow, and by the time Winnie arrives with a mug of coffee, a bottle of her famous jalapeño-infused vodka, and a bag of individually wrapped dark chocolates, Kyoko and I are lying on the rumpled comforter, laughing hysterically. The look of shock on Winnie's face has us laughing harder.

Tears are still spilling down my cheeks, but they're the

kind that feel good. A release. Healing tears. Not quite but almost happy tears.

"I was going to ask if you wanted to start with caffeine or alcohol, but clearly, the answer is chocolate," Winnie says, tossing the bag at me.

No sooner has it smacked me in the chest than I'm ripping it open. I dump the foil-wrapped chocolates in the center of the bed and Winnie joins us so we're sitting knee to knee to knee, tearing open wrappers. The OC, Winnie's one-eyed cat, appears from under the bed and inserts himself in the middle of us, demanding attention. Tonight, probably in honor of the party, he's wearing a bow tie James bought for him.

"Oh! This is the kind of chocolate with special messages," Kyoko says. Then she frowns at the wrapper in her hand. "'You will meet an untimely end stepping in front of a city bus. Avoid jaywalking.' Winnie, what is this? *I love it.*"

Winnie grins, a chocolate smudge at the corner of her lips. "They're called DARK Dark Chocolates. Instead of happy messages, they have twisted ones. I've been saving them for just the right occasion."

"Genius." Kyoko says. "Why didn't I think of that? I'd be rich."

"Probably," Winnie agrees. "This bag was twelve dollars."

Fifteen minutes later, we've been warned about the many creative ways we'll meet our untimely ends (besides hit by a bus, there was an alligator attack and slipping on a spilled mocha) and also been assured that we'll never EVER find luck in love.

"Accurate," I murmur, and Winnie smacks my arm.

"None of that," she says. "This is supposed to be funny. It's supposed to cheer you up so we can get back out to the party."

"Where's Lindy?" I feel bad that I didn't even realize she wasn't here. Probably because Kyoko filled in so nicely. I feel a little guilty at that, then a little sad when I think about how, when I leave, Kyoko will fill *my* empty spot.

That's almost enough to start a fresh round of tears.

"Running late," she says. "Something about a crow emergency?"

"This town is weird," Kyoko says. "I love it."

I get up, straightening my tear- and chocolate-stained shirt. "Okay, I'm better. I can party."

Winnie and Kyoko exchange a glance and then shake their heads. "Not yet, you can't," Winnie says. "We have to fix your face. And … the rest of you. To the bathroom!"

This last part is said like a battle cry, complete with a fist raised in the air.

"But maybe don't look in the mirror," Kyoko says, patting my arm.

I could be offended, but I know from experience that after crying this hard, I look like death warmed over, then frozen again, then burned in a furnace and left outside to rot. So, I don't look in the mirror. I perch on the edge of Winnie's counter and let the two of them fuss over me with products I can't begin to name.

While Kyoko is doing something to my eyes, Winnie says, "You and Chevy looked awful cozy when you walked in."

A warm flush spreads up my neck, and I bite back a smile. "Things feel a little different."

"Underneath all the tears, you've got a glow," Kyoko says.

"Does this mean …?" Winnie trails off, raising her eyebrows as she brushes powder over my cheeks.

"It doesn't mean anything—yet. But I think maybe something's happening. *Maybe*."

"I hate maybes," Winnie says. "You should take that maybe by the horns and make it an absolutely yes."

Winnie probably would do just that. But I'm not sure I'm brave enough to make the first move. Or to bring up the question of whether something is changing between us.

Once my face is done, I let them dress me in some of Kyoko's clothes, which are a bit more to my taste than Winnie's style. According to Kyoko, I look more like an actual human and less like roadkill now, so I'll take it. But the OC runs back under the bed when we leave the bathroom, so it's a toss-up.

The party has grown while we were sequestered in Winnie's room. "Whoa. Where did all these people come from?"

Winnie stretches out her hands. "I wanted Kyoko to get the full Sheet Cake experience."

"This is certainly ... that."

Judge Judie is holding what looks to be a serious discussion with Tank Graham near Winnie's sectional sofa. James is glowering from a chair, beer in hand. Collin is engaged in a fight with the mysterious and terrible girlfriend we've all heard about, and Wolf Waters is playing bartender at Winnie's kitchen island.

One person is conspicuously missing.

"If you're looking for my brother," Winnie says, nudging my shoulder with hers, "he's on the balcony."

I glance away. "Maybe I should get some food or—"

"Nope. You should get out there. And go after what you want."

"Win, I'm still not sure that anything's happening there."

Winnie gives me a knowing smile. "Well, I'm sure enough for the both of you. Maybe it's time for you to make the first move. And I will be the happiest person besides the two of you when Chevy gets his head out of his emotionally stunted—"

"Got it. Thanks, Win."

"Go get him, tiger." Then, as though thinking better of her words, she makes a face. "Forget I said that."

Chevy is alone on the balcony. It's cold, but clear, the air is fresh and invigorating as I step onto the balcony, closing the door behind me. Chevy's leaning on the black metal railing, looking out over the twinkly lights stretching across Main Street. I hope Tank keeps them up all year long. They're quaint and really do a lot to show off the hard work he's been investing to get downtown Sheet Cake back up and running.

It also sets a mood. Maybe THE mood? I'm not so sure after Chevy saw me totally fall apart today. Then again, he never looked shocked or horrified. Only concerned about me.

Maybe this is the true test of love—if a man is still interested after watching you leak tears while sobbing loudly for hours.

"Hey."

He turns, a lazy spin, and leans his butt up against the railing. Lifting a beer to his smiling lips, he says, "Hey, Tiny."

How can men just ... *do* that—look effortlessly sexy in a T-shirt and jeans while leaning casually against anything at all? Chevy would look just as good if he were leaning up against one of the fake animals on a kids' carousel or a scarecrow in a cornfield.

Meanwhile, I just had to have two women work on me to get me looking like I hadn't spent the day crying.

"You okay?" he asks while I'm still pondering the inhumanity of it all. "You're looking a little less puffy."

A little less puffy. All those creams and the stinky serum Winnie insisted I put under my eyes, and I look *a little less puffy*?

I want to lean over the balcony and scream with outrage. But I resolve to be a mature human who has come to terms with how troll-like I look when I've been crying. So, I just stand there, not screaming, but also not answering because what can I even say? I take a step back, because maybe the right thing to do here is to run the other way.

"Aw, I was kidding. Come here."

Before I can make my great escape, Chevy sets his beer down on a table and tugs me toward him. Not just toward him, but into him, curving his arm around my shoulders the way he did at the airport right after we held hands.

I take a deep inhale, relishing in Chevy's clean scent and his warm chest. "Have you recovered yet?" I ask him.

"Recovered?"

"From being in close proximity to a woman who's so deeply in touch with her emotions."

Chevy chuckles. "I have seen women cry. You remember I have a sister. You might know her?"

"Have you actually ever seen her cry? Winnie keeps her emotions inside of a bulletproof locker with a retinal scanner lock."

This draws out more than a chuckle, and as Chevy belly laughs, he pulls me in even tighter, moving me until I'm against the railing directly in front of his body with his arms caging me in on either side.

A girl could get used to this. Me. I'm the girl. *I* could get used to this.

Chevy leans close until his lips are almost brushing my ear. I could get used to this too.

"Today wasn't so bad," he tells me.

The liar.

"At one point, you called Pat for help. You asked him if he knew of any kind of medicine that would help a woman stop crying," I point out. "And don't think I didn't hear you asking if melatonin would knock me out."

If I hadn't been so devastatingly sad, Chevy's frantic phone call to Pat would have made me laugh. It might later, when I've had some time and distance. I'm not sure I've ever seen Chevy panic. But even now, I'm still a little too tender about Mari leaving to laugh.

"I was kidding," he says.

He definitely wasn't.

"Why Pat? Out of everyone in the world, why him?"

"Weird as it may be, Patrick Graham might be the most in touch with his emotions of anyone I know. Besides you, obviously."

"My emotions and I did a lot of touching today," I agree.

"Are you okay?" His voice goes serious, and his lips get a little bit closer to my ear. So close there's a featherlight touch that makes my whole body freeze. "For real—today was a big deal."

I swallow. "Yeah." I don't elaborate on what I'm agreeing with—that I'm okay or that it was a big deal—because I'm not even sure myself.

Chevy's hands slide closer together on the railing so his arms are flush with mine. When he speaks, his lips aren't just brushing my ear. He's practically kissing it.

"Do you have to go?"

"Go?"

If my voice sounds a little breathy, it's just the cold air. That's all. And if I'm struggling to follow the conversation, it's only because it's been a long day. Not because Chevy's lips and whispers have rendered me useless.

"To Costa Rica. I think it might kill me when you leave, Tiny."

Then give me a reason to stay. The words are RIGHT THERE.

In my throat, on my tongue, but my stupid mouth won't let them out. So much for bold Val who held Chevy's hand today. Apparently, she has a short shelf life.

But I stop beating myself up to really focus on what Chevy just said. This is big. HUGE even.

I take a big breath before spinning to look at Chevy. I'm about to ask something or confess something or maybe even DO something like finally freaking kiss him when I catch sight of all the faces pressed up against the glass window behind him.

I mutter a Spanish curse word under my breath, one Mari used to say only when she was really upset about something. Whatever it means, it's so bad she never would tell me.

"What?" Chevy swivels his head enough to see basically the entire party watching us. Then he groans.

The door opens just a crack and Pat sticks his head out.

"Hey, lovebirds. Did you see where you're standing?"

"On a balcony," Chevy says drily, turning back to me and shaking his head slightly.

"Look up, doofus." Pat slams the door as Chevy and I both do as Pat asked, almost instinctively.

A big leafy thing is dangling above our heads. Mistletoe? I'm honestly not sure I've ever seen the real stuff, but I'm guessing that's what this is. Or, rather, what it's *supposed* to be.

My gaze follows the string holding it up. Not a string—a fishing wire. Attached to a fishing pole, which is in the hands of someone I can't see, standing on the roof, just out of sight.

"Really?!" I practically shout. "A fishing rod with mistletoe?"

"That's not even mistletoe," Chevy says. "I think that's a small bush. I see the roots."

Now that he mentions it … I think he's right. The fishing

line dips a little, and a sprinkling of dirt falls over our shoulders.

"It's mistletoe in spirit," a gruff voice from above calls.

"James?!" Chevy and I call in sync.

"Winnie made me. Now get on with it. My arms are tired."

James clears his throat dramatically above, and when I peer back over Chevy's arm, I see the faces in the window. Still watching, though now, a little more restlessly. They're starting to look antsy now, like the line of Black Friday shoppers when the doors don't open right on time.

Chevy maintains his stance, blocking me from view of the people still pressed up against the window. I appreciate the gesture because I feel very much like we're on a tiny stage with the whole world watching.

"Maybe if we ignore them, they'll go away?" I offer hopefully.

"They'll go away if you give the people what they want," James says.

"We shouldn't be surprised by this," Chevy murmurs, low enough that James can't hear. "This is so very Sheet Cake."

"A bunch of Peeping Sheeters," I say, and he laughs.

The balcony door opens again, but I don't look this time, keeping my gaze steadily on Chevy's expression, which I'm finding hard to read.

"The people have spoken, and the people demand a kiss," Pat calls.

Chevy blows a raspberry that turns into a laugh. "Subtle, man."

It is no more subtle when the entire party starts chanting, "Kiss! Kiss! Kiss!" I have to wonder if Winnie is somewhere with noise-canceling headphones on, rocking and telling herself it will all be over soon. She might have set this up, but I doubt she'll want to watch.

The truth is, I want to kiss Chevy badly enough that I don't even care if people are watching. Or that they're pushing this. Sure, I want Chevy to *want* to kiss me. But I'll take whatever I can get.

Chevy raises his voice. "Simmer down, y'all. Why don't you mind your own business!"

They do not hear him or do not care. I'm not sure which, but the chanting continues. The tiny shred of hope that maybe this stupid push from our friends would make Chevy cross this line starts to flicker and fade as we just stand here. Not kissing.

I'm about to give up all hope and collapse in a puddle of self-loathing when Chevy's expression shifts from resignation to something more like determination. And then, suddenly, he's coming in hot.

One of his hands slides around my waist to press against my lower back while the other tangles in my hair. He cups my head gently as he tilts me back toward the railing. He dips me, and I only have time to register the wild way my nerves are thrashing and my pulse is whooshing when Chevy tilts his face toward mine.

I close my eyes, but his mouth never reaches mine. Instead, his lips find my cheek as he whispers fiercely.

"Tiny, if I kiss you for real, it's not gonna be because our friends pushed us into it. Or because we happen to be standing under a fishing rod holding a small shrub posing as mistletoe."

He pauses, and my breath shudders. An electric hum snakes its way down my spine until I feel lit all the way in my toes.

"To all of them, it probably looks like we're making out.

Are you good with that? Because, if so, they'll probably shut up."

"Yes?" The murmured question is about all I can get out right now.

"Good." He pauses. "Because if I kiss you, it won't go down like this. It won't be quick. It won't be sweet. And it won't be with an audience. You got that?"

Oh, I GOT THAT.

A kiss between us won't be quick or sweet.

He doesn't want anyone watching.

I am all about that.

Except ... I don't want to wait. I'm not picky, and I don't care who's watching.

I don't want to take a chance that Chevy might change his mind and backtrack on all of this later. He's planted a seed in my head, and it must be one of Jack's Beanstalk seeds because it's sprouted a vine that has spiraled impossibly far up in the sky.

Chevy shifts, and just when I think he's changed his mind and he's going to kiss me, he tilts his head and kisses the tip of my nose.

You'd think a tiny kiss on the nose would be cute. Sweet. Playful and not really sensual. But no.

Though it's quick, Chevy's lips are soft and gentle. The quick nip of his teeth speaks to his promise for another kind of kiss. It speaks to *more*. To him wanting more. Not just in my hopes and dreams and imagination, but in REALITY.

And it's this tease of a kiss that's the swift kick in my behind, pushing me into action.

I grab his coat in both of my greedy hands and hold him still. I capture his gaze. "No."

"No—what?"

"I don't agree."

He blinks, lips parting in surprise, looking almost a little hurt. "With which part?"

"There's only one word I take issue with in what you just said." I swallow, one half of me really hoping I'm not about to make a giant mistake while the other half doesn't care.

"What word is that, Tiny?"

"If," I tell him, my voice sounding more sure and strong than I feel. "Because there's no *if* we kiss—only *when*. And frankly, I'm tired of waiting for the when."

With a firm tug on his coat collar, I pull Chevy to me until his lips crash into mine.

CHAPTER 24

Chevy

I'VE SPENT a lot of time lately doing mental gymnastics trying to work out how things could possibly work between Val and me. Could I? Should I? Do I deserve her? Could I escape any legacy my father might have passed down in my very DNA? Turns out, those hours were wasted time.

All I needed to allay my fears and answer those questions was a kiss.

And suddenly, there's no room for thinking.

No need to work out the future or deal with my past. I have no interest in trying to second- (or third- or fourth-) guess this.

Because the moment Val's lips meet mine, my world doesn't tilt on its axis; it implodes.

Her mouth, warm and soft and so, so sweet, moves with

no hesitation, no restraint. Val's kiss is sure and without doubts. Her confidence draws out my own.

We should have always been doing this. Always been more than friends.

Okay—once she was old enough that the few years between us weren't weird. But after that, yes.

What have I been wasting years on?

She holds me tighter by the front of my coat. But it's not like she needs to. I'm not interested in going anywhere.

Val may have started this kiss, but the moment her mouth touched mine, I was all in. I'm giving back as good as I'm getting, and what I'm getting is nothing short of life altering.

Me and Val. Val and me.

As if realizing I'm not fighting or running, Val's hands release my coat and begin an exploratory mission. One palm goes flat against my heart, which beats even faster at her touch.

Can she feel that? Can she see how much this kiss is affecting me?

She slides her other hand up my shoulder to the back of my neck where she plays with my hair. Something hot and electric travels straight down my spine from the origins of her touch, like her skin on mine completed a current.

"Tiny," I murmur against her lips as our heads tilt, changing the angle of our kiss. "Tiny, Tiny, Tiny."

Her hair is soft, and touching it now only makes me want to bury my hands in it. To play with the long strands. To comb my fingers through it. To wrap it around my fist as I tilt her head to kiss her more deeply.

Heck—I'd even learn to braid if it meant spending more time with my hands in her hair.

But I need more of her. My hands are eager to move. Greedy, even. I keep one hand on her lower back, sliding it under her sweater until her hot skin brands my palm. I move my other hand from her hair to her face, cupping her cheek then her jaw before I slide it to her neck, feeling her pulse leap against my fingertips.

She makes a humming sound that vibrates through the pad of my thumb, which rests on her throat. I want her to make the sound again, to make other sounds, to experience not only the sound but the feel of them against my fingertip.

She shifts, dipping her head to press hot and hungry kisses along my jaw and throat, then up to my cheeks and back to my mouth, which is waiting hungrily for her, panting breathlessly. For Val. Only Val.

I feel like a man who's been fighting against restraints only to have them snap, and the momentum of my struggle is propelling me forward in a powerful surge. I need Val closer, to hold her tighter. I need more, even as some part of me registers *more* will never be enough.

I won't be satisfied.

Not with this kiss, not with weeks or months or years of kisses. I want them *all*—to own every kiss of hers from this moment on. *Mine*.

That word pulses through me like a drumbeat, then slows and settles over me like a soft, fuzzy blanket. The kind that makes you want to crawl in bed and never leave.

And if there's still some niggling worry that I might not be built for commitment, I'm choosing to kick it to the curb. Right now, there is no room for doubt.

There's a whoosh and then a soft thud as the bush from overhead drops beside us. Val jumps, and we pull apart, foreheads together.

"My work here is done," James says from somewhere above our heads.

I glance at Val, only to see her smiling and biting her lip. Her expression is slightly dazed but happier than I've seen her in a long time. Much happier than she was with Mullet. I frown, remembering how recent their breakup was.

"What?" she asks.

"I don't want to be just a rebound," I tell her, feeling strangely raw and vulnerable even asking the question. So raw, that when she laughs, I start to pull away.

Eyes wide, she grabs me with surprising strength, holding me in place. There's no smile now, only tenderness.

"I didn't mean to laugh. It's just ..." She shakes her head, then lifts one hand to run her fingers along my jaw. "You could never be a rebound, Chevy. If anything, *they* were the rebounds. Every man I've ever dated was only an attempt to get over you."

The words land slowly but with surprising force.

"To get over me?"

"Did you really not know about my feelings for you? It felt *so* obvious. All the time."

I shake my head, trying to wrap my mind—still half mush from the kiss—around this idea. "I mean, I knew when we were younger. But I thought it was just a crush you got over."

"Not a crush. And I did not get over my feelings. They grew into something bigger. But I never thought—you never seemed to—" She stops, glancing away and looking embarrassed. "I thought my feelings were one-way. What with all the women you dated. And then being told over and over that I'm a friend. Your sister's friend. Your roommate. I'm shocked you didn't start moving into other languages. Amigo. Uh ... whatever the French word is for friend. End-fray—is that how pig Latin works?"

"Tiny. Stop." I press a finger to her lips, but let's be honest—it's less because I think it will make her quiet and more because I want to touch her. "For a long time, you were too young. And then, Winnie threatened me, which, it turns out, was about not hurting you, *not* not dating you."

I glide my finger over her bottom lip. Then I slide that same finger over the swell of her cheekbone to the corner of her jaw, not stopping until my finger is just underneath her chin. She blinks up at me with bright eyes. With hope.

There's nothing I want more than to be a man worthy of hoping for. Even if I'm not sure I'm a safe bet.

"I didn't allow myself to have feelings or think about you that way. If I had, I'm not sure how long ago I could trace them back. Because here's the thing, Tiny—I always saw you. Not the way I see my sister. And not the way I see Lindy. Not the way I saw anyone I ever dated either. It's different. You're different." I suck in a breath. "Now that I'm admitting this, I'll admit something else—I'm scared."

Her smile holds the slightest edge of teasing in it, but her voice is gentle. "What are you scared of, deputy?"

"Everything. I've never done this before—something real. I haven't ever felt like the stakes were so high. I don't know what to do or say. But I *do* know I'll probably screw it up. Likely more than once."

"Well, I'll forgive you if you forgive me for all the things I'll mess up." As though she can see the argument forming in my head, she says, loudly, "I *will* mess things up."

I lean forward, pressing a soft kiss to her lips, a feeling of awe channeling through me at the reality of kissing Val. "I'd like to see you try."

———

Once Val and I finally stop kissing on the balcony and walk inside, it's to applause, hoots and hollers, and Patrick Graham trying—and failing—to dump a bottle of sports drink over my head.

"I'm not a coach, this isn't a cooler, and I didn't just win a game," I grunt, struggling to grab the bottle from Pat's hand. Blue liquid is flying in arcs from the bottle, and I'm trying my very best not to get any on Winnie's white couch. Val darts away and out of range.

Pat grins, almost managing to wrest the bottle away. "Oh, I'd say you won big, brother."

"Stop. Both of you." James steps in between us, somehow managing to grab the drink without spilling another drop. He glares at Pat. "Clean it up. Rags are under the sink."

"Aye aye, captain." Pat heads off toward the kitchen, while I brush my hands over my coat.

"I didn't start it," I say when James swings his glare my way.

"I know." He takes a swig of the drink, then makes a face. "Also, in addition to making me provide the mistletoe—"

I hold up a finger. "*Fake* mistletoe."

"Fake mistletoe," he concedes. "In addition to that, Winnie told me to threaten you about taking care of Val. But I don't think I need to threaten you, Chevy. I don't think you'd be stupid enough to break her heart."

"The last thing I want to do in this life is hurt Val," I answer honestly.

"Good." And with a quick nod of his head, James is off.

My eyes scan the room, until they land on Val, who's standing with Winnie and Lindy and Kyoko, watching me. They're ALL watching me. Winnie gives me a head nod, Lindy just smiles, and Kyoko offers me a thumbs up. While Val has a goofy grin and two pink cheeks as she waves. I wave back, and they turn away, probably going back to gossiping about me.

"If my sons are giving you too hard a time, just let me know." Tank Graham is suddenly beside me. And while I'm not intimidated by Collin, Pat, or even James, I find myself straightening my shoulders.

"Yes, sir."

Tank laughs. "We're both adults. No need for formalities."

"Yes, si—*Yes*. Sorry. Hard habit to break." I clear my throat. "As for your sons, I think I can handle them. But I'll add you to the favorites list on my phone. Just in case."

"Good. And while I'm sure my boys have provided congratulations or threats, I'd like to offer something else."

My throat is suddenly dry. My mouth too, when Tank throws an arm over my shoulders and pins me with an intense look.

"I know what it's like to be without a father in your life. Or without a father you can count on." His jaw flexes, and he pauses for a moment, then continues. "If you need support, I'm here. If you need the kind of advice and counsel I keep hoping my boys will ask for, it's yours. Anytime, Chevy. Relationships are never easy. The good ones are worth fighting for, but no one can fight for them alone. So, consider me your backup. Call me anytime."

Val expended enough tears to cover the whole town of Sheet Cake today, and I'm not about to add mine to the mix. And yet I feel a stinging sensation behind my eyes and in the center of my nose warning me that I'm on the verge of embarrassing myself. Especially when Tank squeezes me a little harder, pulling me in close to his massive frame.

I can't manage a response, but he seems to know this. With only a quick nod of his head, Tank crosses the room to talk with Judge Judie and her husband, Burt. While I stand here alone, trying to pretend like not one but two people have knocked me right off my feet today.

I still might feel unsure of myself, but I'm sure that after kissing Val, I won't ever be the same.

CHAPTER 25

Val

IF LAST WEEK I thought Winnie and James walking each other home a million times was disgustingly adorable, I'm not sure what to say about Chevy and me saying goodnight outside each other's bedroom doors a million times every night.

Starting to date a guy you're already living with has its own set of complications. It's a lot of togetherness, which—believe me—I don't mind a bit. Especially because, with his odd work schedule and my rush to finish paintings for Tank, we don't see each other half as much as I'd like. If we weren't sharing a house, I'm not sure we would see each other.

But the house sharing is complicated too because of the whole sleeping situation. I'm not ready to jump from years of pining and just friendship into a relationship and then jump right into Chevy's bed.

And yet ... I have to rethink that every night when he's kissing me up against the wall outside my room. Or pressed to the doorframe to his room. Then back to my room. We have quickly become the disgustingly adorable ones, and *I love it*.

I pull away from Chevy's mouth, where I've been lost for a while now. Kissing my way up his neck, I have to pause for an enormous yawn. His hands, buried into my hair the way they often seem to be, pause.

"Sorry," I say with a giggle, kissing the edge of his jaw. "I'm just"—another yawn—"a little tired."

Chevy's strokes turn softer and slower in my hair. "I should get you to bed, Tiny. Do you have to work early?"

He presses whisper-soft kisses along my cheek and up my temple, making it hard to think about things like schedules. Days. Work. Anything at all but him, pressing me up against my closed bedroom door. When his teeth lightly graze my ear, he must realize that I'm not able to focus, because he pulls back, resting his forehead on mine.

"I go into the gallery at noon, so I need to paint in the morning." I still have a dozen or so paintings left for Tank's lofts before I leave for Costa Rica. Which is something I don't even want to think about. Not when I've got the person I've wanted for so long *finally* wanting me back.

We haven't talked about it yet and we desperately need to, but I'm too afraid. Things feel so perfect now, but also so new and fragile. I'm just getting used to *this*; I'm not ready to think about *that*. And Luis Henry, Mari's artist friend, is flexible. He said anytime. So I'm going to stretch this out a little longer if I can.

"I'd like to see your paintings," Chevy says.

"You've seen them."

"Not enough," he says. "I want to see them all."

This makes a huge smile stretch across my face. Which then gets eaten up by another yawn.

Chevy steps back now, and I feel like all the cells in my body scream in protest, wanting him back, wanting him nearer. "Can I stop by tomorrow morning before my shift?"

"I would love that," I tell him, desperately trying not to get weepy and teary. I think Chevy's seen quite enough of me crying lately, thank you very much.

"Then it's a date," he says. "Now, to bed with you, woman." Opening my bedroom door, he practically shoves me inside, then closes it again behind me. I can still see the shadows of his feet outside though.

I press both palms flat against the door. "Chev? You still there?"

"I'm here."

I can almost imagine him standing just as I am, forehead and hands against the door mirroring me. It has my mind spinning out to some distant—or not so distant?—future. I'm thinking of weddings and those photos capturing the moment where a bride and groom stand on opposite sides of a door before the ceremony. Not wanting to see each other yet but anticipating what's to come.

My heart speeds up at the thought. I barely swallow back an *I love you*. It gets caught in my throat as stupid happy tears threaten again.

"Goodnight, Chevy," I say instead.

"'Night, Tiny. I hope you have sweet dreams. Of me, obviously."

Laughing and wishing I could linger, I step away from the door and head to bed, hoping for exactly the kind of dreams Chevy wants for me.

"I like the direction you're going."

I jump at the sound of Mr. Silver's voice, turning to look at the man who crept into the studio like a silent, art-appreciating assassin. Or maybe like a cyborg or body-snatching alien, as I've *never* heard Mr. Silver compliment my work. Every so often, he's stopped by, giving some constructive feedback. Nothing mean, but also nothing complimentary.

"The color and the composition—very strong," he adds, as I try not to faint from shock.

"Thanks?"

He frowns, so maybe it really *is* Mr. Silver. "Why do you sound surprised?"

I put my brush in water, shaking it a little until the clear water clouds blue with paint. Crossing my arms, I face him again. "Maybe because that's the first nice thing you've ever said about my work."

The frown goes deeper. He steps farther into the studio, walking along the wall where I've got a whole row of finished canvases, ready for Tank to pick them up.

"I only ever saw the pieces you showed me back in December," Mr. Silver says, tilting his head to examine one in a series of blues.

"And do you remember what you said about them? Because I do." His words are carved somewhere deep within me. "I think one of the words you used was *uninspired*."

He grimaces, then moves on to the next painting. "That may have been … undeserved. And a little harsh."

"If this is your way of apologizing, you're not very good at it."

Sighing heavily, Mr. Silver turns to face me with a look

like I'm his dentist about to perform a double root canal. "I apologize. You caught me on a rough day with the boys and, well, I wasn't in a place to say a word to anyone about anything. I am sorry. Truly."

I think I may have swallowed my tongue. That's why I can't respond.

Then he says, "I looked up Luis Henry Aguilar, by the way. He's good, and I think it will be good for you. That kind of apprenticeship always is. But I hope you don't lose your sense of your own style. You're really coming into your own. When are you planning to leave?"

I gulp, because going soon is the last thing I want to think about. Couldn't he have just stopped with the kind words and compliments and the sudden showing of a softy under the hard exterior?

"I'm still not sure," I hedge.

"I wouldn't want to see you give it up because of a man."

"I won't," I say, but the words are hard-fought. I *need* to go to Costa Rica. I know this. It's a sense I have deep within my bones that it's the right choice. I wouldn't let a relationship—even one as blissful as mine is with Chevy—make me change my plans.

And yet ... I can hardly stomach the thought of leaving him.

As though conjured by my thoughts of him, Chevy appears, knocking on the already open door. A smile is on his lips until he blinks, his eyes darting to all the paintings that he helped carry in while they were still wrapped up and the new ones I've done since.

His eyes and his expression are filled not with appreciation but pure awe. "Wow, Tiny. Look at these!"

My blush is immediate and hot, not creeping but zooming

up my neck and cheeks. My smile is just the same: fast and wide. "Thank you."

Mr. Silver gives Chevy a nod, then leaves without a goodbye to either of us. Unexpected compliments and apologies, he's still Mr. Silver. Brusque. Judgy. A little harsh.

Though I want to throw myself in Chevy's arms every time I see him now that I CAN throw myself in his arms, I stay by my easel, watching him walk through the room. Each time his gaze lands on a painting, I feel as though it's on me —his eyes traveling over my bare skin. My blush stays, joined now by goosebumps climbing my arms and legs.

When he finally finishes his perusal, I'm shaking where I stand. Chevy stares at me, like I'm someone he's never seen before. A stranger he greatly admires—and maybe wants to ravish.

That last part I'm basing on the way his eyes darken as he stalks across the room. He stops just short of me, his chest mere inches from mine. The air between us and around us feels suddenly charged. I halfway expect my individual hairs to start lifting from my head like they're being pulled by static electricity.

"Valentina," Chevy says, my name on his lips a caress. "You are so beautiful. And I'm completely blown away by the way you can take your beauty and push it out onto a canvas." He shakes his head, and I resist the urge to grab him and pull his mouth to mine. "I don't really *get* art, so I don't know the right words to say but—"

"Your words are just fine, Chev. More than fine. They're ... everything."

The tension building between us reaches an almost unbearable level, a full-body throb. But still, neither of us makes a move, letting the electric hum in the air rise and crest around us.

"Can I watch you?" he asks, his voice husky and unsure.

"Watch me paint?"

He nods, then tilts his head toward the big canvas I've nearly finished. "You were working this morning. I'd love to watch."

I shift my weight between my bare feet. "You want to watch me? It's pretty boring."

"There's no way I'll be bored watching you, Tiny."

I expect him to kiss me first, as there's no way I'm the only one feeling this palpable buildup. But maybe because he knows that kissing right now would lead to *not* painting right now, he backs up and settles on a nearby stool.

"Pretend I'm not here," he says.

Impossible.

And yet, within a few minutes, I'm lost again, only stepping back when my arm is cramping and I have that sense of completeness about my canvas. I blink, coming back to myself, to the room, to Chevy. When I glance over at him, seated on a stool nearby, I almost drop my brush.

If I thought his gaze was appreciative before, it's absolutely adoring now. My instinct is to shrivel up in embarrassment, to start to babble. But instead, I let myself feel proud. Of myself. Of my work. I bask in the warm glow of Chevy's gaze.

"Come here," I tell him, a brash confidence in my voice I hardly recognize.

He responds immediately, closing the gap between us. Just as before he keeps the slightest amount of space between us.

"You always have paint somewhere on you," he says, and that embarrassment I fought off only moments ago rises. I examine my hands, then rub one over my face, wiping away any bits of stray color or flecks of blue. Chevy catches my hand, holding it between us. "Don't. I like it."

His eyes rove everywhere over me. Though I'm wearing my usual coveralls and tank top underneath, my sweatshirt discarded by the door, I feel bare before him.

"I like looking at you, studying you. Searching for paint on your cheeks, your hands, your hair." His thumb grazes the inside of my wrist, and my pulse practically beats through my skin to reach him. "It's you," he says. "Completely you. And I happen to really, really like you, Tiny."

Feeling emboldened in a way I never have before, I say, "Bring the stool here. Sit."

Chevy raises an eyebrow but does as I ask. When he's seated again, legs angled wide and hands resting on his thighs, eyes curious, I step closer. Plucking a fan brush from my jar of dry brushes and palette knives, I step closer still, my heart ramming against my ribs.

I'm not the kind of woman who usually takes initiative with the men I date. Not to say I'm some passive, wilting flower. But I'm not bold. And I've never been particularly creative or innovative. I've certainly never done anything like this.

"Close your eyes," I tell him. He does, but only after giving me a smoldering expression, one side of his mouth turned up in a smirk.

I start there. With the brush angled comfortably in my hand, I sweep it oh-so lightly over the corner of his mouth. The smirk disappears, his lips parting as his breath quickens. I brush up over his cheekbone and then up to his temple and across his forehead. Down the slope of his nose, slightly crooked from that time he broke it playing football, and over the other cheek. Slow, slow, slow.

Without lifting the soft bristles of the fan from his face, I skim over one eyelid, then the other. Along the edge of his jaw, which clenches, and then down his neck. His Adam's apple bobs when I pass over it, and when I dip just inside his collar to the hollow between his clavicles, he grabs my wrist, nostrils flaring.

"Tiny." The word strangles its way out of him, like he's on the very verge of losing control.

I lean forward, kissing the spot where my brush stopped.

And then Chevy does lose control.

Or at least, that's how it feels as he stands, sweeping me up in his arms. My brush falls to the ground, and I'm only slightly aware of it because everything else is homed in on Chevy. He's the beat of my heart. The breath in my lungs. Is it too dramatic to say he's the completion of my soul?

Yeah, probably. But also … very true.

Our mouths meet messily, driven by something deeper than hunger. His stubble adds a rough edge while his lips are so soft, even in their intensity. All the tension building since Chevy walked into the studio has exploded in the very best way. I'm not sure I can come down from this, not when his hands grip my waist fiercely, like he wants to consume me but also protect and keep me safe.

My back arches, body bowing forward like I'm a whole field of flowers, tilting toward the sun as it crests the horizon. I'm lost. I'm found. I'm *his*.

Yet I'm more fully *myself* than I ever have been.

He pulls back, letting us both catch our breath. Gently lowering me until my feet touch the floor, he drops his forehead to my shoulder, sliding his hands up my back until he's hugging me tightly.

"I have a new appreciation for art," he says, finally, turning his head to nuzzle my neck. When he smiles, I can feel it against my throat. "A new appreciation for you."

"Good," I tell him, "because I hope we can do a whole lot more appreciating in the future."

That is … the relatively near future and then when I come back from Costa Rica. But for now, I let those words and my fears about the distance and the time and everything else stay unspoken.

FROM THE NEIGHBORLY APP

Subject: Congratulations, Coach!

BobToo

I'm usually not one to gossip, but let's all give our congratulations to Sheet Cake High football team's assistant coach Chevrolet Boyd as he and Valentina Ramirez are officially in a relationship!

1BigBass

You're totally a gossip, Bob. But also, congrats to the happy couple!

BagelBytes

I think it's highly inappropriate to discuss people's personal lives here. Just let them live!

DeltaDeltaDelta

I mean, I guess congrats? But watch out, Val—he'll be on to someone new next week.

Cal_45

Back from your suspension, DDD, and you're already running your mouth.

TheRealBob

Don't get me started on you, DDD. And don't think I don't know who you REALLY are. Say anything else negative about Chevy, and I'll be sure to docks you.

Vanz

That's dox. Not docks. And we all know DDD is really Tabitha Waters Graves.

BagelBytes

It's really unfair to share real contact information when people have chosen anonymity for a reason.

Vanz

They choose it so they can be bullies. No sympathy.

Chels

More importantly, what should Chevy and Val's couple name be? I'm voting for Vevy.

Danielle_L

How about Cheval? It sounds sophisticated.

Bob1

Cheval means horse in French. How about Valvrolet?

MegaB

I vote for Cheval!

TheRealBob

Another vote for Cheval

Vanz

Why do couples need names? But if they do need one, how about Chevrotina?

Cal_45

Vevy

BobToo

Cheval

SweetPea43

Cheval

BagelBytes

I don't approve of the idea, but I really hate Cheval, so if I did vote—which I'm not—it would be for Vevy.

The_Real_Shell_E

Cheval!!!!!!!!

WayneNGarthBrooks

Cheval

Chels

VEVY. Would YOU want your couple name to mean horse?

BagelBytes

I wouldn't want a couple name to begin with.

Vanz

I guess Cheval is okay if no one else likes Chevrotina.

Neighborly Mod

The comments on this thread have been closed. But let the record show that Cheval earned more votes. Please remember to be kind and above all, Neighborly!

CHAPTER 26

Chevy

"YOU'RE HUMMING AGAIN."

Blowing out a frustrated breath I drop my pen and glare at Grant, sitting one desk away, a similar stack of folders in front of him. "Yeah, and?"

"This paperwork doesn't seem likely to inspire humming."

It normally wouldn't. A pretty riled up and boozed up farmer named Butch got a little rowdy while being brought in last night and knocked over a file cabinet. Today, Grant and I have the pleasure of going through and making sure all the paperwork is in the right folders. So, yeah—it sucks. But I'll see Val later.

My fellow deputy is grinning. The kind of grin that says he knows why I'm grinning because he's all caught up on

Neighborly gossip. Which this week has largely centered around Val and me.

We're suddenly the Brangelina of Sheet Cake—hopefully with a more promising future ahead. Our couple name is worse. In a Neighborly poll, the votes went in favor of Cheval, which sounds like a French perfume designer and is only slightly better than Vevy.

You'd think the family of football players moving to town and falling in love with Sheeters would garner more attention. And while the Grahams certainly have held their fair share of the small-town spotlight, the interest in Val and me is greater.

Part of it is because we both grew up here. Part of it is probably the betting, which has been going on for longer than I want to know.

"Aw, I think your humming sounds nice," Charlotte calls from the receptionist's desk. She's watching a soap opera on silent, reading the closed captioning because her hearing isn't the best. Though she doesn't answer phones anymore for that same reason, we all love Charlotte and will keep her so long as she'll show up to smile at people coming in the door.

"Thank you, Charlotte."

"And I'm happy for you and Val," she adds. "Took you long enough."

Yeah, it did. And other than some lingering doubts that flare up from time to time, I can't remember the last time I was happy like this.

I'm humming again without realizing it until Grant huffs.

"Fine! You want to make any requests, newbie?" I ask him. "And don't say *Freebird*."

"How about some Zac Brown band?"

"Now *that* I can do. If you can get back to work and leave me be."

He does. And I start to hum through "Toes," more than a little surprised when Grant starts humming the harmony along with me. We're halfway done with the song when the phone rings. As the newest hire, Grant gets the honor of answering the call.

I ignore his chorus of *yes ma'ams* and *mm-hms*. From his tone, this is a complaint, not a real call. My hands go back to the papers; my mind stays on Val.

When I'll see her next. What she'll be wearing. If she's making dinner. When I can pull her close and kiss the daylights out of her.

Grant hangs up, shaking his head. "That was Mrs. Fleming. She said you were going to come clean out her cannons?"

It's clear from the question in his voice, Grant has never met Mrs. Fleming. Or her cannons.

"Is that, like, a secret code?" he asks.

"Nope. She has actual cannons. Some kids have been stuffing trash in them. It's a whole thing. I meant to take care of it, but I forgot."

"Can I come?" Grant's floppy golden hair and wide, hopeful eyes give him a golden retriever vibe.

"Sure. Just don't mention her cat." I close a folder and move onto the next.

"Why?"

"Because it's actually an opossum."

Before Grant can ask follow up questions about *that*, someone pushes through the double doors and into the station. He's a dark-haired guy I've never seen before. Looks to be about Grant's age, fresh out of college.

"May I help you?" Charlotte asks.

"Yeah, um." The guy shoves his hands in his worn jeans and glances past Charlotte. His gaze hops right over Grant and lands on me, holding. I can't read the expression in his eyes, but it's intense. I glance back down at the folder in front of me, feeling unease spreading in my gut. Something about him seems familiar.

"Chevrolet Boyd?"

"You know Chevy?" Charlotte asks, glancing my way.

"No. Well, sorta. I was hoping we could talk."

Though I can't shake the disquiet, anything's better than paperwork. I push back my chair and stand, gesturing to the chair near my desk. "Come on back."

He glances between Charlotte and Grant. "Do you have anywhere, um, private?"

More dread. More worry about what this guy wants with me that he doesn't want anyone else hearing.

"Sure." I lead him into the conference slash interrogation slash break room and close the door behind us. It always smells like burned coffee in here, which, considering all the options, isn't all that terrible. I start to pour myself a cup.

The guy has his back to me, looking around the room like he's taking in every detail. "Is this where you question criminals?"

"Suspects. And yeah, when we need to. Coffee? It's terrible. Might kill you."

"Sure. Let's live dangerously." When he turns back to me his smile is barely there, then gone. But even in that quick flash, my unease turns to something worse: dread.

Because I think I recognize that dimpled smile. And I think I know why he looks familiar.

I keep my eyes down, trying to keep my hand from shaking as I pour. I'm mostly composed when I set it down in front of him. He's seated in the chair I usually would use, and I sink down into the one that's normally for suspects.

He takes a sip. Makes a face. I lift the Styrofoam cup to my lips. Drink. Taste nothing.

Setting down his cup, he crosses his arms. "I've been trying to reach you, but you keep sending my letters back."

"Charlie," I say. My stomach churns.

"So you know who I am."

"I didn't at first."

We stare at each other across the interrogation table with matching blue eyes—my half-brother and me. We have similar coloring, different face shapes and different bodies too. He's tall and angular, long lean legs stuffed into faded jeans and sneakers.

He looks away first, staring down at his knuckles, which don't look all that unlike mine the night Val bandaged me up at CVS. Even thinking about her right now makes me feel even sicker. I shove thoughts of her away.

"Are you in trouble?" I ask. "Is that why you're here? Do you need help or something?"

"You really didn't read any of my letters?"

"Nope."

Not entirely true. I started reading the first one until I got to the part about *his*—our—dad. The thing with letters is they're so much more personal. Knowing the person writing touched the same paper, folded it up. Seeing their handwriting and how they write. It's so much more invasive than sliding into someone's dms. Also, you can't block letters the way you can a phone number—you have to return them to the sender.

Until the sender seeks you out.

"I'm not in trouble," he—Charlie—says. "I just ..." Lifting

one of his hands, he drags it through his hair, which is longer than mine and a few shades darker.

"I just don't know what to do or how to process this, you know?"

I do know. And I'd rather not be processing anything with this stranger. My ribs feel like they're cinching in, squeezing my lungs and heart in a vise grip.

Charlie leans forward, his elbows on the table, eyes flashing. "I don't even know where he's buried. Didn't get to attend the funeral. He was never there a lot, but then he was just gone. And, I mean, I should hate him. Right? Do *you* hate him?"

I've read about panic attacks. Witnessed a few. And I refuse to have one right now, so I take a moment to steady my breathing. Nice and slow through the nose, then out. In and hold ... then out. The tightness in my chest eases. Slightly.

"I'm still trying to figure that out," I tell him. "But yeah— I think I hate him a little. Probably only because I loved him so much first."

We sit there in silence after what may be one of the most raw and honest things I've ever said. I don't know if I should ask him questions, or even if I want to. Maybe I should comfort him, but I don't know how because I've had no comfort myself. I never read his letters, so I don't know if he has some kind of endgame or something he wants. Maybe money like his mama did.

I reach for my coffee, seeing the slightest tremor in my fingers. As I take a sip, Charlie lifts his cup and drains it, then slams it on the table like he just won the battle of the bad coffee. The Styrofoam crumples, and he stares at it like he's shocked somehow.

Just as I'm about to ask maybe a little too bluntly what he

really wants, the door to the room flies open. Val stands there, grinning at me and obviously not reading the room. She doesn't even seem to see Charlie, but I notice how he straightens in his seat.

Val dives forward, giving me a hug around the neck from behind. My whole body hardens, like I was just filled up with quick-drying cement.

"I was just running an errand and had to say hi," Val says. She kisses my cheek, loudly, then must notice Charlie. "Oh. The new guy said someone stopped by, but I didn't realize you were doing official police stuff. Sorry!"

I don't say anything as Val stands, squeezing my shoulders once before backing toward the door. I can't even turn to look at her.

"Sorry again to interrupt. Anyway. I'm making dinner tonight. Just let me know when you'll be home. Bye!"

And as fast as she rushed in, Val rushes out. I feel like the wreckage left the morning after an F4 tornado ripped through a small town.

Charlie blinks at me. "You're in a relationship?"

I nod, barely moving. "Yep."

His eyes dart around the room, like he's collecting data and still not coming up with a final conclusion. "Wow."

"Be careful or I'll get a complex about my good looks." I force a grin that wouldn't fool any of my friends. I'm not sure if it will fool Charlie either.

"I just mean ... I haven't been able to really date ever since I found out." He shakes his head, looking down at his empty coffee cup. "I'm angry with him. Angry with women. Angry with you. Angry with myself."

I know the feeling, even if I've done my best to pretend I don't feel anything.

Maybe I should tell him that I understand. It might make

me feel better to open up because even more than Winnie, I think Charlie would get it. But I don't say anything at all.

Things I'm only now realizing I shoved down deep instead of actually dealing with are bubbling up like some kind of backed up sink. My thoughts are muddy and sticky and heavy, while my heartbeat seems to have slowed, thudding in my ears like the ticking of an oversized doomsday clock.

I find myself rubbing my cheek where Val kissed me, like I'm trying to wipe off a stain.

You're in a relationship?

I don't even want to think about Val right now, the very person who consumed my every waking thought for days now.

Was I really just humming? That feels like a different day, different life, different man.

Charlie's face swims before me, and I squint. Doesn't help.

"You okay?" he asks.

No. "Yes," I grit out.

Charlie stands. "I should go."

He is my half-brother. My blood. My family. I should stop him. Or exchange phone numbers. Emails. *Something*.

I don't, though. A tingling numbness spreads through my limbs while I stay seated in the uncomfortable metal chair. Charlie leaves, maybe saying goodbye. If he does, I don't hear it. I do see him scrawl his number on a piece of napkin and shove it across the table.

I'm not sure how long I sit. Staring. Forcing myself not to think.

"Chevy?"

I look up, and Grant stands in the doorway. With great

effort, I stand. Put on a smile that might be passable. Remind myself to be cool, man. *Be cool.*

But it all falls away as Grant blinks his golden retriever eyes at me and asks, "You have a half-brother?"

CHAPTER 27

Val

WHILE I'VE GOTTEN USED to Chevy sitting at the island, watching me cook as I talk his ear off, tonight is different. First, Mr. Clean Freak kicked off his boots and left them in the middle of the living room instead of lined up neatly by the door. Somewhere, a pig sprouted wings and flew. And then, rather than greeting me with the kind of kiss that could make a girl burn dinner, he barely reacted as I kissed him—okay, maybe he flinched, but that can't be right—and slumped onto a stool.

I burned dinner anyway. I'm too distracted by his uncharacteristically silent demeanor and the rigid line of his shoulders. Tonight, my talking isn't the typical flow of words because I like talking. It's more like word vomit. And I've got a bad case of the talking flu.

"Sorry about this. I guess we'll just get takeout if that's

cool. My treat! Anywhere you like. Burning happens to the best of us. Once when I was in, like, seventh grade, Mari left the stove on too long and it—"

"When do you leave for Costa Rica?"

The question is jarring. Not only because we haven't discussed this yet, but because of his tone and *how* he's asking.

I don't answer right away, scraping the charred chicken and onions from the pan onto the trash. Might as well toss the pan, too. It won't ever be the same. But it's not mine, it's Chevy's, so I'll do my best to salvage it. Carefully, I set it on the stove and grip the edge of the counter.

Chevy's face is impassive. He's staring intently at the napkin he shredded while I was busy burning the heck out of dinner.

"I haven't bought my ticket yet. I was tentatively supposed to start my apprenticeship or mentorship or whatever in a few weeks. Or a month. Luis Henry is flexible. And Mari says my room there is always open, so it doesn't matter when."

Chevy says nothing.

"Why do you ask?" My words sound pitiful. Soft and vulnerable and embarrassingly raw.

Because I'm getting a terrible sense about where this is going, and my tear ducts are already gearing up for mass production. My nose stings, and I clench my jaw, trying to hold it together and not assume the worst.

"I think it would be good to take a break when you go," Chevy says.

We were on a break! The quote from *Friends* is my very first thought, and it isn't at all funny in this context. But a choked laugh bubbles out of me anyway, turning into a sob.

"That's it?"

Chevy drags a hand down his face, swiping it across his mouth. His eyes still don't meet mine.

"I'm not saying it's over, just that … maybe a break would be good for us."

"You mean for *you*. Because a break certainly doesn't sound good to *me*. We barely got started, Chevy. What happened? We can figure this out. Relationships take work. That's okay. We can work through whatever it is—together. But you have to talk to me."

I hate how desperate I sound. But the thing is—I'm not just fighting for our relationship here. I'm fighting for *Chevy*. I can feel the hurt practically radiating off him, and I remember what Winnie said about him being as emotionally available as an old boot. She was wrong, though. He's more like a squished cockroach stuck in the tread of a boot at the bottom of a lake.

But I don't want to leave him down there. I want to help him up. Because, our short-lived relationship aside, we were always friends. And friends don't leave friends at the bottom of a lake.

"Chevy, talk to me. *Please*."

He doesn't move.

Something happened between the last time I saw him and now. It had to have. This didn't come out of nowhere. But what? I trace back the day in my mind while my tears keep falling. This morning, he insisted we try making out on every single chair, couch, and stool in the house. Then I stopped by his work and—

My mind slams into that moment. *There*. I was in such a hurry that I barely registered anything other than Chevy, but now that I'm thinking back, something was off. He didn't move in that chair. Didn't try to pull me in his lap and kiss me. Which I didn't think too much about because he was at work, and I was in a hurry. But he wasn't himself.

Who was the guy he was talking to? I barely glanced at him and can't remember his face now. But he wasn't familiar.

"What happened today at work?"

He gives his head a slight shake, and I swear he tenses up even more.

"Let me help you."

I'm back to begging. Which I wouldn't do for me. Nope. In the past, when I've been broken up with, I pretty much ran off with my tail between my legs. I didn't beg. I didn't push for more. I didn't argue about why. This is different. It's not just a breakup.

Before me, I'm seeing a broken man. A man I really, really, REALLY love. And think I have for a long time.

This is about *him*. Not me. Not us.

I wish that made it hurt less.

His jaw flexes, and it makes all his gestures tighten. "I don't need help. I need a break."

Somewhere in me, an alarm is clanging because there is a breach. My heart just cracked wide open. And now the sadness is flowing out freely by way of tears and a runny nose. I plug it with a napkin as I round the counter, grabbing my purse.

Chevy grabs my wrist, and I pause, turning my ugly crying face in all its glory toward him. His blue eyes are a stormy ocean. They glisten, but no tears fall.

"I never wanted—I didn't mean—" He stops. Swallows hard. Drops my wrist. "I'm sorry, Tiny."

I walk away before I collapse, stepping over his discarded boots on my way to the door. As I close the door, I say, "Call me Val."

But I'm not sure it was loud enough for him to hear.

Within an hour, I'm safely on Winnie's couch, falling apart while sandwiched between her and Kyoko with the OC offering his one-eyed support by loud purrs. I'm translating his kittyspeak into veiled threats to make Chevy pay.

"The thing is," I say, my voice hoarse from all the crying, "I'm not just hurt and mad and all the breakup feels. I'm *worried* about him."

"As you should be," Winnie says through clenched teeth. "I did warn him."

"I didn't mean worried about you. Worried about whatever had him practically frozen."

"There are no excuses for this," Winnie says.

"I'll only help if no jail time is involved," Kyoko says. "My specialty is in long-term prank warfare."

I'm quite sure I don't even want to know what that means.

I touch Winnie's arm, making sure she meets my gaze. "Will you check on him? When you go get my stuff?"

Her eyes narrow. "Oh, I'll check on him, all right."

"Win, I'm serious."

"So am I."

I pause to blow my nose. Half a tissue box has been sacrificed to my sadness already. "I think something happened today. There was a guy with him at the station. And now that I'm thinking back, there was this vibe. I kind of ignored it because I was in a hurry but ..."

Winnie blows out a breath, then rolls her eyes. "Fine. I'll check on him. In a nice, caring, sisterly way." She stands, then mutters under her breath, "And then I'll check on him the way I *really* want to."

"Need help?" Kyoko asks.

"You stay with Val. Keep her hydrated to replace all the liquids she's losing. Feed her if she'll eat. Don't let her near her phone, and no watching any sad or romantic things and no sad ballads of any kind. Sarah McLachlan is off the table. Same with Nick Drake and—"

Kyoko waves a hand. "I got it."

Before she leaves the loft, Winnie kisses the top of my head. "I love you, Valley Girl. You'll always be my sister."

What she doesn't say—but I hear anyway—is that I'll always be her sister, even if I'm never her sister-in-law.

"I'm going to get snacks," Kyoko says. She adjusts the headband holding back her short, dark hair. "The kitchen is stocked, but we can also order out. What do you want?"

"Pizza," I tell her. "Stuffed crust. I don't care about toppings. And garlic bread. And chocolate."

"A mountain of pizza and a river of chocolate coming right up."

The moment Kyoko dashes off to order, I slide the phone she forgot to confiscate out of my purse. After checking to make sure I haven't missed any calls or texts from Chevy—I haven't; of course, I haven't—I book the soonest plane ticket I can get for Costa Rica—one way.

CHAPTER 28

Chevy

AFTER MY SISTER moved out of my guest room, the quiet felt strange at first, like an old friend I was happy to see but had to get used to again. The silence felt like a soul-deep sigh.

Val left only hours ago, and my house feels all wrong. It's haunted by the ghost of her, like Val's absence isn't something missing, but something extra added into the space. A wart. A skin tag. A tumor.

I hate it.

I want to go back to the world before, when an empty house felt right. When I hadn't had to face my father's *other* son. When I hadn't known what it was like to have Val, to hold her, to call her mine ... and then break her heart.

Just like I always feared I would. Call me Deputy Self-Fulfilling Prophecy, I guess.

"Please don't take it out on my baseboards," I beg, as Winnie violently drags one of Val's wheeled suitcases toward the front door, letting the wheels knock into the white trim I painstakingly painted myself a few years back. I already see a scuff.

"I make no promises," Winnie says, glaring with enough anger to light a fire. "Something we apparently have in common."

The door slams behind her. With a sigh I swear I can feel in my bones, I get up from the couch and walk into Val's room to help with the bags and boxes. The moment I step inside, I falter, grabbing the door frame to steady myself.

Val's scent is in the air. Warm vanilla and sugar, like someone's been baking cupcakes. I squeeze my eyes closed, trying to stuff down everything that's been rising up since that guy—Charlie—my half-brother—walked into the station.

Clearly, stuffing things isn't working. Because that's what I'd been doing. And the moment I saw Charlie and had to think again about my—*our*—dad, it all rose back up again. Making me doubt. Filling me with fear. Reminding me of all the reasons I never dated seriously.

I meant what I said to Val—I wanted a break. Not to break up. But it didn't come out right. I couldn't say the words or answer her simple questions. There's the general sense that I can be an idiot about women, just like many men before me, but I think I'm a very special kind of idiot to have wrecked things so completely.

Something knocks into my hip, hard, and I stumble. "Hurts, doesn't it?" Winnie asks, shoving past me and into the room.

"I've been hip checked by you before. I can take it."

"I didn't mean the hip check," she says, picking up

another box and giving me an icy stare. "Oh, and I brought help."

James appears beside me, and though he doesn't hip check me like my sister, the look he gives me assures me he'd like to do worse.

"Winnie—"

"Don't speak if you're gonna give me some lame excuse. Just … don't."

I swallow, but when she tries to pass me and head through the door, I put a hand out, grabbing her arm. "Our half-brother came to see me today."

Winnie's eyes go wide behind her glasses. James steps between us, taking the box from Winnie's hands. He says nothing, walking by us to take things to the car.

"What did he want? Money?" Winnie asks. When I shake my head, she scoffs and says, "So, he just showed up out of nowhere?"

"He's, um, been writing me letters for a while now."

"You've been in contact with our half-brother and didn't think to tell me?" Winnie's voice is rising to a level that could be described as shrieking eel with an edge I might describe as borderline murderous.

"I sent them all back without opening them. I just couldn't deal, you know?"

Winnie backs up and sinks down on the bed, stunned. "Why didn't you tell me?" Her voice is softer now. "I thought we were done with secrets."

Stepping further inside the room, I lean up against the dresser, thankful I collected real wood furniture from thrift and consignment stores. I'm not sure cheap, fake wood could hold the weight of me right now. I'm pretty sure my blood has turned to something heavier and denser. Any minute now, I'll drop through the floor, leaving only a sinkhole behind.

"I don't like talking about it. About any of it. I've been trying—"

I pause when James comes back in the room. He still says nothing, which is scarier than James saying just about anything at all, but he sits down next to Winnie and presses a tender kiss to her temple. Then he pulls her right into his lap.

The sight makes my chest throb like an angry bruise. Because that could be me and Val. If I were like Winnie, better at loving. Being loved. Dealing with my stuff. The tightness that's been crushing my chest ever since I realized who Charlie was presses in harder until each breath takes maximum effort.

"I can't do what you do," I say quietly, gesturing between them. "I'm not good at … feelings."

James makes a sound that's somewhere between a laugh and a scoff. "You think Winnie is good at feelings?"

"Hey!" She tries to shove him, but he just bands his arms tighter around her.

Raising one brow, James pins her with a look. "You really want to argue this?"

"Okay. Fine. But you're not so hot at feelings either, big guy."

James only grunts. Then he turns to me. "So, this is why you broke Val's heart?"

I wince, and my mouth goes dry. "Is she okay?"

"I'm not giving any information to you, pal." Winnie glares. "I get that this is hard. Having a half-brother show up is a blindside. But do you know what Val did when she left here, what she said? She was worried about *you*. She is crushed and confused and, frankly, devastated, but she wanted me to make sure *you* were okay."

The thought of Val caring about me while she's in pain makes me feel literally ill. I bend over, putting my hands on my knees as I fight for breath, hoping I don't barf right on the refinished hardwoods.

"I think I need to see someone," I say when I can speak, still bent in half and panting.

"Like … a wizard? A claims adjuster? A lawyer?"

My sister the comedian. "A counselor," I say. "Or therapist? Psychiatrist or -cologist or whichever one. I don't know the difference between any of those. But I think I need one."

"That may be the smartest thing you've said in your whole life," Winnie says. "I think it's a great idea."

James clears his throat, and from my bent-over position, I can see him squeeze her knee with one of his big hands. "I think it would be a great idea for *lots* of people," he says pointedly.

"Like you?" Winnie quips.

"Maybe me too," James says.

With a heavy sigh, Winnie climbs off James's lap and walks to me, rubbing my back. "Fine. Maybe we should go together, Chev. Talk about our feelings and all that gross stuff."

"You'd go with me?" I ask, straightening up and eyeing her to see if it's a trick.

She takes her hand off my back long enough to pinch my side. "Of course I would, you big dope. Now, when do I get to meet this half-brother? Is he coming back?"

"I have no idea. But I have his number if you—if we— want to call him sometime."

"Okay. But first things first—when and how are you going

to fix things with Val? Do you want me to tell her about this or are you going to?"

"I'll tell her. But I need a little time." My head still doesn't feel right. Neither does my heart or anything else. And I'm not going to apologize or try to win her back unless I know I'm really ready and able to commit without breaking her heart the first time something difficult is thrown my way.

That's *if* she'd even take me back. But I have to reserve hope for her, for us. Otherwise ... I'm not sure what I have left.

Winnie narrows her eyes before hoisting up another box of Val's. "Tick tock, brother. Your secret won't keep in this town for long."

———

She's right about the secrets. By the next morning, news not only of my breakup but rumors of Winnie and I having a half-brother are being discussed. Though I don't deserve it, I kind of expected a call from Val once she found out about Charlie. Knowing my sister, she might have smashed Val's phone with a sledgehammer to keep her from calling or texting me first.

I roll up to Mrs. Fleming's house feeling like a ghost of myself. Sleep was a joke, with stressful dreams punctuating the little sleep I did get. Not even a cold shower could draw me out of this exhausted funk. When I arrive—late—Mr. Silver sits on the hood of a sleek black Mercedes with his arms crossed, and the three boys are waiting on the sidewalk next to Grant.

Mrs. Fleming brandishes a wicked looking rake, and glares at all of them from her front porch. Grant and the boys seem more alarmed by the opossum and her bedazzled leash than the rake.

"Thank goodness you came," Mrs. Fleming calls to me. "These punk kids look like they're up to no good."

Mr. Silver opens his mouth, but I hold up a hand. "Now, Mrs. Fleming, you can't go around calling people punks. These boys actually volunteered to come help me clean out your cannons today. They weren't the ones who put this trash in, but they're still here to help."

I choose my words carefully, because at one time, two of them did put *some* trash in the cannons. Just not THIS trash. "And this is Grant. He's one of our newer deputies."

"Fine," Mrs. Fleming says, setting down the rake and tightening her hold on the possum's leash.

I pull two trash bags from my truck as well as some rubber gloves. I may feel only halfway here, but I came prepared.

Brady looks horrified. "What kind of trash is in there?"

I shrug and give the best grin I can manage as I snap on a glove. "Don't know. But I'm not about to stick my hand in someone's chewed up gum. Or worse. Are you?"

All three boys shake their heads with comic force and speed. Grant bites back a smile. And then we get to work. Brady and Bryan take one of the cannons while John and I take the other. He yanks out trash while I hold the bag open. Grant starts pulling weeds from Mrs. Fleming's cracked sidewalk, keeping one eye on the possum.

"They don't carry rabies, you know," I tell him in a low voice.

"Why doesn't that make me feel better?" he asks.

Ten minutes, a pair of broken glasses, and a losing lottery ticket later, we're just about done. Both trash bags are almost full. Cannons can hold more trash than you think.

"Ours is empty," Brady says, tossing his gloves in the trash bag.

John peers into ours. "I think there's a soda can or something still back there. I can't reach."

"I'll get it," I say, and John steps aside. I try not to think about all the gross junk we've already pulled out. Or the fact that my arm is inside a CANNON. The final bit of trash, which does feel like an aluminum soda can, is really jammed in there. I can't get a good hold.

"Where'd you get these cannons?" Grant asks, leaning against the porch railing, still watching Genevieve like he fully expects her to do a WWF body slam on him any moment.

Mrs. Fleming pats the back of the cannon I'm working on. "My Nate bought these for us when we moved in. He was a navy man," she tells him. "It was his little taste of the sea."

"Do they still work?" Brady asks, looking a little bit too interested.

"No," Mrs. Fleming says.

"Are you sure?" Grant asks. "Because that might be a hazard if they do."

"They shoot cannonballs and aren't loaded," Mrs. Fleming says. "Plus, they wouldn't fire without gunpower packed in. See?"

Something about that last comment makes me jerk my head up. Just in time to see Mrs. Fleming holding a lighter near what must be the fuse. I yank my arm out of there faster than I would from a lion's mouth, but John who must not have seen the lighter, steps closer, peering inside, just as there's a loud sizzle.

Sparks fly. Genevieve the possum falls over fake-dead. And I only have time to shove John out of the way before there's a deafening sound, a blast, and something collides with my chest.

I'm flat on my back on the sidewalk. My ears are ringing. My nose burns. And there's an overwhelming pressure and burning in my torso.

The last thing I hear before things get really dark is Mrs. Fleming saying, "I guess they do fire! Oh my—that's a lot of blood."

CHAPTER 29

Val

I DON'T WANT to answer when Winnie calls. I REALLY don't. Definitely not when she calls immediately again. And then a third time.

She and James and Kyoko left for some kind of craft brewing thing in San Antonio this morning, and I've been peacefully wallowing in my misery on her couch ever since. Not answering calls. Not checking Neighborly to find out what people think about my breakup. My main goal is to create an actual rut on the couch before they get back tomorrow.

It's a lofty goal, but I have faith in my wallowing abilities.

When Winnie calls a fifth time, then a sixth, I finally cave, pressing pause on *Criminal Minds*. I've gone back to bingeing the show that scares the heck out of me, but makes my life feel like a carousel ride with cotton candy by comparison.

"Yes, I'm fine. And no, I don't want to talk," I say instead of hello.

Winnie's response is breathless and shaky. "Val, it's Chevy."

My whole body seizes up. Because I know this tone. I've never heard it from Winnie, but I know the panicked sound of an absolute emergency.

"What happened? Is he okay?"

"Yes? I don't know. He had an accident of some kind on the job—I don't really understand what happened. But we can't get back for a few hours, and Chevy's all alone at the hospital. Val—I know this is awful of me to ask, considering, but would you please go? I need someone to tell me he's okay. He was in surgery when they called me."

Surgery? My stomach is a tightly wound coil of dread.

"I'm on my way." I'm out the door before we hang up, still in my wrinkled wallowing clothes because what I'm wearing doesn't matter when Chevy is *in surgery*.

Right now, not even the tattered state of my heart matters, because when push comes to shove, Chevy still owns whatever shreds are left of it.

———

The hospital is a shiny cube in the new part of Sheet Cake, and I definitely break some laws to get there quickly. It takes a few arguments, several smallish lies, and one threat to find Chevy. I might have said I was his sister. (Ew.) But I'm a woman on a mission, and I can't fully breathe until I open the door and see Grant standing by his bedside.

Chevy looks ... alive. And that's the best thing I can say. Right now, I'll take it.

His shirt is gone, and his whole chest is wrapped in

bandages. He's blinking sleepily, and there's something that looks like blood on his chin. Grant, who looks more than a little relieved to see me, has blood all over his shirt.

"What happened? Is he okay?" I ask Grant, trying to ignore the adorably sleepy smile Chevy's giving me. And the resulting feelings unfurling in my chest without permission.

Relieved. You are ONLY allowed to feel relieved.

"Valentinnnnnnnna," Chevy singsongs. "My love."

Grant gives me an apologetic look. "He'll be fine. But he's a whole lot loopy between coming out of the anesthesia and the pain meds."

I'm trying to ignore the way Chevy's looking at me. It's not him. It's the meds smiling and looking me up and down appreciatively. And it's my stupid ovaries responding with glee.

"I got shot," he says. "I deserve a medal. Will you pin a medal on me, Tiny? But not on my chest. It's all busted up."

"You let him get shot?!" Eyes wide, I stare at Grant.

"Not with a gun."

"Oh, good." I sag, my hand pressing against my sternum, like it has any ability to slow my racing heart.

"With a cannon," Grant says.

I smack him in the arm, and he winces. "You let him get shot with a cannon?! That's so much worse!"

"It wasn't loaded," he says, like this makes it all okay. "Mrs. Fleming doesn't even have cannonballs."

I cross my arms, wishing I could shoot Grant out of a cannon. "So, why is he in the hospital? Why did he just have surgery if it wasn't loaded?"

"Dr Pepper, baby," Chevy says. He laughs, then groans, then laughs again.

Grant rubs the back of his head. "He was struck by a can of Dr Pepper—or, the shredded pieces of a can of Dr Pepper.

Shards of aluminum came apart and embedded in his skin. Turns out, none of them went too deep, except one. That's why they put him under. They were checking to make sure it didn't damage any tissue or, uh, organs."

Suddenly, Grant looks a little green. How can a cop get squeamish? Isn't there some class on getting used to blood and guts as part of their training?

"My organs are just fiiiine," Chevy says, winking.

I can't help it. I giggle. The heartbreak and stress and emotional turmoil of the last twenty-four hours has left me raw and hollowed out. Whatever cord held my emotions in check has frayed and now snapped.

I giggle again. Then I snort.

Grant eyes me with suspicion and inches toward the door. "Now that you're here, I should probably, uh, head back to the station."

"Workman's comp, boiiii," Chevy says, then tries to lift his hand, flashing a peace sign, only to be stopped by a sling holding his arm in place. Probably to stop movements just like this one. "Am I in a straitjacket?"

"Nope."

"Why can't I move me?" he whines, looking so pitiful that I can't help but step closer to the bed. I catch a flash of move-ment as Grant darts out and slams the door. I'm not sure if it's my presence or the talk of Chevy's injury, but the man departed like he was on fire.

I stop right next to Chevy's bed, curling my hands into fists at my side so they don't go rogue and do something like smooth out his tousled hair or take his hand.

"Come here," he says, and I take the teensiest step closer.

Mistake! Because now, I'm in striking distance. Chevy clasps my hand and—well, folks, that's the end of my ability to hold back. I let him link our fingers, then don't stop him when he—*oh no, oh no, BIGGER MISTAKE*—lifts my hand to his mouth for a kiss.

Only, he misses my hand and kisses his knuckles instead. His brow furrows and he turns our hands, trying again. He still gets his own hand.

Oh, my heart. This man is THE man I want. He's it for me.

Except I have to remember that he wants a break. At least, the Chevy not on painkillers does. This version of him is flirty and sweet and determined—trying until he finally places a sloppy kiss on my fingers.

For the sake of preserving what's left of my heart, I should move away. I should go. I mean, no one knows this yet, but I'm leaving tomorrow. Actually, Mr. Silver, of all people, does because I had to ask if he would arrange for Tank to pick up my paintings. But I didn't tell anyone else. I'm scared I won't go through with it if I do.

"Blue paint," Chevy says triumphantly. "You've got blue paint right here."

So I do. "Yep."

"I love finding paint on you."

He really needs to stop with the sweetness. But he doesn't. Instead, he leans his face into our clasped hands and closes his eyes.

I wish things were different. If I just close my eyes, I could forget yesterday even happened.

Yesterday? Nah. Never heard of the guy.

The thing is—Chevy could have DIED. I don't understand how the cannon went off but it's a CANNON and being hit by *anything* at close range is not good. The idea of losing Chevy only highlights the ways I've already lost him.

I feel my face stinging, but I don't try to fight the tears. Why bother?

His eyes open suddenly, still hazy and heavy lidded. "I got shot by a cannon," he says, sounding like a little boy telling his mom he got to meet his favorite superhero at a convention.

"I heard. With a Dr Pepper can, no less. Solid choice of sodas."

His eyes brighten. "Maybe they'll put my face on the can?"

"I wouldn't hold my breath. But you're really okay?"

"Doc says I'll be just fine." Chevy angles his head, trying to peer down at his chest. "I'll have a wicked scar though. The can gave me a lassie—a laser—a lizardation?"

I can't help but smile, despite every moment here making my heart feel like it's cracking open more. "Laceration?"

He nuzzles into our clasped hands, then frowns when he realizes more of his cheek is touching *his* knuckles. He lets go. And though I shouldn't, I cup his cheek. He pushes into my hand like a needy cat, and though I REALLY shouldn't, I start playing with his hair. His eyes flutter closed again.

"They say ladies like scars. Do you like scars, Tiny?"

I want to kill Winnie for not being here. For sending me to this hospital room when I'm feeling so emotionally fragile and Chevy is being all endearing after what could have been a terrible accident but now will live on as a joke or meme.

"I'm just glad you're okay."

"I'm more than okay now that you're here."

"Chevy," I groan. "You can't say things like that."

"But it's true. You're my favorite person." He lowers his voice and tilts his head, his lips brushing my palm. "Don't tell Winnie. She probably thinks it's her."

Breathing steadily takes so much effort. Almost as much effort as it takes to hold in my tears. The only upside is that in Chevy's state of mind, he doesn't seem to notice my attempt not to fall apart. And I'd bet money he doesn't remember this later.

By then, I'll be a country away.

"I won't tell," I manage to say, and my laugh is at least fifty percent a sob.

"Am I *your* favorite?" he asks, opening his eyes a slit and giving me a boyishly hopeful look on his face that is TOO MUCH.

"Always," I tell him. I dig my fingers in just a little more on his scalp, earning a groan from him. His eyes close again.

I massage his scalp, trying to memorize the feel of his soft strands on my fingertips. This might be it. The last time.

As much as I felt like Chevy and I had something more than all his fast and furious relationships (if they can be called that), in the end, maybe he just can't do commitment. Or, at least, doesn't think he can.

I still don't know what changed so suddenly. If Winnie found anything out when she came back with my stuff last night, she didn't say anything. But if I take in the evidence—years of Chevy casually dating, the lack of any significant romantic relationship *ever*—am I really so surprised? Maybe I'm his favorite person, but I don't know that it matters if he can't make a commitment that lasts longer than a week.

Winnie may have been right about her brother being emotionally unavailable. And me? I'm the glutton for punishment rubbing his head while silently crying at his bedside.

Yep. Definitely time to flee the country.

"I'm leaving tomorrow, Chev," I whisper, and in response, he snores softly. "And though it's dumb, I love you. I have for the longest time, and if all I ever get from you is the short time we were together, they were the happiest days of my life."

I bite my lip, my chest aching. People get over heartbreak

though. All the time. I'll go to Costa Rica, focus on painting, get to know my family, and then ...

The rest is just too hard to think about.

Though I should probably stop touching him, I keep rubbing Chevy's head through the nurse coming in to check his vitals. Through a doctor stopping in to tell me—the person he thinks is Chevy's sister—that Chevy's stitches will dissolve on their own and that we need to watch for any signs of infection after they release him tomorrow.

I stay long enough to fall asleep, waking to see Winnie peering down at me, where I slumped against Chevy's unbandaged shoulder. And once I know he's safe with Winnie and James, I excuse myself, giving Chevy one last, likely horribly embarrassingly desperate look of longing, then head back to the loft so I can finish packing, do some more crying, and prepare to leave the country.

CHAPTER 30

Chevy

I WAKE to someone poking me in the shoulder. Before my eyes are even open, I'm aware of just that: Poke. Poke. Poke. Only one person in my life has ever woken me like this.

"Winchester," I groan, trying to crack open my eyes. They're gritty. My eyelids are heavier than normal. And the light's weird. Things smell funny and—

My brain suddenly jolts into consciousness and my eyes fly fully open. I'm in the hospital.

The cannon—the stitches.

And ... Val? Was Val here?

I squint at my sister, who looks like some kind of avenging angel in the harsh lights of the hospital, all angry face and golden hair. I shift a little in the bed, feeling the ache and sting in my chest where I received some amount of stitches earlier today.

Was that today? The light from the window is really bright. Looks more like morning. So—yesterday?

My brain feels cottony and slow, and a headache is building right behind my eyeballs. Pain meds and I aren't the best of friends, and that's the normal over the counter stuff. I'm not sure what they've given me, but I can feel the impact.

Winnie pokes me one more time.

"Stop," I tell her, starting to swat her away until the pain radiating through my chest stops me. I groan, glancing down at the bandages and sling. "Why are you harassing me? Shouldn't you be bringing me flowers and chocolates?"

"Not when you do stupid stuff like getting shot by a cannon and almost die."

"I didn't almost die."

"No, you didn't. But you could have. And then I'd be all alone. It's simply not allowed."

"Noted."

Winnie sighs and sits down on the edge of my bed, carefully, like she thinks I'll break. Which makes me think again of Val. There's a chair by the bed. Did she sit there? Was she even here or did I dream it?

"Is Val here?"

"No." Winnie pauses, and I'm not sure what kind of look it is she has on her face. "She left last night when we got here."

So, she *was* here. I can't quite grasp the memories. They feel almost like cobwebs blowing in a strong breeze while I try to gather them in my fist. Lifting the hand on the good side—or, better side, anyway—of my body, I rub my forehead. My face even hurts.

"Are you okay?" Winnie asks, and her tone is gentler now. Very un-Winnie. When I nod slightly, she sighs. "You really did scare me, Chev."

Her voice is wobbly, and Winnie *never* wobbles. When she takes my hand, though, that's when I squint at her.

"Who are you and what have you done with my sister?"

"It's me, you big dork."

"My real sister wouldn't hold my hand." When she tries to pull away, I squeeze, holding on tighter. "Only an imposter. Or maybe you're Tom Cruise wearing one of those realistic faces like in *Mission Impossible*."

Winnie snorts. "You wish I was Tom Cruise."

"A little bit. But seriously—no need to worry. It was an accident. Not even a hugely serious one."

Winnie tips her chin toward the bandages on my chest. "The doctor said you got seventy-two stitches. Seems pretty serious to me."

"Meh. Minor flesh wounds."

"Chevy, you had a crushed Dr Pepper can embedded in your chest. It's kind of a big deal."

"Did they save what was left of the can? I could make a trophy out of it."

"I'll ask. But I doubt it. I think it was mostly shrapnel. You're officially good to go. We're just waiting on the doctor with official discharge and instructions. Mostly—go easy and try not to rip your stitches or reopen any of the cuts. Watch for infection. Take pain pills as needed. Blah blah blah."

"Thanks for that very medical explanation," I say drily.

Winnie's quiet for a moment, and since I doubt that will last long, I try to focus my thoughts and remember Val's visit. What did we talk about? Did I do or say something stupid? Most likely. But what?

Thinking of Val makes a very different part of my chest ache. A deeper than my Dr Pepper injury part.

I miss her.

I miss having her in my house, leaving toothpaste in the

sink and long, dark hair everywhere. I miss her laugh. The sight of her in my kitchen, whether that's yawning and messy-haired in the morning or bright-eyed and telling me some story while cooking for me. I miss kissing her in various rooms of the house—because we absolutely did kiss in every single room. And the front and back porches. I'm nothing if not thorough.

Then I think of Charlie, his face with features similar to mine, to my dad's. I allow that pain to sink in deep, below the mild throb of my injuries. For the first time in a long time or maybe ever, I let it hurt.

The grief over losing my father—not to death, but as my childhood hero. Living years with his lies. Carrying them as though they were mine too, being crushed under the weight of that burden. Forcing myself to shut it all in, to protect Winnie from it. Fearing I will be no better.

That something in me, inherited from him and inside my cells like some kind of virus, would make it impossible for me to commit. Like I would be forced somehow, from my genes, to be unfaithful.

I open my eyes. Man, are those thoughts stupid. *I'm stupid.*

My dad's choices aren't mine. And though I still feel a deep sense of hurt and anger I should probably still work through with a therapist like Winnie and I talked about, a deadweight has lifted from my chest.

I am not him.

Which means I pushed away the one person who means more to me than anyone in the world because of a lie I told myself.

"Idiot," I mutter.

"You're the one who's got a Dr Pepper related injury," Winnie says. "Don't call *me* an idiot."

"Oh, I definitely meant me. I'm the idiot. Move."

Winnie hops off the bed. "Are we leaving?"

"I need to see Val."

The white curtain between my bed and the next one jerks aside to reveal James Graham. He's lying in the hospital bed with one hand behind his head like he was sleeping, his motorcycle boots on the floor next to him. He's wearing socks with Roy Kent's face on them, which have to be a gift from my *Ted Lasso*-obsessed sister.

James and Winnie exchange a look.

"What?" I ask.

"Seeing Val might be ... complicated," Winnie says.

"Spit it out, Win."

"Kyoko texted me a while ago. Val is on her way to the airport. I guess, with all your aforementioned idiocy, she decided to leave sooner than later."

Moving as quickly as I can while testing my limbs and the pain in my chest, I sit up, swinging my bare legs over the side. "No time to waste. Let's go. We've got to get to the airport."

"To stop her from going?" James asks.

I slip carefully off the bed, wincing at the cool floor and the slight pinch in my chest. "No. She needs to go. But I need to talk to her first. To apologize, to explain. To tell her ... things."

I'm not about to say that I love Val for the first time in front of Winnie and James.

Winnie covers her eyes at the sight of me in just boxer briefs and tosses my jeans onto the bed next to me. "I approve. But if you want to grand gesture her, Casanova, you need pants."

"Grand gesture her?"

"Don't even pretend like you didn't read the romance

novels I left all over your house. Did you think that was an accident?"

"I just thought you were messy," I say.

"I'm not a mess. I'm a *mastermind*."

My sister might be a mastermind, but I'm a man who can't put on his own pants. With the sling and the limited movement of my upper body, there's no way.

Winnie darts out the door. "I'll get the car. James, you want to help my brother put on his pants?"

The very last thing I want is James Graham putting on my jeans for me. No—make that the second to last. Because the VERY last thing I want is to get to the airport too late to speak to Val.

I eye James, then give him my very best smile. "You ready to take our relationship to the next level so I can win back a woman?"

James only grunts in response. I take that as a yes. And I guess it's finally time to put him out of his suspense and give him my blessing.

It's the least I can do if the man's going to help me put on pants.

CHAPTER 31

Val

I'M NOT scared of flying. I'm *not*. At least I didn't think I was.

No—I am an adult woman, and I am not afraid of the plane blowing up mid-air or crashing in a fireball, sharing my last moments with complete strangers.

Nope. Not scared.

Of course not! That would be silly.

Telling myself this doesn't make me move any closer to the check-in area where I watched Mari do this exact thing not long ago. I'm standing in the middle of the airport lobby —is this called a lobby?—trying to psych myself up to approach the counter.

I have my passport. I have my driver's license. I have my carry-on stuffed as full as it can be and my massive rolling bag with all the things I think I'll want for the next ... however long I stay.

Maybe I'll stay forever? What kind of visa could I get if I wanted to stay? Because staying means I wouldn't have to do this again and get on a plane. Ever again.

No more planes. No more airports.

"No more cowardice."

I say this one out loud. Maybe with a little too much force, because a few people turn and look my way. I thought airports were the kind of place where no one pays you any mind.

Unless you talk out loud. To yourself. About cowardice.

"I'm not a coward," I whisper, and no one looks up this time.

Still, I call Mari through the app I downloaded so we could talk internationally without paying exorbitant fees.

"Am I doing the right thing?" I ask the moment she says hello.

There's a soft chuckle, the kind that makes my heart squeeze with affection. "What *thing* is that, princesa?"

"Leaving Sheet Cake. Coming to Costa Rica. Getting on a plane that could crash and leave me a charred pile of bones at the bottom of the ocean."

Mari *tsks*. "Ah. We're being dramatic today. It would be very hard to burn up under water."

"Thanks for that assurance."

"Well," Mari says, and it sounds like she's switching the phone to her other ear, "talk me through this decision. Why do you *want* to come? Why do you *not*?"

Tears spring to my eyes, despite my very vivid and silent threats for them to stay put inside my tear ducts. Because yes —I am scared to fly. I didn't know this until this moment, facing my very first flight all alone—and out of the country to boot.

But that's not the real reason I can't just walk up to the counter.

"I don't know," I whisper.

"Does it have to do with being scared of doing something new?" She pauses. "Or leaving what you know?"

"Both?"

"And what about your deputy?"

With Pavlovian precision, an image of Chevy in the hospital, shirtless and smiling goofily at me flashes in my mind. "He's not mine anymore," I grit out. "He wanted to break up before I left."

"He broke up with you?" Mari sounds shocked.

I pick at a loose thread on my purse strap. "Technically, he asked for a break while I was gone. But it turned into a very real breakup."

"I'm sorry. Is that why you changed your ticket to leave so soon?"

"Yes." My lip starts to tremble. "And what if I come back and he's with someone else?"

Mari sighs. "I have faith in Chevy. And in you. If it's meant to be, distance won't be the end of your story."

I want to cling to that, to hope in it. If drug-addled Chevy showed me a glimpse of his real feelings, maybe there is hope. But not if fully-awake Chevy is going to push me away for reasons he can't even voice.

He's the coward. Not me.

"You know what?" I say, feeling a sudden surge of confidence. I tighten my grip on my wheeled carry-on and begin marching to the ticket counter. "I'm getting on the plane. I'll see you soon." Then I remember this is a long, overnight flight with two layovers. The best I could get last-minute. "Or—I'll see you tomorrow. Whatever."

"I'm so proud of you," Mari says. "And I miss you. Everyone here is so excited you're coming."

That's good. Because what I'm feeling as I hang up is anything but excited. Determined, maybe. Disappointed? Definitely.

"Ticket and ID," the unsmiling woman at the counter orders.

I can feel my sweatiness growing in proportion to her irritation. I wipe my forehead with the sleeve of my jacket as I grab my phone. "Sorry. Hang on."

I manage to pull up the ticket on my phone and pass over my driver's license and passport because I don't know what she needs. I also have my birth certificate and my very last high school report card tucked in my purse. I'm not sure why I even still *have* it, or why I brought it, but BETTER SAFE THAN SORRY.

A few sweaty minutes later, my big bag is rolling away on a conveyor belt, and I'm checked in—no need for my report card, as it turns out—and headed toward security when I hear a familiar shout.

No—I *imagine* a familiar shout.

Because there is no way I actually hear Chevy shouting. He's in the hospital. And even if he weren't, he pushed me away just days ago. No way is he going to chase me down in the airport now.

Unless …

Unless he realized he was being an idiot and DID show up here.

No way. Again: he's in the hospital.

And maybe the person was shouting Sal or Hal. Not Val.

I keep shuffling forward with the rest of the people

through a zigzag maze rivaling an amusement park line. This is far from amusing.

I hear another shout, this one shouting a word I can't possibly mistake. "TINY!"

My head whips around.

I spot a shirtless and still bandaged Chevy all the way across the terminal just as two beefy and out of breath security guards reach him. My eyes meet his across the crowded space, and something inside my chest locks into place.

He's here. He came!

Those thoughts are quickly followed by questions: Where's his shirt? Did he escape the hospital?

I stand there, still staring dumbly, as two airport security guys say something to Chevy I can't hear. It doesn't look pleasant, based on their expressions and the way they grab his bare arms.

Even from here, I can see the way Chevy winces at their rough hold.

"HEY!" I shout, and now everyone's turning to look at me. I start working my way backward through the line, never taking my eyes off Chevy. "Excuse me. Excuse me. Sorry. Could I get by?"

People grumble as I fight my way past, trying to keep my wheeled carry-on from whacking people in the shins. The security officers are yelling at Chevy now, which allows me to catch pieces of conversation, like about how he needs a shirt and needs to leave.

"Chevy!" I call, right as a large motorized trolley thing stops right in front of me, letting a handful of older men and women pile off with their carry-ons, almost completely boxing me in.

I hoist my bag in my arms and hop onto the trolley, cutting right across one of the rows.

"Hey!" the driver shouts. "You can't be on here."

"Just taking a short cut," I call, making my way across and hopping down.

Now, James and Winnie have joined the fray, and while one of the security guards still has Chevy by the arm, Winnie is shouting at the other, channeling all her fierce Winchester Boyd indignation.

"Can't you see he's injured!" Winnie shouts. "He's a cop and was injured in the line of duty, so hands off and back up!"

"Let's all calm down," James says, just as another security guard with a bristly mustache appears in front of me.

He holds up two placating hands, which are anything but placating at the moment. "Ma'am, I'm going to have to ask you to stop running through the airport."

"I'm not—"

His hands go up higher, much closer to my face. If he doesn't watch it, I'm going to take a bite out of one of his fingers.

"I saw you going the wrong way through the line and using the trolley as a springboard."

"Are either of those things crimes? Are you going to put me under airport arrest?"

"No, but—"

"I'm coming, Tiny! Hang on!" Chevy cries.

I peek around the security guard's shoulders. From somewhere, James has procured a wheelchair, and is gently shoving Chevy into it. Then, in a move so smooth it belongs in a movie, James rips off his shirt.

I swear I hear the collective dropping of jaws all around the terminal at the sight of James Graham's bare torso. He should come with a permanent warning label like the one you're never supposed to remove from mattresses. Only his would say something like, *Look, don't touch, or my girlfriend will claw out your eyeballs and feed them to the crows.*

With a gentleness I've only seen James direct toward Winnie, he helps Chevy into the shirt. Chevy's arm in the sling can't move, so there's one empty sleeve hanging there.

One hundred points for James Graham.

The security guards, however, do not appreciate his act of kindness. Or his model-worthy bare torso. It's only a matter of time before—

"Is that one of the Grahams?" I hear someone ask.

Guess the time for James to get recognized is now. I sometimes forget how famous the Grahams are. They're all so *normal*. I mean, no—the abs that all of them possess are in no way normal. But I mean, they're so down to earth, I forget unless I see them in a public space how well-known and respected they are. Even James, who never got to play pro ball.

I step around the security guard, who is now distracted by the people gathering, phones lifted to take pictures and video. James continues to provide a distraction to the security guards by standing firm in his shirtless Graham glory while they yell at him about proper airport attire. Winnie takes this opportunity to bolt, pushing Chevy in the wheelchair at a dead sprint.

In pink peep-toe heels.

Chevy clutches the armrests with both hands, looking as though he might regret this whole endeavor. Or, at least, the part where Winnie got control of the wheelchair.

Until our eyes meet again. And then, his expression shifts to something totally different. It's the way I've always wanted someone—for most of my life, wanted HIM—to look at me. Like I am worth being pushed through an airport in a wheelchair. Worth all of this fuss and the scene he and Winnie are making. And the million stitches he might be ripping open with all this movement I *know* he shouldn't be doing.

One of the security guards is trying to escort an unmoving James out of the building, while the other runs after Winnie, who ditched her heels somewhere for better speed. The security guard in front of me clears his throat and raises his eyebrows at me.

"Friends of yours?" he asks.

"Yes. I'm sorry for running and climbing over the trolley," I tell him, then ask, "Have you ever done something stupid for love?"

His mustache twitches, and I'm not sure if it's because he's uncomfortable talking about his feelings or trying not to laugh at me. "Who hasn't?"

"Me," I tell him. "I've done a lot of stupid things for a lot of people who weren't worth it, but until now, I haven't really done anything stupid for love."

His eyes narrow. "Is the stupid thing you're thinking about doing against airport policy?"

I shake my head. "Nope. My stupid thing is giving this guy a chance to redeem himself. Even though he was a total idiot."

The security guard turns then, just as Winnie and Chevy reach us. My friend is panting and leans on the back of the wheelchair for support, while Chevy gets unsteadily to his feet. The security guard who's been chasing Winnie finally catches up, too out of breath to even say anything to her yet.

My mustachioed security guy sighs, mutters, "Only at airports," and walks away to help his friend deal with Winnie. I'd offer to help, but she doesn't need it.

"Tiny." Chevy stands in front of me, looking tousled and funny in James's too-big shirt and empty sleeve dangling there. "I'm so glad I got here in time."

"I still need to go soon if I want to make my flight." His face falls, and I barely stop myself from reaching out to touch his good arm. "Are you okay?"

"Physically—I might have pulled a few stitches. But that doesn't matter. Because I'm not okay otherwise."

His expression takes on an intensity I've never seen before. They're sparking with determination, but he drags a hand through his hair, looking like he's fighting to find the right words. My instinct is to fill pauses like this with words—lots and lots of words—but I bite the inside of my cheek to stay quiet.

"I'm bad at this," he says. "I'm so good at the light words, the ones that stay up near the surface. But I don't know how to do these kinds of words."

"What kinds of words?" I ask.

Tentatively, like he's scared I'll pull away, he reaches for my hand. I let him, and his shoulders sink with relief. "The heart kind of words," he says.

"Is that why you're here, Chevy—to talk about heart words?"

I'm afraid for a moment he's going to say he's here to stop me from going. Despite my fears about flying, nervousness about moving to a whole new country with a lot of unknowns, and the temptation it might be if Chevy asks me to stay, I can't escape the sense that I *need* to go. For *me*. I don't want him to make me choose.

Though if he asks ... the temptation to NOT get on the flying metal death sausage will be very, very real.

Chevy takes a step closer until we're toe to toe, my hand still in his. He squeezes my fingers, and I suck in a breath, clinging to what I hope isn't a foolish hope.

"I've made a lot of mistakes in my life, Tiny. I'm sure I'll make a million more. But I can't let you leave without telling you how I feel—how I *really* feel—and what I want for us."

US. He said us! There is still an us!

"I'm listening," I say.

Chevy licks his lips and shifts, wincing slightly. "I've had a lot of hang-ups because of my dad. I know it's dumb, but I really believed I couldn't—or *shouldn't*—have a committed relationship because of *his* mistakes."

"Chevy—"

"I know. It's stupid and untrue, and I should never have thought that. The other day at the station, my half-brother tracked me down."

I gasp. "That guy was your half-brother?"

He nods, jaw clenching. "He's been writing me, and I returned all the letters. That's what you saw in the kitchen. I thought I'd processed a lot of this when you and I started dating, but really, I just stuffed it down and tried to ignore it. Seeing him brought it all back to the surface."

Oh, Chevy. I've had my own fair share of angst because of my mom leaving and my sisters pretty much wanting nothing to do with me. But I also had Mari, sure and steady and so full of love. Whenever I did want to talk about Mom or was sad about her leaving, Mari talked me through it and held me while I cried. I didn't stuff it down. I worked through it.

Chevy lost his mom, and his dad was living a huge lie. I know he and Winnie both didn't tell anyone at first when they found out—not even each other. I can't imagine all the hurt that might be stored up inside him.

Now, I'm the one squeezing his fingers. My lip trembles as I say, "I'm so sorry, Chevy."

"I know. And I know if I'd told you that day instead of freezing you out, you would have been there for me. I've just never been good at this. Relationships. Talking about feelings. Even admitting my feelings."

He pauses, then lets go of my hand to tenderly brush his fingers over my cheek. His hand slides back to cradle the back of my head.

"Even good feelings." He licks his lips, looking suddenly nervous. "Like, for example, I haven't told you I love you, Tiny."

I'd love to say I play this cool. But instantly I'm smiling and crying at the same time.

Not cool, Val. Not even a little cool.

I sniff. "Happy tears. Go on. You were just saying that you love me?"

"I do," he says, grinning. "I love you. I really, really do. And being a man not very in touch with his emotions—"

Somewhere behind him, Winnie snorts. I glare, realizing there is a whole crowd of people standing around, listening and watching. My mustachioed security guard shushes Winnie, whispering, "Don't ruin the moment."

"But that's my brother," she says. "It's my familial obligation to give him a hard time."

I catch her eye. "And you're my friend. And you have a friend obligation to not ruin this. I know where all your bodies are buried."

There are a few gasps, and the security guard nearest Winnie takes a step back.

"Not real bodies," I add. "Metaphorical ones. *Anyway.*"

"Where was I?" Chevy asks.

"You were about to tell me about your emotions."

"Ah, right. Yes. Emotions." His smile tilts, making him look boyish. Not just boyish, but the kind of boy who just got caught with both hands in the cookie jar and isn't even a little sorry about it. "I love you, Val. But I'm not good at saying how I feel, much less acting on it. I don't know how to do relationships. My instinct is to run when I'm scared. To stuff things down and pretend they don't exist."

He trails off, the happy, boyish look fading into something so deeply painful that I wrap my arms around his waist, careful of his injuries.

"Is this okay?" I ask.

Chevy rests his chin on top of my head. "This feels like how I want to spend the rest of my life. Without the seventy-two stitches and the sling, that is. I could also do without the audience," he says as someone in the background says, "Awwww."

"Chevy, about your dad …" He stiffens, but then exhales deeply and nuzzles his head into my neck. "You have to know that just because he's your dad, it doesn't mean that you're going to be like him in that way. You are a great guy, Chevy. Faithful. Constant. Amazing."

"Why, Valentina—it almost sounds as though you love me."

I pull back, meeting those deep blue eyes. "I do. I love you, Chevy. I have for … well, I don't know when this turned from a crush into what it is now, but it's been a long, long time."

"Same," he says with the kind of flirtatious smile that gets my heart racing. "Only I didn't really allow myself to look at you that way, to admit the things I felt."

I smile. "So you stuffed the good feelings right down there with the not-so good?"

"Yep. And now, before you go, I need you to know how I feel. I don't know how to do this, but I want to do this."

"To make sure we're on the same page—what's the *this* you want to do?"

His look turns downright wicked, and I feel a blush coating my cheeks. "I want to do *lots* of *this-es*. But to start with, I'd like to ask you to be mine."

"No break?" I ask.

"No breaks. Other than the distance, which might kill me. But I know this is a great opportunity. Personally and professionally. You have to go. Heck, maybe I'll finally get a passport and come visit sometime."

"I'd love that."

"And meanwhile, Winnie and I agreed to start therapy to deal with all our stuff."

"I think that's a really good thing, Chevy."

"Hey kids," Winnie interrupts. "I hate to do this, but Val—what time is your flight? Because I think it's boarding and you aren't through security."

Chevy reaches his good hand up again, tucking my hair behind my ear before tracing my cheekbone. "I'd love nothing more than to ask you to stay, but I love you too much to be selfish with you."

"We can write letters," I suggest. "Emails. And there's an app I use to talk to Mari. We can call and even video chat."

"We'll need to do all that. And then you need to come back home, Tiny. Come back home. Home to *me*."

"Yes," I tell him.

He grins and presses his lips to mine. So soft it's almost a question, and I can't help but wonder if all this vulnerability has left him needing more assurance. Trying to be mindful of his injuries, I pull him tighter and let my mouth reassure him. Then reassure him some *more*.

When we pull away—only because Winnie says something else about missing my flight—Chevy and I are both panting and breathless and smiling big, goofy, in-love smiles.

"Is this really happening?" I ask Chevy.

He leans close, his breath warm on my cheek as he murmurs, "This is happening, Tiny. And I can't wait to see where we land."

FROM THE NEIGHBORLY APP

Subject: Real Cannons?

BagelBytes

In case you haven't heard, Deputy Boyd was shot by one of Mrs. Fleming's cannons yesterday and suffered critical injuries. I'm attaching a petition to have the cannons removed. They're clearly unsafe and a danger to the community.

JB

RIP Chevy

Vanz

He didn't die, JB. He was shot with a coke can. It was stuffed inside the cannon.

Cal_45

I thought it was Dr Pepper

Vanz

That's what I meant. A coke can of Dr Pepper

Chels

That makes no sense. I grew up calling it pop.

Vanz

Go back to the midwest and take your pop with you! It's Coke. And the best Coke is Dr Pepper.

1BigBass

Hey, maybe we should petition to change it so instead of calling them all Coke, we call them all Dr Pepper

DeltaDeltaDelta

????

1BigBass

For example, normally if I want a fountain drink at a restaurant, I'll say I want a small Coke. When they ask what kind, I'll say Dr Pepper. Maybe instead, we should start saying, I want a Dr Pepper. And when they ask what kind, we can say Sprite. Or Coke. (But honestly, we all just want Dr Pepper, so it's a moot point.)

Cal_45

I don't like Dr Pepper. It's made from prunes. I do drink it when I'm blocked up.

JB

DDD, weren't you banned?

DeltaDeltaDelta

Just suspended. Now I'm back. But you better believe my lawyer plans to bring legal action.

LindyLouWho
Good luck with that.

Chels
I vote to change Coke to Dr Pepper.

Vanz
I vote we ban Coke and ONLY serve Dr Pepper in the Sheet Cake city limits. I'll send a note to Tank.

JB
Send it to Billy Waters! He'll be running for mayor soon, and would love to run on a Dr Pepper platform.

BagelBytes
The important part was that a MAN WAS SHOT BY A CANNON. An officer of the law. One of our own. The cannons need to go.

SweetPea43
Mrs. Fleming also has a pet possum. I'm pretty sure that's illegal too while we're on the subject. Maybe she shot Chevy when he was trying to take her possum away?

MaddieDVM
It's actually called an opossum. And yes, they are also illegal to own. Opossums and owls can only be kept by licensed people who have proper permits. Does Mrs. Fleming have a permit?

Vanz

She has a leash for it.

Chels

Once I saw it with a bow

TheRealBob

We're going to be collecting donations for Coach Chevy to offset his medical bills. See the link to the GoFundMe I set up to help cover his hospital bills.

Vanz

Workman's comp should cover it if he was on the job.

Bob1

I heard he dove in front of it to save a kid's life. He's a hero!

BigBass

I heard he flew ten feet and caught fire

SlimShabby

I heard they were going to put his face on a Dr Pepper can.

Vanz

As long as it's not a Coke can

Chels

Dr Pepper 4life

BagelBytes

Doesn't anyone care about REAL issues? A man was shot! By a cannon! Which is still on Mrs. Fleming's front porch! Does someone actually have to die for anyone to care????

WayneNGarthBrooks
I say we also take up a collection of Dr Pepper for Deputy Boyd. Can anyone make a Dr Pepper bouquet—like those chocolate and fruit bouquets?

CraftyCarol
I never have before, but give me a glue stick and I can make any kind of bouquet!

Vanz
Does that include taxidermied chicken feet?

CraftyCarol
No. Sorry.

Vanz
Then you probably shouldn't say "any kind" of bouquet. False advertising.

Neighborly Mod
The comments on this thread have been closed. Please remember to be kind and above all, Neighborly!

EPILOGUE

Val

I'M AN ANXIOUS, sweaty mess when I get off the plane in Austin-Bergstrom. Because, as I realized on my first-ever flight, I'm not just a nervous flier. I'm the kind who jumps at every bump, who screams at strange noises, and who uses multiple barf bags. A panicked flier. And, of course, a cheap flier, which means I had two layovers.

But I came prepared! No way am I going to see Chevy for the first time in months looking like death warmed over and then flambeed. True to his word, he came to Costa Rica a month ago. The visit took the edge off the distance, but barely. I mean—letters, calls, video chats, and the visit were great, but nothing will beat finally being home for good with Chevy.

Six total months away, and I'm ready to be back with the person who is my home.

It only takes a few minutes in the airport bathroom to freshen up—new shirt, freshly applied deodorant and a new perfume I found in Costa Rica, and a little bit of mascara. I'm giving my reflection a silent pep talk—since I'm not alone—when the woman washing her hands next to me meets my eyes in the mirror. She has blond hair and the kind of tiny lines around her eyes that say more about her propensity for smiling than her age.

"You've got that look about you," she says with a smile. "A glow. Coming home to a boyfriend?"

"It's probably just remnants of nervous sweating from the flight," I say, zipping up my makeup bag.

She laughs at this, and I hand her a paper towel since I'm blocking the dispenser. "No—it's definitely that love glow," she says. "Enjoy your reunion."

I know I will. And it's thoughts of the reunion that have me power walking once I'm through customs. We're supposed to meet at baggage claim, and I'm straining to see a familiar cowboy hat or those warm blue eyes or the crooked grin.

Instead, I spot a different familiar face.

"Lindy?"

She envelops me in a hug so tight I think she realigned my spine. As glad as I am to see her—especially with the new, rounded belly I can't help but get teary over—she isn't the person I wanted to see.

"I know," she says, patting her belly. "I'm huge. I'm a whale. A double decker bus."

"Hey! Stop talking about my friend like that. You look perfect. But, um, where's Chevy?"

Lindy's face falls. "He couldn't come." Trying to brighten her expression, she grabs my hand. "But Pat and Jo are out in front waiting."

I force my disappointment down, down, down. Because I am excited to see Lindy again, to see Jo and Pat, to be *home*. But I ache for Chevy in a way that I don't for anyone else, and I'm going to be in a constant state of buried frustration until I'm in his arms.

Per the usual, Pat provides an epic distraction.

"What are you *driving?*" I ask as he hops out of a sleek black minivan at the curb.

"Don't ask me," Lindy mutters. "I wanted a suburban."

"Aw, you know you love the heated seat massager." Pat gives me a big hug and a kiss on the cheek. "Looking good, Val! Don't be too mad at my boy for sending us to pick you up. It kills him not to be here."

I swallow down a sudden lump in my throat. "Thanks."

Pat pulls away, then pushes a button that makes the automatic door slide open. Jo leaps out and practically knocks me flat on the sidewalk.

"Did you grow, Jojo?"

"I did. Dad says I get my height from him." She gives Pat a quick glance and then lowers her voice. "But I know that's not how DNA works. I just play along. Here's your card!"

She shoves a construction paper card in my face. There's a crow on the front with a shiny something in his beak. "Great drawing! Did you ever get that charm bracelet yet from the crows?" I touch the shiny silver pieces jangling on her wrist.

Pat scoops her up before she can answer and holds her above his head—those Grahams and their biceps!—spinning her until she squeals. "The crows still come and demand food, but as far as them bringing gifts, so far, it's a bust," he says.

"I'd offer you the front, but I get carsick," Lindy says. She glares down at what has to be the cutest baby bump ever bumped. "Bad baby! Bad!"

"You know by this stage of development, the baby can hear you," I point out.

Lindy blinks at me. "*I* know that. But how do *you* know that?"

I shrug. "I've been reading this mom blog so I can be the most supportive friend possible."

For a moment, Lindy's jaw goes slack. Then her eyes get watery, and she wraps me up in another hug. At this rate, I'm never going to see Chevy again.

"That's so nice," she says, sniffling.

"Mom's crying again," Jo says with a sigh.

"Better adjust the board," Pat says, setting Jo down. She hops in the car and pulls out a small dry erase board that says, *Number of Hours Without Tears*, and erases the two to write in a zero.

"I can't help it!" Lindy says through a sob. "I hate crying! It's the mean baby!"

"I know, darlin'. I know. Now, let's get you in the car." Pat gently peels Lindy off me, then winks as he walks her around the front of the car. "We've got places to be!"

Places to be and Chevys to see! Pat doesn't need to tell me twice.

"This isn't home," I say as Pat pulls up to the curb downtown. I can see a lot of signs of change. More people. More businesses open. Definitely no open parking spaces. It's dusk, and the strings of lights are just winking to life.

"Consider yourself kidnapped," Pat says, winking at me in the rearview mirror.

Lindy turns around and hands a bandana to Jo. "Blindfold Val, would you?"

"Gladly," Jo says, unbuckling her seatbelt.

"Is this really necessary?" I ask.

"Yes," all three say at once. In utero, the mini-Lindy is probably nodding along as well. A minute later, Lindy takes my arm, helping me out of the van. I stumble a little, and Pat takes my other arm.

My stomach is full of all kinds of nervous flying things: butterflies, birds, and maybe even a dragon or two. "Can I ask for a clue?"

"Nope," Lindy says cheerfully. "Step up."

Carefully, Pat and Lindy lead me somewhere, and I can feel a blast of air conditioning as a door opens. "Another little step," Pat tells me as I take probably too large of a step over a threshold. "And now's the time we let you go."

"Let me go? But—"

"You can take off the blindfold, Tiny."

That familiar voice, laced with a smile, sends a thrill through me. I rip off the blindfold and blink—my eyes and brain both trying to adjust to what's before me.

Chevy—in his uniform, standing in the middle of Mr. Silver's gallery, grinning at me. I'm about to launch myself into his arms when something snags my gaze. I suck in a breath.

Every painting hanging up is one of mine. Luis Henry promised to pack and ship them after I left, claiming he was more familiar with how to pack for shipping and how to deal with the postal service. Obviously, he was in on this.

Aside from my paintings, the room is also full of people. Winnie and Kyoko. The entire Graham fam. The ladies from the LLLS. I'm happy to see Charlie too, standing between Winnie and Tank, looking like he always belonged.

And … is that Mari?

She gives me a smug look that then turns soft. I'm

confused for a second, but I bet, unlike me, she didn't skimp on plane tickets and flew direct, beating me back to Texas.

All my friends. All our family. All smiling.

I falter, wanting to rush forward into Chevy's arms, but suddenly feeling overwhelmed by all of this. Tears, which never falter, prick my eyes. I try to breathe because I don't want to have a whole breakdown.

"What is this?" I whisper.

Chevy grins his signature crooked grin with an added side of tenderness he only reserves for me. "This is your gallery show."

"Oh."

Chevy drops to one knee pulling what looks like a ring box from his pocket. "And your engagement party."

I bite my lip, the tears winning the battle as a few escape down my cheeks. "So cocky," I say. "You planned a party without even waiting for me to say yes?"

A few people chuckle, and Chevy's grin widens. "I have many faults, but I've never claimed to suffer from a lack of confidence. Now, get over here, Tiny."

Chevy holds out his free hand, and I feel a soul-deep sigh the moment my hand slides into his. He gives me three squeezes, which is a code he and his mama used to say *I love you*. More tears fall.

"You know I'm not great with words about feelings," he says, looking up at me. "So, I'll keep this short and sweet. Valentina, you're it for me. I love you. I'm nowhere near good enough for you, but I'll spend the rest of my life trying to be. I promise to be faithful."

He pauses here, his lips trembling for a moment before he gains control. I know just how much that promise means to him.

"I'm yours. Everything. The good and the bad."

"And the ugly," Pat says under a cough from nearby.

Chevy shakes his head. "I can't get through one simple proposal." There's soft laughter from around the room, and then Chevy's attention zeroes back in on me with renewed intensity. "While I was visiting you in Costa Rica, I asked Mari for permission. And, with a few stipulations, Mari offered her blessing."

The fact that Chevy did that, somehow without me knowing when I swear we spent every minute of his time there attached at the hip, means so much to me. More tears. More butterflies. And more of my heart being owned by this man.

"Tiny, will you do me the honor of becoming my wife?"

I don't even look at the ring in the small box he's holding. I don't need to. It's about the man, not the token of his love. *"Yes."*

The word has barely left my lips when Chevy stands, throwing his arms around me—*finally!*—and picking me up off my feet to spin me around. People around us cheer and I'm crying even harder with a smile that cramps my cheeks.

"Look up!" someone calls, and I glance up to see a small bush hanging above our heads.

"For old time's sake," Chevy says, and with tears streaming down my face, laughing and crying, I press my lips to his.

My palms glide over his chest, feeling the raised skin of his scars. He calls them ugly, but I kissed every single one on a beach in Costa Rica, while a band of monkeys jabbered at us, shaking the trees. We couldn't decide if they were impersonating an angry mob or cheering crowd, but in the end, kissing eclipsed the argument.

Though we've spent precious little of our actual relationship in person, he wrote me surprisingly romantic love letters in a script as tidy as his house. We called every day, video chatted as often as we could, and messaged constantly. Now, we have endless days ahead together, and the anticipation bowls me over inside, as a shudder of happiness goes through me.

My Chevy. My best friend. My fiancé.

Finally, and maybe for the first time in my life, I'm *home*.

THE END

———

BONUS EPILOGUE

Collin

When my office door slams behind Liza, I stay seated behind my desk, head in my hands. I should feel upset. Sad. Maybe I should chase after the woman who is now, officially, my ex-girlfriend and ex-employee. I bet Liza expects me to follow.

In fact, her footsteps clanging down the metal steps to the main gym floor are slow. Hesitant, like she's waiting for me to yank open the door and beg her to reconsider. But there is no way I'm going after her, and by the time she reaches halfway, she's stomping quickly.

Clang! Clang! Clang! Probably every person in the gym is looking. Drama—Liza's favorite thing. And my least.

Despite the ugly conversation we just had and her current dramatic exit, I am relieved. No matter how much I defended Liza to my brothers and sister, she was unpleasant. At best. I can admit that now. She was not a great girlfriend, overly possessive and self-centered. Maybe she's not a great person, period.

But I *wanted* her to be. Is it wrong to believe in people? To give them plenty of chances? Isn't that what relationships are about: working hard, trusting the other person, giving it your all?

Maybe I know as little about relationships as I did back in junior high, when I asked Jordan Luckey to go out with me, then immediately tried to kiss her. For the record—that didn't end well either. Though it did teach me an important lesson about consent.

My phone buzzes, and I pick it up. Even if it's my most annoying brother. "Hey, Patty."

"Ding, dong—the witch is dead! You finally did it!" he cries, loud enough I pull the phone away from my ear.

"Did what? And stop yelling."

"Broke up with your terrible girlfriend!" he says at only a slightly softer volume.

I'm mid-eye roll when his words hit me. "Wait—how do *you* know we broke up?"

"She posted on her Instagram stories," Pat says, his voice turning hard. "And believe me, it is not good stuff. Did you fire her too?"

"Fire her? No! She broke up with me and then quit when I didn't beg her to take me back. How is she already posting? She literally walked out of my office not two minutes ago."

"Dude," Pat says. "*She* broke up with *you*? That's … wow. Her video looked like she was in her car. Maybe she's still in the parking lot. Check the security cameras."

I open my laptop and click to the app, scanning until I find a camera pointed right toward her pink VW Beetle. And yep—she's apparently still filming, gesturing wildly and holding her phone a few inches from her face. She pauses for a few moments to reapply lip gloss and practice smiling at herself.

I scoff. "Yep. She's in the parking lot, still going."

"You might want to do something," Pat says. "She stopped just short of claiming sexual harassment."

That has me freezing in place. False claims of harassment or assault make me madder than most things in the world. Because I know legitimate claims are underreported, and any time there is a proven false claim, it undermines the real victims.

"I can send security out, but that might make it worse," I tell Pat.

"Make sure you save any video footage you might have. Just in case she actually tries something legal."

Worry replaces the relief I felt moments ago. I move to the window overlooking the gym that is pretty much my life. A large portion of my savings went into this business, and every member of my family has a little something invested. My sister Harper and her husband both work here as trainers. The last thing I want is to see our good reputation ruined because Liza didn't get her way. Thank goodness I do have cameras everywhere, including my office.

It will be fine. It'll blow over. Won't it?

"I should go," I say.

"Let me know when you want me to set you up with someone," Pat says.

I make a face, even though he can't see it. "Pass. The last thing I need is to hop into another relationship doomed to fail."

"They wouldn't be doomed to fail if you stopped choosing the wrong kind of woman."

"Yeah, yeah, yeah. I'm starting to think all women are the

wrong kind," I tell him, and before Pat can argue, I mumble a quick goodbye and end the call.

My eyes snag on Harper down below. She's working with a UT football player who's flipping a massive tire across a stretch of Astroturf. When he stops, head down and looking ready to quit, Harper steps in and flips the tire twice. She glances back at him with hands on her hips. Clearly issuing a challenge. I smile as the guy gets back to work. That's my baby sister.

And this is the gym I've built. I'm proud of it. But as I survey the room, I feel a gnawing in my gut that it's not enough. It's never enough. My success here is great, but I want something more. Love. Family. A house that doesn't echo with emptiness when I walk in at the end of a long day.

My phone buzzes with a text. Pat. Again. Probably threatening to set me up on a dating profile.

But it's worse.

Didn't Liza have access to the financials? Better check that, his text reads.

My stomach sinks, and within seconds I'm in Quick-Books, scanning data. When Harper got too busy, Liza volunteered to help. And, like an idiot, I let her.

It takes me a minute, but then I see it—Liza's been messing with payroll, basically giving herself a raise for the last two months. Not enough to break us or anything, but it's not good. At least it's one more piece of proof just in case, as Pat suggested, she does try to come after me legally with her lies.

There's a knock, and Harper steps in, closing the door behind her. "Are you okay? I saw Liza stomp out of here throwing a true toddler tantrum."

"We broke up, but I'm fine," I tell her as she takes the

seat across from me. "But Liza's been stealing money, and she's posting a bunch of lies online. So, that's not great."

Harper frowns. "No. It isn't. Want me to sic Abby on her?"

I snort. One of Harper's best friends, Abby is absolutely the kind of person you could count on to exact revenge. "Nah. I'll hope it dies down and chalk the loss up to my stupidity."

"You're not stupid," Harper says.

"And you're not a good liar."

Sighing, she says, "Okay, fine. You're not stupid in general, but you *are* stupid in love."

"How can I be stupid in love when I've never been *in* love?"

"Stupid in *relationships*," Harper clarifies. "Is that better?"

"Yes. Thank you."

She smirks. "Now that we've resolved that issue, how about we get out of here? I have something that will make you feel better."

I sit up straighter, a goofy smile taking over my face. "Does it involve petting baby goats?"

Thanks to her friendship with a local woman who raises goats and a few other animals, Harper has anytime access to a number of adorable furry friends.

She jumps to her feet and reaches out her hand. "Duh. Baby goats are the answer to most of life's woes. You can quote me on that."

"I'll do you one better—I'll make you a T-shirt."

"Deal."

I slide my hand into my sister's, feeling a sudden tightness in my chest. A happy, warm kind of pressure. Harper gives my hand a squeeze, smiling as she tugs me toward the door.

"Do you think the baby goats can cure my relationship stupidity?" I ask as we start down the stairs, still hand in hand.

Harper laughs. "I'm not sure even baby goats can fix that, brother. But I believe in you."

I'm glad someone does. Because to be honest, I'm not sure anyone besides Harper—including me—does.

———

A Free Sheet Cake Novella!

I've got a special FREE Sheet Cake novella for you! This one takes place between The Pocket Pair (book #3) and The Wild Card (book #4) but will act as a standalone or an introduction if you haven't read the series yet!

There are minor spoilers (mostly who ends up with whom) … but if you're okay with that, you can sign up here! https://emmastclair.com/ante

A NOTE FROM EMMA

Hello, you amazing reader, you! This is the part of the book where I share a little bit of the behind-the-scenes and maybe some TMI.

Ever since Brooke (*Insta handle: a_brooke_and_her_books*) won a contest and chose to name a character after her late brother, I've been itching to write Chevy's story. It feels like an honor to be able to use his name, and I hope I wrote a worthy character.

If you didn't get the Pocket Pair reference (*because I think all of these have been pretty subtle*), the pocket pair is a pair you have from the very start of the game. And though Chevy didn't return Val's feelings from the start, I sort of feel like these two had their roots wayyyyy back at the start and were always the pair in the hand. :)

I chose to have Val's from Costa Rica because my sister-in-law married a Costa Rican (hi, Sergio!) and they raised their amazing kids there. I loved getting to bug Sandi with my questions. Next time, I'll go visit for research!

Val is kind of living my other dream life. In high school, art—not writing—was my main thing and what I was known for. I considered going to art school and actually originally planned to double major in art and English. For a time when Rob and I were first married, I sold paintings (*mostly of cows or bell peppers*) and hand-painted children's furniture as well as painting several murals in local YMCAs. (*If you're in Houston, I*

THINK mine is still up at the Clay Road Y, but not sure about the others.) I never really knew how to sell my own art either, but still do paint from time to time, so it was fun to write someone who really IS dedicated to it.

I was realizing as I wrote that a LOT of my characters have messy families. Though I have much to be thankful for with my own family, I doubt ANYONE is without some wounds due to family. So if that's you, I see you, and I'm sorry.

As a note, sheriffs and deputies and police and constables all kind of vary state by state and so the way it works in Sheet Cake may not be true to your town. Sheet Cake lives by its own rules!

Right now, there are two more planned books in this series, Collin's story, and Tank's story. I hope to have these completed by the end of 2023 or early 2024!

Acknowledgments...

A massive thanks to Jenny Proctor for seeing me through this book. Your feedback has become SO vital. I don't know what I did before you!!!

A big thanks to Owen (a friend from alllll the way back in high school) for giving me details about things like radar guns and cop stuff.

I am so so so so very appreciative to **every reader**, for every review, and for every kind email I receive or every time I hear someone recommending my books. This never gets old, and I never take it for granted. THANK YOU.

If you want to connect other places, you can find me hanging out on Instagram or in my Facebook reader group.

A final big thanks to Rita, Ruth, Lyn, Marsha, Teresa, Nicole, Rosalynn, and Lori for being my early eyes. <3

Happy reading!

-Emma

WHAT TO READ NEXT

The Appies

Just Don't Fall- Emma St. Clair

Absolutely Not in Love- Jenny Proctor

A Groom of One's Own- Emma St. Clair

Romancing the Grump- Jenny Proctor

Runaway Bride and Prejudice- Emma St. Clair

Love Stories in Sheet Cake

The Buy-In

The Bluff

The Pocket Pair

Sweet Royal Romcoms

Royally Rearranged

Royal Gone Rogue

Love Clichés

Falling for Your Best Friend's Twin

Falling for Your Boss

Falling for Your Fake Fiancé

The Twelve Holidates

Falling for Your Brother's Best Friend

Falling for Your Best Friend

Falling for Your Enemy

Oakley Island (with Jenny Proctor)

Eloise and the Grump Next Door

Merritt and Her Childhood Crush

Sadie and the Bad Boy Billionaire

Izzy and Her Off Limits Love

ABOUT THE AUTHOR

Emma St. Clair is a *USA Today* bestselling author of over thirty books and has her MFA in Fiction. She lives in Katy, Texas with her husband, five kids, and a Great Dane who doesn't make a very good babysitter. Her romcoms have humor, heart, and nothing that's going to make you need to hide your Kindle from the kids. ;)

You can find out more at http://emmastclair.com or join her reader group at https://www.facebook.com/groups/emmastclair/

Emma is represented by Kimberly Whalen, The Whalen Agency.